Hunters Moon

Lynda Renham

To Shelagh

Lots of love

Lynda Renham

xx

About the Author

Lynda Renham is the author of the best-selling psychological thriller *Remember Me.* Lynda is also the author of a number of popular romantic comedy novels including *Croissants and Jam, Coconuts and Wonderbras, Confessions of a Chocoholic, Pink Wellies and Flat Caps, It Had To be You, Rory's Proposal, Fudge Berries and Frogs Knickers, Fifty Shades of Roxie Brown, Phoebe Smith's Private Blog, Perfect Weddings* and *The Dog's Bollocks*.

Lynda Renham

ISBN 978-1-9998299-0-2
first edition

Printed for Raucous Publishing in Great Britain by
4edge Limited

www.raucouspublishing.co.uk

Prologue

Professor Dorcas teaches philosophy. He likes to talk about errors of judgement. His lectures are popular. He's patient with his students. They all like him. Sometimes they will ask him a question that is too difficult to answer and a mask will cover his face, his expression hidden. Professor Henry Dorcas talks about errors of judgement. Henry Dorcas is a fine one to talk.

Chapter One

Sunlight cut through the gap in the curtains, the rays slicing across the crisp white sheets and caressing the sleek body that was wrapped within them. She watched as he dressed, her pale blue eyes embracing every part of his body. He carefully retrieved the starched white shirt from the back of the chair and covered his muscular torso with it. She wanted to make love again, to feel his hot body on top of hers. She opened her mouth to speak but the words she wanted to say wouldn't come. Instead she said,

'Can you pass a cigarette?'

He gave her a disapproving look.

'You should try and stop. It's bad for you.'

He threw her handbag on to the bed, the contents spilling out on to the floor. She sighed and leant down to pick them up.

'I'm going to give it up,' she said, tapping a cigarette from the packet.

He checked his reflection in the dressing table mirror. Satisfied, he grabbed his wallet and phone.

'Do you have to go?' she asked sullenly.

She hated herself for pleading. Worse still, she despised herself for being in this situation.

'Yes, I do.'

He leaned towards her and gently kissed her on the lips.

'I'll be in touch,' he said as he turned to the door.

There was something in the way he said it, the offhand tone in his voice.

'I'm pregnant,' she said. She hadn't planned on telling him like this but what was she supposed to do, she thought. She probably wouldn't see him for weeks.

He stopped, his hand frozen on the door handle. She waited, her heart hammering in her chest. It seemed an eternity before he turned.

'But you're on the pill,' he said finally.

'I think I missed a couple,' she stammered.

The lie slid easily off her tongue.

'Is this some kind of joke?' he asked, his eyes hardening.

'I've been trying to find a way to tell you.'

'You're telling me you're pregnant and you're smoking?'

His lip curled in disgust. She shook her head. Wisps of blonde hair struggled to escape the neat bun at the nape of her neck.

'I wouldn't joke about something like this,' she said, pulling herself up in the bed. 'I'm going to stop. I just felt a bit anxious.'

She held her arms out to him but he ignored them. She suddenly felt vulnerable and stupid and covered her breasts with the sheet. She stubbed out the cigarette and climbed from the bed. He watched as she elegantly pulled on her clothes. His face softened and he stepped towards her.

'I'm sorry,' he said, gently taking her into his arms. 'It was a shock. Don't worry, we can sort it out. Money's no object, you know that. We'll get you the best there is.'

She pulled back, the words cutting into her.

'I'm not getting rid of it,' she said forcefully. 'I already thought about that but I can't, you know that. Our baby was conceived out of love and ...'

'For Christ's sake,' he said angrily, letting her go. She stumbled and fell on to the bed.

'I just want us to be a family,' she pleaded. 'You, me and ...'

He frowned in disbelief.

'Are you out of your mind?'

She stood up and clung on to his arm.

'You love me. Only an hour ago you said you adored me. You said you would get a divorce. After all, you ...'

He scoffed loudly.

'You really are out of your mind.' He turned away from her and made for the door. 'Get rid of it. I'll pay.'

He opened the door and stepped out to the landing. This wasn't how she'd imagined it. She rushed out after him and grabbed his arm.

'You can't just walk away,' she yelled. 'I only want us to be a family.'

He shook her hand roughly from his arm.

'You're being melodramatic. There is no way I am getting divorced.'

Anger engulfed her. How dare he dismiss her like this.

'I'll tell her,' she said menacingly.

His face darkened and for a moment she felt afraid.

'Don't threaten me,' he warned.

'I can't get rid of it. I'm already sixteen weeks. I'm surprised you didn't realise. You kept on enough about how big my tits were getting.'

'There's still time to get rid of it,' he snarled. 'We both know that. Get it sorted.'

'Please,' she begged, 'let's just talk about it.' She gripped his arm with both hands.

'Stop this,' he said angrily, pushing her away. 'I'm running late.'

She stumbled and struggled to regain her balance. She flailed for something to cling on to but there was nothing. He stepped forward to take her arm but in her fear she grabbed him roughly by the shirt. He was pulled forward and had to reach back for the banister to stop himself from falling. When he reached out for her again, it was too late.

'No,' she screamed, her eyes wide with fear.

He watched in horror as she bounced unmercifully down the stairs. The brutal thumping of her body against the steps seemed never-ending. The shrill ringing of his mobile made him jump. He ignored it and stepped slowly down the stairs. She wasn't moving. He could see, even before he reached the bottom, that her neck was broken.

*

I wake with my heart pounding. I look around the room with bleary eyes and exhale when I focus on the familiar outline of the dressing table. My hand rests tenderly on my abdomen and I remind myself it was just another dream. Even kicking the duvet off doesn't stop me from sweating and I wipe the perspiration from my forehead. Then I feel it, the all too familiar cramping. I close my eyes and try to ignore it, pretending it isn't happening but ten minutes later it is all-consuming and I feel the dampness between my legs and have to fight my disappointment.

With a heavy heart I stumble in the darkness to the bathroom where hunched over the toilet I let the tears flow. The silence of the night seems to suffocate me and the feelings of loss are too much to bear and sobs take my breath away.

Why? I plead. Why us, why is this happening to us? Finally, I reach into the bathroom cabinet and remove the tampons. Maybe next month I tell myself. Maybe next month you'll be in a new home. Surely a new beginning can only mean good things.

Carefully closing the bedroom door, I slip back into bed and hug my sore abdomen. The painkillers will work soon and I'll get back to sleep, but I know the disappointment will be even harder to bear in the morning. I remember the dream. I'd been pregnant. I could feel the baby moving inside me. It had seemed so real. I pull my knees up to my chest and close my eyes. It hadn't been real at all.

2017
Professor Dorcas

'But it doesn't always end in tragedy does it?' asks Zoe, a pretty red-haired student sitting at the back.

'No, but every action has its consequences,' replies Henry. 'Before we know where we are we find ourselves in a tangled web of deceit. One mistake can, and often does, lead to lies and more deceit. Then our moral judgement starts to elude us. Just one error of judgement can have devastating effects. It can destroy our dreams and our futures. It can make a person desperate and this often leads to further errors of judgement.'

'A domino effect,' says the young man to Henry's left.

'Indeed,' smiles Henry. 'And why do we make errors of judgement?'

There's silence and Henry waits for an answer.

'In moments of weakness?' suggests one student.

'To make an impression,' says another.

'Pride, envy, greed, lust, wrath, gluttony and sloth. The seven deadly sins,' adds Henry.

'It's not always easy to own up and tell the truth,' says Zoe.

'Every action has a consequence. Every action has a price to pay. Some errors of judgement can affect the rest of our lives, and the lives of those around us. But think about it, you make a mistake. It's your own fault and you can't undo it. What do you do?' asks Henry.

'You try to duck out of it.'

'Exactly, you try to cover up. You attempt to save face. Maybe you lie. You do things to hide your mistake and in doing so you make more errors of judgement.'

'We weave a tangled web of deceit,' says Zoe thoughtfully.

'Thank you, Zoe, for that quote from Walter Scott,' Henry smiles.

'Have you ever made an error of judgement Professor Dorcas?'

Henry's face clouds over.

'Can anyone here say they haven't?' he answers.

Chapter Two

May 2017

Malcolm drives along the tree-lined lane which cuts through the woods. As the car turns the corner a field with horses comes into view. We wind our way down the lane and finally turn on to a gravel driveway. The house is fronted by high iron gates. A plaque next to the gates reads *Hunters Moon*.

'This is it,' Adam says.

I peer through the rain-speckled windscreen at the foreboding building in front of me. Adam's phone trills and I try not to sigh.

'Sorry about this Flora,' he apologises as he clicks into it.

'It's okay,' I say, turning in my seat to glance at the Range Rover that had pulled up behind us.

'You'll get used to it,' Adam says, following my eyes before speaking into his phone.

'I'm looking at a house with Flora, what's so urgent Lucy?'

I fiddle in my handbag to find my phone. I idly check it. There's one text. It's from Laurie, checking we're still on for lunch. I throw it back into the bag and look at the house. It's not at all what I'd been expecting. Adam clicks off his phone and follows my gaze.

'What do you think?' he asks with a smile.

'It's big,' I say.

'It's perfect', he replies. 'It's overpriced but I've been assured we can get a drop.'

It's far too big. The gothic oak front door is uninviting.

'Assured by whom?' I ask.

He taps his nose with his finger.

'I've got my contacts,' he smiles. 'We'd be mad to let it go.'

Heavy clouds linger over the house and I shiver. It looks imposing and not like the other houses we'd looked at. I stare up at the peeling window frames and dark stone. Ivy has grown wild and unchecked and covers the side of the house

'Are you okay?' he asks protectively.

I fight back a sigh. I know he means well but I don't know how he expects me to recover if he keeps reminding me how fragile I am.

'I'm fine, Adam.'

'Right,' he says decisively. 'Let's take a look inside. I bet you can do wonders with this.'

A pretty woman in a soft camel coat skips down the steps to greet us. Her carefully coiffured hair is protected from the rain by a red umbrella.

'Hello,' she smiles. 'I'm Sienna. Welcome to Hunters Moon. I'm afraid Vikki Merchant, who normally handles the house, isn't able to show you around but I'll do my best.'

'I'm sure you'll do great. I'm really sorry but I've only got thirty minutes before I have to leave for a meeting,' Adam smiles.

He turns his soft brown eyes to me.

'Let's check it out.'

Two men from the Range Rover quickly follow. Sienna looks at them uncertainly and then holds out her hand to me.

'Nice to meet you,' I say, 'I'm Flora Macintosh.'

She nods knowingly. It was stupid of me I suppose. Of course she knows my name. My husband's the Home Secretary and one day, if his ambitions are realised, he'll be the Prime Minister.

'I'm not used to them either,' I say nodding to the bodyguards, who I privately call Tweedledee and Tweedledum. 'But apparently we now have to have them.'

Adam has been Home Secretary for six months and I'm still finding it hard to adjust. It wasn't so difficult when he was on the back benches. Life had seemed normal then.

'Are you coming?' Adam calls impatiently.

I follow Sienna up the steps and stand on the threshold. The entrance hall is not what I expect and far from being dark and imposing it is bright with large airy windows. A chandelier hangs from a high ceiling and a long carved staircase stands in front of us. It's bright and cheery but a shiver runs through me all the same.

'It's one of those damp chilly days isn't it? I'm afraid the heating is only on low,' Sienna apologises. She leads us down the stone flagged hallway and into the lounge. There is a scent of roses around us and I inhale the fragrance.

The walls are painted in damask red and I try not to grimace. Soft white couches covered with gorgeous print cushions surround the room. They seem too modern somehow and don't fit with the character of the house. The windows are draped in heavy maroon brocade curtains and look frayed at the edges. Tacky candleholders litter the windowsill. The room needs a good dust but I don't say anything.

'We will need a drop,' Adam says. 'It's over our budget.'

'I can certainly ask for you. What were you thinking?'

'I'd say two hundred and fifty thousand less,' says Adam.

'I'll put it to the vendor,' Sienna says without batting an eyelid.

Adam studies the walls and glances at the ceiling.

'It needs some renovating,' he says.

In the corner of the room is a piano. I wander over and tinkle on it. It's out of tune.

'The owner is Gerard Meyer, the actor,' explains Sienna. 'The house hasn't been lived in for a while. It will be cleared, obviously. Let me show you the kitchen.'

'Gerard Meyer lives here?' I say surprised. I'd seen him in several films. He was being hailed as the next Brad Pitt.

'Yes, he's made it big in the States hasn't he?' says Sienna.

'Didn't his wife die?' I ask, but Sienna pretends not to hear me.

'It's perfect,' Adam says. 'It's just what we've been looking for.'

I turn and stare at him.

'But you've only seen one room.'

'The location is perfect. It has a long driveway, secure gates and it's an ideal country getaway for us.' He climbs the stairs to the first floor while I follow Sienna to the kitchen.

'It is a good location,' she agrees. 'An hour and a half from London and you're in the heart of Oxfordshire. It's a sought after village and property rarely comes up for sale here.'

'My husband makes snap decisions,' I say feeling irritated with Adam.

'Oh,' she says, raising her eyebrows.

'Not in his job,' I laugh.

'That's a relief,' she grins.

'I can smell roses,' I say as the scent of roses wafts over me again.

Sienna sniffs.

'I can't smell anything,' she smiles.

The kitchen is beautiful with every possible mod con. A large oak table is perfectly situated at the far end overlooking a pair of French doors. A shiny Aga sits centre stage.

'It's in working order, but you have an induction hob too', she assures me.

I look out of the window. 'There's a lake,' I say.

A little rowing boat bobs on the water.

'Yes, technically it's a large pond, man-made, but all the same it's lovely isn't it? The grounds have been well kept. I believe there is someone from the village who comes in ...'

I turn to her.

'Why is he selling it?'

She shuffles through her notes.

'This is so embarrassing,' she says blushing. 'Vikki knows everything about Hunters Moon. I'm so sorry about this.'

'It's okay.'

'His wife died didn't she?' I repeat, 'Was it in this house?'

'I know she died a year ago. He'd just been nominated for an Oscar,' says Sienna.

'Was it here?' I ask, feeling myself shiver.

'Oh no, I don't think so,' Sienna assures me. 'I don't know the full story. Vikki could tell you more. She knows the history of this house. It isn't one of the houses I manage I'm afraid. I'm so sorry.'

But her face tells me she knows more than she is letting on.

'I'm just standing in for her this morning. She would be able to tell you a lot more than I can. I only know that the owner, Mr Meyer, spends most of his time in the States now and has decided to finally put the house on the market. We've been custodians of the house for the past six months. I imagine he's keen to get shot of the place now. It's a bit neglected as you can see.'

'It's huge. I imagine it has a limited market.'

'Yes, it's a bit out in the sticks.'

Sienna bites her lip and looks past me to the burly bodyguard before saying quietly,

'You'd feel safe here. The house is very secluded.'

'Are you coming up?' yells Adam.

Sienna and I look at the ceiling.

'He's only got thirty minutes,' I smile. I glance back at the lake.

'I don't feel comfortable here,' I confide. 'I don't know why. It's bigger than the other houses we've looked at, but it's more than that.'

I think of Laurie and how she would love this house. She'd be picking up vibes all over the place. The smell of roses has followed us into the kitchen and I look around expecting to see a vase of them but there are no flowers anywhere.

'We're handling other houses in the Cotswold area if you'd like me to send you other details. This village, Penlyn, rarely has property and it is a beautiful place,' says Sienna. 'I don't think you'll get another house like this one unless you look further out.'

'North Oxfordshire is my husband's constituency so we have little choice. We've got a flat in Oxford but we need something a bit bigger.'

'You're an interior designer,' says Sienna. 'I saw your work on television last week. You'll transform this place.'

I smile. It would be a good project for me, this is true. I need something to focus on right now and the house is ripe for my ideas.

'For Christ's sake Flora, you know I've only got a small window. Can we get on with this?' Adam says, bursting into the room.

'Sorry,' I mumble, following him upstairs.

'It's ideal,' he says to Sienna. 'When will it be available for possession?'

'Immediately,' she smiles. 'Mr Meyer isn't living here. We'd just to need to arrange for the house to be cleared.'

'I don't want us to lose it. Can I put a deposit on it now?'

I reel around to face him.

'Adam, may I have a word?' I say sharply.

He shrugs and follows me into the master bedroom. Before I can speak he checks his watch.

'Adam, I know you've got a lot on but I'm really not sure about the house, especially not enough to put an offer on it. I just sense ...'

He raises his eyebrows.

'Sense?' he smiles. 'You're sounding like Laurie.'

'I know. I just don't feel comfortable. I can't really explain it ... Did you know that Gerard Meyer's wife died? And probably right here in this house.'

'Did the agent tell you that?'

'No, but obviously it happened here, that's probably why he'll take a drop.'

I realise I'm sounding ridiculous. I'm a thirty-six-year-old successful woman. I'm married to a man who one day may be the Prime Minister and I'm rambling on like a five-year-old.

'I think you listen to Laurie too much.'

'Plus it's huge and really expensive,' I add, lowering my voice. 'Can we afford this and the flat in London?'

'Of course we can. I can get the mortgage and besides, it's a good investment. We can get a drop, the place needs renovating. You keep saying you want to get out of the Oxford flat and you know how much you hate London.'

I sigh.

'I do, but I was hoping for something a bit more modern.'

'This has character,' he says taking my hand. 'It's the type of house where you work your magic best. This is our dream home, Flora.'

I nod.

'You're right,' I say. 'It is the perfect house. I'm sorry. It's probably just me.'

He pulls me to him. The roughness of his suit chafes my cheek.

'It's okay. You'll get pregnant here, I know it,' he whispers. 'We'll go into Number Ten in six months' time with you huge. This will be a great place for us to escape.'

'Not with Tweedledee and Tweedledum around I won't, and I don't think you'll be in Number Ten in six months, but I agree it is good to have ambition.'

He laughs.

'A lot can happen in six months, and I promise Tweedledee and Tweedledum won't be in our bedroom. What do you say? Shall I pay the deposit?'

I sigh.

'Okay,' I agree, glancing at the bedside cabinet. A young woman stares back at me from a silver frame, large hooped earrings dangle from her earlobes. She looks happy and vibrant. She was far too young to die. I recognise the man at her side as Gerard Meyer.

'Right, I'd better get back,' says Adam, breaking into my thoughts. 'Do you want a lift with me or shall I get Malcolm to drop you off in town?'

'I'm meeting Laurie, so if Malcolm wouldn't mind.'

'Malcolm does what we tell him, darling. That's his job. No worries. I'll go back with the boys.'

I nod.

'Don't forget tomorrow we've got the fundraising do. All eyes will be on us. Get yourself a nice dress.'

He pushes a credit card into my hand.

'I love you,' he says kissing me warmly. 'I'll get the deposit sorted.'

I take a last look at the photograph and meet Sienna on the landing.

'Congratulations,' she says beaming widely. 'I just know you'll be happy here.'

'My husband's got to leave now but can you show me the rest of the house?'

'Of course,' Sienna says, looking relieved. 'Let's finish up here, and then I'll show you the grounds.'

I watch Adam from the landing window. He waves from the car and then is gone.

'There are three more bedrooms,' Sienna says. 'This is the master bedroom with an en suite and the middle bedroom also has an en suite plus there is a separate bathroom along the hall. His and her bathrooms,' she laughs. 'You can't beat that can you?'

I agree it does sound like heaven. I look up at the yellowing ceiling.

'There is some roof damage. I'm sure we can get you a drop,' she says.

The smell of roses wafts over me again. Sienna leads me back downstairs.

'There's a cellar here,' she says pointing to a door. She struggles with the handle but it doesn't budge.

'It seems to be stuck. We can get someone to look at that,' she says helpfully.

We step into the next room. A study lined with bookshelves. I picture Adam working in here and feel a sudden affinity with the house. Another set of French doors look out on to the lake. The light in the room is amazing.

'This is a great place to work,' I say.

'Let me show you outside,' Sienna says, clearly pleased with having made such an easy sale. I catch a glimpse of my reflection in an ornate mirror over the fireplace. I look gaunt. My woollen jumper seems to hang off me. I fluff up my fringe and push stray strands of hair that have escaped my bun, behind my ears. I look older than my thirty-six years. Maybe Adam is right, perhaps we do need this house. Perhaps it will be lucky for us. Maybe I will get pregnant again. I stifle a sigh. When did getting pregnant define me? I was a confident, successful career woman until Adam and I decided to start a family. Now I'm obsessed with cycles, hormones, temperature charts and fertility books. It seems I can think of nothing else these days. My thoughts wander and I have to force my mind back to the house.

The lake ripples as a gust of wind passes over it. Sienna hurriedly guides me to the boathouse to take shelter from another downpour.

'What a day,' laughs Sienna, shaking the rain from her hair.

The boathouse smells musty. Two tatty sofas and a rainbow rug are the only furnishings. They look lost in the large room. Colourful throws cover parts of the sofas, a weak attempt to hide their shabbiness.

'This is so romantic isn't it?' says Sienna. 'It's my favourite part of the house. I bet it's lovely on a summer's evening. You could do a lot with this.'

I visualise the boathouse with large cosy sofas and rocking chairs covered in warm throws. We could even install a log burner so that we could sit here during the cooler weather. I feel that little tingle of excitement that I always get when planning a house's interior.

'Is there a rose garden?' I ask.

Sienna shakes her head.

'Not that I know of, but there's plenty of space to make one.'

Behind the lake and boathouse are acres of woodland.

'Is that part of Hunters Moon?' I ask, pointing.

'Yes, spectacular isn't it? You've got four acres of woodland. Marsham Woods joins on to your land but everything is walled off. There are security cameras on the perimeter. There's a gate keypad and camera at the front of the house and there's also a gate from Chatterpie Lane into the woodland but that is securely locked. The house is amazingly secure.'

The wood looks menacing under the leaden clouds. A storm is brewing and the last place I want to be when it does is here. I look to the house, its stone walls cold and commanding. The ivy had been pernicious and its long strands were now encroaching on the house. It's far too big for two people. We'd rattle around in it and never see each other. It will be a nightmare to heat.

'It will be so cosy in the winter,' says Sienna as though reading my mind. 'It will be gorgeous with the open fire in the lounge.'

I smile.

'Your husband said he'll be in Number Ten by the end of the year. I'm sure he'll make a better Prime Minister than Ralph Meadows.'

Only if Ralph bows to the pressure and I know he won't. Adam is going to be so disappointed.

'It's not guaranteed by any means,' I smile.

Adam becoming Prime Minister is not something I relish. I know from other politician's wives, that the more powerful their husbands become the harder it is to have a normal family life. Sienna locks up the boathouse as I hurry back into the house. The dark clouds in the sky resonate with a strange sense of doom that I feel. I hug my arms around me to warm my chilled body.

'Thanks so much,' I call over my shoulder.

Malcolm turns the Range Rover around. I look back at the house. It looks cold and unfriendly. A figure at one of the upstairs windows catches my eye. I wave but she doesn't wave back.

'The Grand Café in town please, Malcolm,' I say.

I take one last look at the house and see Sienna locking up. She couldn't possibly have got downstairs that quickly. I glance back to the window but the figure has gone.

June 1997
(Twenty years earlier)

It was a humid night and a thunderstorm was forecast. Kate didn't like thunderstorms and was keen to get home before it began. It was her eighteenth birthday in two days. She was excited. She had so many plans and so many dreams.

The bus pulled into the lay-by. She thanked the driver and stepped off into the warm night. The heavy scent of honeysuckle hung on the air and she sniffed the fragrance appreciatively. She clicked on her torch and began to make her way along the country lane. Her cottage was a ten minute walk from the bus stop. He had jumped out of the bushes. She had recognised him immediately and a tremor of fear ran through her body. He lived with his mother in a ramshackle cottage on the edge of the village. Everyone said he was strange, 'like his mother', they said. He smelt of alcohol and she backed away.

'I thought it was you,' he said, stepping closer.

'Hello,' she said making an attempt at friendliness.

'You look nice,' he said, licking his lips.

'My dad is expecting me,' she said, side-stepping him, but he met her step and blocked her way.

'Fancy a walk?' he asked with a grin.

She was conscious of her skirt. It wasn't that short but it came above her knee. She felt uncomfortable.

'No thank you. I have to get home,' she said, pushing past him.

She would forever regret that push. Maybe she should have talked to him, been a bit nicer. Perhaps he wouldn't have turned the way he had. Maybe it had been her fault. She'd tried to escape and struggled for release, but he was too strong. She was pushed on to the ground. She'd opened her mouth to scream but he had covered it roughly with his hand. It smelt of tobacco and beer and she felt the bile rise to her throat. She prayed someone would come but no one did and no one heard her whimpers of anguish.

It was an hour later when she stumbled into the village hall, her skirt ripped and her face bruised. A meeting was just ending. Blood trickled down her thighs and she wiped at them with trembling hands.

'Help me,' she pleaded as she fell at the feet of Henry Dorcas.

Chapter Three

'It sounds idyllic,' says Laurie, sipping her cocktail. 'What a great name, *Hunters Moon*. It sounds like something out of a gothic novel.'

'It looks like something out of a gothic novel too.'

'Cool.'

'It's too big,' I say. 'I wish Adam wasn't so impulsive.'

The Grand Café is busy and the crashing of crockery is adding to the headache that started at Hunters Moon. Laurie watches as I pop two painkillers.

'He really wants to please you, Flora. It's been a tough time for him too.'

'I know,' I say.

'If you want my advice, you should take the house. It will be a great project and you keep saying how you need to get back into the swing of things. I know things have been hard but this could be your saving grace. You can get involved in village life, Women's Institute and all that malarkey and you can really focus on your work ...'

I nod in agreement.

'I know. A project would be great, but Women's Institute? Don't you think I'm a little young for that? Do you really think that's me? I just don't think this is the right project.'

'Well maybe not the Women's Institute,' she laughs.

The waiter brings our salads and I look enviously at the next table where they are tucking into steak.

'You could have had one,' smiles Laurie.

'I want to keep to my healthy eating regime. I know I sound boring but I'll try anything that will help me carry a baby. That's if I can get pregnant again.'

She looks sympathetically at me.

'That's why this house is exactly what you need. The grounds sound idyllic. You can forget the flat, forget the miscarriages and focus on positive things. It's the only way you'll get pregnant again. You should get a puppy.'

'A puppy?' I laugh, cutting into a slice of smoked salmon.

'Yes, it's a great idea. You can't have one in the flat, but with those grounds you could. Leave it to Adam. He's good at these things. Focus on yourself. If he says you can afford the mortgage then you can. You still earn good money too.'

I sip my cocktail and say gingerly,

'I sensed something in the house.'

'You mean like a presence?' She says with her eyes widening.

'I don't know, it was probably all in my head.'

'Oh my God,' she gasps.

'I knew you'd get excited. It was just me I'm sure. Adam didn't seem to feel anything and ... well I don't believe in that stuff. You know that.'

Laurie leans across the table knocking over the salt cellar in the process.

'What did you sense?'

I exhale.

'I smelt roses. No one else did but I definitely could. I was sure there must be roses somewhere but I couldn't see flowers anywhere. Even the garden doesn't have a rose bush.'

'What's the history of the house?' Laurie says, pushing her plate to one side.

'The estate agent didn't know much ...'

'How come?' she interrupts.

'The woman who usually handles the house wasn't in today.'

'But ...'

'There isn't a but, Laurie,' I say.

I realise I've finished my cocktail and beckon the waiter.

'Do you want some water?' I ask Laurie.

'No, I want to hear more about what you felt.'

I sigh. I consider telling her about the figure at the window and then dismiss it. It was probably just a reflection.

'Okay, don't get excited, but the house is owned by Gerard Meyer the actor ...'

She wrinkles her brow.

'Should I know him?'

'Well, he's not George Clooney, but there's a buzz around him. He won an Oscar for his role in *The Loner*. He's the new fresh face of Hollywood. I only know this because Jan is big on her films as you know. His wife died. She was really young. I don't know quite what happened and I don't know if it was in the house.'

Laurie's eyes widen.

'Can we have a jug of water?' I ask the waiter.

'Oh my God, you so have to take that house. I can't wait to see it. You must ask the estate agent more about it.'

I wave my hand dismissively.

'I don't believe in ghosts, you know that.'

'I'm not saying you have ghosts, but it is exciting.'

'Anyway, we're not buying it. I'm going to talk to Adam tonight. It's far too big for two people ...'

'It won't be once you have your puppy and a couple of kids,' she smiles.

'I'd rather have a modern house.'

Laurie huffs.

'Who wants a modern house? Seriously, I do think you need a project like this and I'll help. I can organise the housewarming party.'

Visions of people milling around the lake with glasses of champagne enter my head.

'Well, you know how determined Adam is,' I smile.

'So, are we going to have dessert? Or are we straight out to find you a dress for the fundraiser dinner?'

'The dress I think. It will no doubt take me ages to find something.'

'Great. I've got all afternoon.'

'No events to organise?' I smile.

'I've left Helen holding the fort. I pay her a bloody fortune so she might as well do some work. I've got a big celebrity do coming up. Shall I try and wangle an invite for you and Adam?'

I wrinkle my nose. Adam loves that kind of thing. Anywhere he can network and he is in his element. I prefer quiet intimate dinner parties.

'That would be great, thanks Laurie.'

'No problem, just hand my card around to your friends and make sure I'm the one that organises the housewarming.'

I smile.

'That's if we take the house.'

'You've got to take it. The house will be full of secrets. Imagine what fun you'll have finding out what went on there.'

I make a mental note to phone the estate agent when I get back and have a chat with Vikki.

2017
Los Angeles

He was deep in concentration. It was an important role and he wanted to be perfect. There was the chance of another Oscar in this one. The ringing of the phone made him jump.

The voice at the other end sent a chill through him. Memories of an old life forced their way into his mind. The fear and panic he'd known returned, and it was like he was back there all over again.

'I'll be brief. I know you're a busy person.'

His stomach lurched.

'Someone came to look at the house. They want it but they need a drop of two hundred and fifty thousand.'

He let out a breath.

'Why do you care?' he asked.

'I don't think that's for you to worry about. Things are going well for you aren't they? You know the house is overpriced. You want rid of it don't you?'

'I'll take the drop,' he said in reply.

'Good. Our business is done.'

'That's it?'

'That's it. Your debt is paid. I think you've learnt your lesson.'

The phone went dead and Gerard Meyer sat staring at it. After a few minutes he picked it up again to make a call.

'Lauren and Michael's estate agents, Sienna speaking, how can I help?'

'I'd like to speak to Vikki please?'

'She's not in today. Can I help?'

'It's Gerard Meyer, I was wondering if there had been any interest in the house.'

Her voice seemed to rise slightly and his lip curled in pleasure. A fan no doubt.

'Hi, Mr Meyer, we were going to contact you later today. I was taking into account the time difference ...'

'Yes, has there been any interest?'

'Yes, there has, but the interested party are asking for a significant drop.'

'I'm happy to drop,' he said, fiddling with a ballpoint pen on his desk.

'They're asking for a two hundred and fifty thousand drop.'

'That's fine,' he said, feeling his chest constrict.

'That's great,' said Sienna. 'I'll let them know and get back to you.'

He hung up and dropped his head into his hands. Some minutes later he got up and poured himself a large whisky. Three glasses later and he had numbed the pain that came with the memories of Hunters Moon.

Chapter Four

'Fancy a whisky before we leave?' Adam calls.

I purse my lips and carefully apply my lipstick as Adam bursts into the room carrying two glasses.

'You smell gorgeous,' he says. 'Here, I thought these would get us in the mood.'

'Great,' I say, although I won't drink it, not now that I've got my make-up on. My stomach is churning with nerves. It's been three months since I attended a function with Adam and I know everyone is going to ask me how I'm doing. The press will be there with their photographers. Adam's fundraising committee had raised thousands for a new infertility unit but I'd been so full of my own pain that I'd not shown any interest in it. The thought of having to put on a show for Adam's political friends fills me with dread. Everyone knows how much I wanted a baby and how I had miscarried for the second time at five months and everyone will be gushing with superficial sympathy. I'd do anything to get out of the evening.

Adam strokes my hair and kisses me softly on the neck. I can smell the whisky on his breath.

'That perfume always turns me on,' he whispers, 'but there's no time now. Put some on when we get back.'

Guilt punches me in the stomach.

'Do you mind awfully if we wait a few days. I'll be ovulating then and I'd rather get the ...'

'Full potency,' he smiles, fumbling around in the jewel case.

I nod.

'I'm sorry. I know it's all clinical but ...'

'You shouldn't wear that perfume then.'

I glance at the bottle of Artemisia Eau de Parfum and remember the smell of roses at Hunters Moon.

'Have you heard any more about the house?' I ask.

'They're putting it to the owners. Hopefully they'll accept our offer.'

'It smelt of roses,' I say.

'I'm not sure about this shirt,' he says, checking his reflection in the mirror. 'Have you seen my Pierre Cardin? It's not in the wardrobe. I don't know what Jan does with my laundry.'

'She gets them dry cleaned is what she does,' I smile. 'I'm sure your Pierre Cardin is in the wardrobe. Do you want me to look?'

'No, I'll put the black Gucci on.'

He pulls off his shirt and I admire his fit body.

'Where's your chain?' I ask.

He puts a hand to his chest.

'I don't know,' he says. 'The clip was faulty. I should have had it repaired. It must be somewhere in the flat. It's silly I know but I don't feel right without it. I keep expecting things to go wrong. I feel like I'm not protected.'

Adam is superstitious about the St Christopher his parents bought him before his gap year. It was especially engraved on the back to wish him safe travels. He feels certain it brings him luck. I smile at his naivety. You make your own luck, my mother used to say. Besides, a pendant can't possibly protect you but I don't say that to Adam.

'It can't be far. I'll ask Jan to keep an eye out for it.'

'I don't want our luck changing,' he jokes. 'Not now.'

He unbuttons his shirt and I admire his perfect features. His strong jawline twitches as he studies himself. I wrap my arms around his waist. I still find him as handsome as I did when we first met. It was his warm brown eyes that attracted me and the way he stood, proud and confident. I knew then that he was going to be special in my life.

'I'm going grey,' he says as he ruffles his hair with his hand.

'I still love you,' I say, kissing him.

'What was that about roses?' he asks.

'Did you smell roses at Hunters Moon?'

He shakes his head.

'No.'

I look at him through the mirror and think how lucky I am.

'The house is okay,' I say, hugging him close to me. 'I know I've been unbearable the past few months but maybe the new house will help.'

'It will be good for you. You need something to help you heal. Getting the house nice for us will be the perfect therapy.'

He kisses me on the cheek.

'We should get going,' he says.

'Laurie said we should get a puppy.'

He shudders.

'God preserve us.'

'She thinks it will help,' I say reaching for my clutch bag. 'It will run around the grounds and keep guard for us.'

'We'll talk about it later. Let's go.'

I check my reflection and dab a bit more blusher on my cheeks. I look longingly at the whisky. It would help calm my nerves. I consider it and then take a long gulp before throwing my lipstick into the clutch.

'Flora,' calls Adam. 'The car's here, hurry up.'

I take a deep breath and follow him out.

*

'You look amazing,' says Philippa Mann, the Chancellor of the Exchequer. She leans closer and whispers, 'Adam told me what happened. You just need to push on. There'll be other babies.'

I feel tears prick my eyes. Push on? What does she know?

'Yes,' I mumble, looking around for a drink.

'How long has it been?' she asks.

Talk about tactful, I think.

'Three months,' I mumble.

I really don't want to talk about it.

'It must have been difficult. I'm so sorry.'

'Thanks,' I say, fighting back my tears.

'Have you bought a house yet? Adam said you had been looking?'

'Not yet,' I say. I don't want her gossiping to all and sundry about Hunters Moon.

'Trust me, once he's in Number Ten, you'll be grateful for somewhere to escape.'

'We can't be sure that's going to happen,' I say with a smile.

'No, Ralph is a stubborn old dog. He'll stick it out. But, you never know. The tide is turning, my dear, the tide is turning.'

I take a drink from a passing waiter as the gong sounds for dinner. I look around for Adam.

'Abandoned you has he?' says a voice behind me.

I turn to see Ralph Meadows, the Prime Minister. His piercing blue eyes penetrate me.

'Hello Ralph,' I say.

'May I escort you into dinner?' he smiles.

There's no warmth in the smile. I look for Adam but there is no sign of him.

'He's abandoned you. He's probably found someone that can help further his career. He puts that before anything doesn't he?'

I shake my head.

'Not everyone is as ruthless as you, Ralph,' I say, feeling my anger rise.

'I'm only ruthless when I want something and when I want something I go all out to get it, whereas your husband is a little more deceptive.'

I bite my tongue. How dare he criticise Adam. If it wasn't for Adam, Ralph Meadows would have been out a long time ago. I wish Adam wouldn't cover Ralph's back so much. I let out a small gasp as he rests his hand on my hip.

'So, how are you, lovely Flora? We don't see you anywhere near enough in London.'

'I've been busy house hunting,' I say, edging away from him.

'Ah yes, that quiet place in the country that Adam hankers after.'

'Flora,' cries Felicity Meadows as she approaches us.

'Darling,' smiles Ralph, stepping back and removing his hand. 'I've been looking for you. I was just about to escort Flora into dinner.'

'Well, now you can escort us both,' says Felicity.

She pecks me on the cheek and then puts her hands on my shoulders.

'How are you?' she asks intensely as we walk into the dining room. I feel sure everyone is looking at me. I can almost hear their whispers, *'There's Flora Macintosh, she had a second miscarriage, Took her forever to get pregnant too. It's a terrible shame for Adam don't you think?'*

'I'm fine,' I say casually.

'You sure?' she asks, looking into my eyes.

I feel like I'm going to scream. Voices seem to penetrate my brain and a burst of raucous laughter makes me jump. I'm not ready for this. It's too soon.

Adam waves from our table.

'Where have you been?' I ask, more harshly than I mean to.

'I went to the loo,' he says looking at me oddly. 'Are you okay?'

I nod. He pulls a chair back for me and I sit down.

'Great to see you,' says Felicity. 'And I'm pleased to hear you're doing well.' She taps me on the shoulder before walking to her seat.

'I wish you wouldn't abandon me,' I say to Adam. 'I got caught by Ralph and Felicity. He's very scathing of you.'

'He's feeling insecure,' says Adam, offering me some wine. 'Don't let him bother you.'

'I feel sorry for Felicity,' I say, glancing over at her. 'He's a sexist pig.'

I shake my head to the wine and pick at my food, waiting for Adam to make his speech. Half an hour later some people step outside for a smoke. Adam joins them for a cigar. The evening drags. I would leave early if I could but I know Adam would never forgive me. I stroll on to the terrace at the back of the hotel and breathe in the fresh cool air. The sky is clear and the stars are brilliant.

'Not a smoker then?'

I turn to the blond-haired man behind me.

'No, are you?'

'No. It's bad for you.'

I'm feeling chilly but it seems rude to go in now.

'You're cold,' he says.

'A little.'

He removes his jacket and places it around my shoulders. It smells of his aftershave.

'Simon Kingsley. Your husband kindly raised a lot of money for my infertility unit.'

'Yes, I recognised you.'

'I hear you're thinking of buying a house in Penlyn.'

'Oh, did Adam tell you?'

'I've heard it's a pretty village. So, when can you come and see me?'

I'm taken aback and fail miserably to hide it.

'Oh,' I say.

'Adam tells me you have an appointment in six months' time. That's a long way off.'

'You're a hard person to see,' I say shyly.

'I'll get my secretary to call you. I'm sure we can get you in sooner than that.'

'It's very kind but ... well it seems wrong of me to jump the queue.'

'I assure you that you will pay like everyone else.'

'Monopolising my wife again Sir Kingsley?' says Adam jovially, as he joins us. He has had too much to drink. He's loud and jolly.

'Not Sir yet, Adam,' smiles Simon Kingsley.

'It's in the bag, old man,' says Adam, slapping him on the back.

I feel myself blush at the realisation that Adam may be responsible for Doctor Kingsley's knighthood.

'I'm trying to give her an earlier appointment but she's not having it, says she doesn't want any preferential treatment.'

'What! Of course she does. I've just raised thousands for this guy's clinic. Of course he can see you, Flora.'

Not to mention the fact that you've organised his knighthood, I think cynically,

'If you can get this baby business sorted you'd be doing us both a big favour. It's playing havoc with our sex life, know what I mean?'

Adam nudges Simon in a familiar fashion. I feel myself blushing.

'Adam,' I say firmly.

I let the jacket slide from my shoulders and hand it back to Simon Kingsley.

'My secretary will be in touch,' says Simon before walking back into the dining room.

'That was embarrassing,' I say.

'You should get an appointment. It's the least he can do. Let's go inside. I've got to make my speech.'

He takes my hand and leads me back into the dining room.

'Come and sit with us,' says Philippa, grabbing my hand.

I'm ashamed to say I missed most of Adam's speech. I drifted off and was thinking about Hunters Moon and the tragic death of Gerard Meyer's wife. I think back to the lake. What if we had a child? The lake would be dangerous. What was the shadow at the window? Did I really see someone or was it just a trick of the light? I jolt in my seat as Philippa nudges me. My attention is drawn back to Adam and I realise everyone is looking at me.

'She's been my rock for the past two years,' Adam is saying, 'I don't know how she has put up with me being away so much and always seeming preoccupied with things. It was Flora that gave me the insight into how important this charity was. I love you darling and I'd like to propose a toast to my wife, Flora. I wouldn't be the man I am today if it wasn't for you.'

I stupidly feel tears well up and Philippa hands me a tissue.

'Hear hear,' she calls.

I blow Adam a kiss and tell myself how lucky I am. If Adam wants Hunters Moon, the least I can do is support him.

2017
Professor Dorcas

He thought about the question again.

'Have you ever made an error of judgement Professor Dorcas?'

Had he? No, he assured himself, he hadn't. He could say with hand on heart that he'd always made the right decisions. Was it his fault that those around him were weak? He should have let them ride the devil. That's what they deserved. But how could he? How could he watch those with such glittering futures lose everything? You can't go back. It wouldn't have been possible to change what had been done. What would it have meant? Scandal, shame, their names tainted forever. No he was right not to let that happen.

One bad decision, that's all it needed.

'I don't think I've ever made an error of judgement,' said one of the students confidently.

Henry had hid his smile. It was only a matter of time, he thought. With that arrogance an error of judgement is bound to happen. I wonder who'll cover for you, he wondered.

'How can we not make bad decisions?'

'Ah,' said Henry, stroking his chin. 'Know your weaknesses.'

They'd all nodded. They weren't going to make any errors of judgement. Not today anyway. But Henry knew that sometime, sooner or later, they would. For some it will be easy to untangle their web of deceit but others would weave a web from which they would never be free.

November 2015
An Error of Judgement

It had been a wild night. Ben's parties were always a riot and this one was no exception. Shame the barn got raided at 3 a.m. They were having a great time and things were only just hotting up. Ben had got totally wasted and insisted they drive back in his vintage Aston Martin.

'Here you drive. You're more sober than me,' Ben had said, throwing the car keys to him. The truth was he was just as wasted, but it didn't take much to persuade him to do it. He'd wanted to get behind the wheel of Ben's Aston Martin for some time. After all, he told himself, the roads would be empty and there are never any police on the country roads outside of Oxford and it was only a short drive. It would be a laugh. Ben cradled a bottle of champagne on his lap and complained that 'the bloody seatbelt wouldn't fit.' They had laughed and sung along to the booming stereo, a stupid song, which had seemed great at the time but he couldn't even remember it now. He only remembered they were happy. He'd floored the accelerator, screeching the tyres on the wet road. He glanced in the rear-view mirror to her curled up body on the back seat, the result of too much champagne. But they'd had a lot to celebrate. He was on cloud nine. He couldn't have been higher if he was on crack cocaine. It was raining lightly, but nothing to worry about. He loved the car and was determined to show Ben that he could put it through its paces. The Ecstasy pills that he had taken earlier made him feel invincible.

The lane widened slightly and he swerved to take a bend. Then out of the darkness a figure materialised in front of him, her eyes wild in the glare of the headlamps. She came out of nowhere, what the hell was she doing on the road at that time in the morning? He stamped on the brake and skidded, narrowly missing a tree. The thud of the body as it bounced off the bonnet was followed by screams from the back seat.

The music was deafening and he fiddled with the volume control to turn it off.

'Oh God,' someone moaned. It may have been him that said it, he couldn't remember. The steering wheel seemed to be dragged from his hands. He screamed as the car careered out of control but the sound was lost as a tree rushed towards them. He squeezed his eyes shut as the Aston Martin piled into it. Everything suddenly stopped and there was just the eerie hiss of steam where the overheated engine met the rain. He twisted his neck around, pain searing through his head. He fought back a retch at the sight of Ben, his head embedded in the windscreen, his eyes vacant.

'Oh Jesus,' she said from behind him. 'You killed him, you fucking killed them both.'

He followed her eyes through the rear window to the road where the lifeless body of the woman lay. He blinked, hoping it was a dream but it wasn't a dream, it was a nightmare.

'Jesus, she came out of nowhere.'

'You have to phone for an ambulance,' she wailed.

He fumbled with trembling bloodied hands in his pocket for his phone. This would be the end for him. The future that had looked so rosy just a few hours before would be peeled away and he'd be left with this. Her sobs jarred on his nerves. He couldn't think clearly.

'For God's sake, phone for help,' she cried.

'I am,' he replied hoarsely.

He looked again at Ben. He was dead there was no doubt about that. There was nothing he could do for him now. The roads were quiet. No one had seen the accident. He couldn't just throw it all away. Everything he'd dreamt of, everything he'd worked for, gone in a second. He couldn't do it. He couldn't let it go. He couldn't allow his life to be over because of one mistake. There must be a better way. Feeling sick in the pit of his stomach he punched in a number. It was the only number he could think of. Surely he would know a better way.

Chapter Five

'Can I speak to Vikki please?'

There is a pause and I wonder if we've been cut off.

'Hello?' I say.

'Who's calling?'

'Flora Macintosh, we're buying Hunters Moon.'

'Yes, hello, it's Sienna. I was going to give you a call this afternoon.'

'I was hoping to chat with Vikki.'

She seemed to hesitate.

'Vikki's not in I'm afraid. I can add you to her messages.'

'I phoned yesterday and I've been added to her messages already.'

'Oh right. Sorry, we're not sure when she's coming back. There are some personal problems.'

'Okay not to worry. Thanks for all you've done.'

'You're taking possession next Wednesday aren't you? I imagine you must be very excited.'

'Yes, it's all happened so quickly.'

'That's the pleasure of no chains and the best solicitors,' she laughs.

And the fact that your husband is the Home Secretary, I think.

'I was going to phone you actually. Most of the house is clear now. There are a few items of furniture that have been left. They are rather nice pieces which Mr Meyer has asked us to sell. I thought I'd check whether you'd like to hang on to them. There's the super king size bed in the master bedroom and the king size in the middle bedroom. There is also a lovely dressing table in the main bedroom. It's an antique.'

'How much are they asking for them?'

There's a rustle of papers.

'It's open to negotiation. I'd suggest two hundred and see what Mr Meyer says.'

'We'll take them,' I say impulsively. 'Can you have the mattresses removed?'

'Oh yes, of course.'

Adam won't disagree. He's more than happy for me to take care of the interiors. Our own king size bed would be lost in the master bedroom. It's worth hanging on to the super king size until we decide what we want. I'll arrange to have new mattresses delivered along with some Egyptian linen. I've always been keen on old vintage style dressing tables and I remember the one Sienna was talking about. It was gorgeous.

'I'll get rid of the boat, unless you want to keep it?' says Sienna.

'Oh yes, it would be a shame for it go. I'm sure Mr Macintosh would want it to stay.'

'That's lovely,' says Sienna. 'If you ever need to pop in, you know, to measure up or anything, I'd be happy to meet you there with a key.'

'That's great thank you. Is there anyone else I can talk to about the history of the house?'

'Vikki has all the information. I'm so sorry.'

It seems ridiculous to me that they can't get the information off her. I bite my tongue and say nothing. Adam will be cross if I push things too much.

'Okay, thank you Sienna.'

I hang up and wander back to the bedroom where Jan is helping me sort out the contents of the wardrobe.

'I'll finish this and then I'll get dinner on,' she says.

I look at the bundle of clothes and suddenly feel overwhelmed.

'You know what, Jan. I think I'll take the lot and sort them out in the new house.'

She smiles.

'That sounds like a good idea to me.'

'I just don't think we have enough things to go in this huge house.'

'You'll soon fill it up. When Fred and I bought our house I thought the same. Twenty-eight years later and we don't have enough room for it all.'

I laugh and give her a hug.

'I'm so glad you're coming to the new house with us. There is going to be so much to do.'

'I'm dead excited. It's not often you get to clean a film star's house.'

I laugh.

'Ooh, look at the time. I'd best get the potatoes on,' she says.

I hang the clothes back in the wardrobe and then tidy the dressing table. I scoop up the bracelet I'd worn yesterday and drop it into the jewellery box. My eyes land on the diamond studs that Adam had bought me after I'd announced my last pregnancy. I grip the dressing table stricken suddenly by longing. Self-pity pushes into my consciousness and I quickly shove the earrings to the bottom of the box and slam the lid down. With a sigh I pull the creases out of the duvet cover and make my way downstairs. I go through to the kitchen where the phone is ringing.

'No, I'm the housekeeper, just a moment,' I hear Jan say.

She hands me the phone. 'Doctor Kingsley's secretary.'

'Oh,' I say.

I really hadn't expected him to remember me. The fundraiser had become quite raucous after the speeches. A lot of alcohol had been consumed and I'd convinced myself that Dr Kingsley would forget all about me.

'Flora Macintosh speaking,' I say.

'Doctor Kingsley asked me to arrange an appointment,' the secretary says briskly. 'Is next Friday afternoon at four o'clock suitable? Doctor Kingsley has a clinic in Oxford on Fridays. He thought that might be easier for you.'

My heart quickens in anticipation.

'That's amazing. I know how busy Doctor Kingsley is.'

'I'll pencil you in then Mrs Macintosh.'

I feel suddenly guilty. What if they've cancelled another woman's appointment just to fit me in?

'That sounds perfect, thank you.'

'That's booked for you. We'll see you then.'

I replace the receiver with trembling hands. Surely if anyone can help me hold on to a baby it will be Doctor Kingsley.

October 1997
Peter Snell

Pete was having a peaceful pint in the local. After all, he had no reason to hide. A court of law had found him not guilty and he sure as hell didn't fear no hillbilly. She'd been a good fuck. She'd been gagging for it. He doesn't care what anyone else says. He'd heard her moans of pleasure. She'd led him on with that short skirt of hers. It wasn't right for a hillbilly like her to dress so provocatively around red-blooded men like him, and then to cry rape. She'd got exactly what she'd deserved and bloody enjoyed it too. He was entitled to drink wherever he chose. It was certainly a peaceful pint alright. No bugger in the pub had spoken to him. He took a final swig and slammed his glass down on the table. Eyes followed him as he stepped to the bar.

'I'll 'ave another of those,' he said. 'It's a warm night. Makes a man thirsty.'

'I don't think you need any more,' said a deep voice behind him. 'Not in this pub anyway.'

He turned and grinned at the man. He recognised him. He was the one that lived in the big house on the hill, Henry something or the other.

'I like the beer in this pub,' he said, turning back to the bar.

'You know you're only here to cause trouble.'

'I ain't caused any trouble,' he retorted angrily. 'I'm the innocent one. A court of law proved that.'

There was a collective scoff from the other patrons.

'This is a village pub, and some of the villagers would like to come in here and have a pint but not while your foul-smelling body is in here,' said Henry.

The words had fallen like acid drops. Pete gritted his teeth. They're not fucking worth the aggro, he told himself. He'd made his point. He might as well move on to a friendlier place.

'Fuck the lot of you,' he said throwing a handful of loose change on to the counter. 'I'm going. This place sucks anyway.'

'Might be best if you don't come back,' said Henry, a subtle threat in his voice.

'You can't threaten me. I'm an innocent man. The court said so, remember?'

'The court made a mistake.'

'She was up for it. She just doesn't want you lot to know that.'

There was a scuffle behind him and he clenched his fist in readiness. Henry held up his hand.

'We don't want any trouble with you. We just want you to leave.'

'Fucking hillbillies,' he muttered, grabbing his jacket. 'Don't worry, I'm leaving anyway.'

He began walking to the bus stop, whistling a tune that had been stuck in his head all day. He'd go into town, have a few pints there. Except he never got to the bus stop and he never made it to town. Barbara Caldwell, the library assistant from the next village, saw him at six the following morning. She was walking her dog, Bella. She liked to go through the woods. There was a path that took you all the way to Penlyn from Ambleside. It took her about forty-five minutes each way. She'd stop at the village shop for a gossip and then make her way back before getting ready for work. Bella had run ahead and was barking excitedly.

'What is it girl?' she called.

The sun was still low and she had to squint to see what was ahead. She stopped abruptly and opened her mouth to scream but it was as if an unseen hand was clutching her vocal chords, preventing them from working.

Peter Snell's body hung motionless from the branch of the old oak. Barbara fell back in shock, her hands reaching behind her to soften her fall. She closed her eyes, strained, and forced her vocal chords to release the scream that had been paralysing her.

He'd hung himself out of shame, they said. But one person knew better. He knew what really happened. He knew it was an accident, that they never meant it to go that far. It was meant to frighten him that was all. Make him leave the village. That's all they wanted to do. The police didn't take it further. It was suicide, plain and simple the inspector had said. No doubt the guilt and shame had taken its toll. His suicide note said it all. Yes, everyone agreed, good riddance to bad rubbish.

Chapter Six

It's a beautiful day and Hunters Moon is bathed in sunlight. There is an air of impregnability about the building. I ought to feel safe and protected here but I feel the opposite. I shiver and pull my woollen shawl around me.

'Are you cold?' Adam asks as he steers the car on to the gravel driveway.

'Just a chill,' I say looking up at the house. A removal van is parked outside and Jan rushes to greet us.

'It's a fabulous house,' she enthuses. 'I've just made everyone tea.'

'Great,' I say grabbing a couple of bags from the boot.

I stop and look at the security cameras on the wall.

'No one is going to come in here without us knowing,' Adam smiles.

Adam looks admiringly around the hall.

'Some grand paintings on these walls are what are needed.'

I look up at the dusty outlines where Gerard Meyer's paintings had been.

'We need to decorate first,' I remind him.

'You could have a painting party,' suggests Jan.

Adam grimaces.

'That's not one of your best ideas Jan,' he smiles.

'God, this place is amazing,' he exclaims, looking up to the large rectangle window on the first floor landing. 'What a shame I've got these bloody meetings in Brussels the next few days. I'd loved to have played around here with you.'

He laughs and squeezes me around the waist.

'We'll have to christen the place later.'

'Do you have to go to Brussels?' I ask, knowing full well what the answer is.

'If there was any way of getting out of it I would.'

'I know.'

I glance into the lounge where our two small couches look alone and isolated.

'Well, we certainly need more furniture,' I smile.

Four hours later and Hunters Moon is packed with my neatly labelled boxes. Jan and I find the ones marked *bed linen* and make up the bed in the master bedroom.

'It's funny making a bed that belonged to someone else,' Jan says. 'You never know what went on in it do you? Especially these celebrities, there were probably all sorts going on.'

I giggle like a schoolgirl.

'Jan, you make me laugh.'

'Well, you never know,' she says softly as if someone might be listening. 'Lots of babies could have been conceived on this bed. It might be lucky for you.'

'I hope so,' I grin.

Half an hour later and both beds made, Jan makes a final pot of tea.

'I'll see you on Friday,' she calls.

I look at a pile of unopened boxes. Adam joins me and whistles.

'Wow, where did all this stuff come from?'

'I've no idea,' I laugh.

'I'll phone for a takeaway,' he says, kissing me on the cheek. 'Apparently there are a couple of good ones in the next village. I saw one of the locals earlier. By the way, they have a village guild here. Maybe I'll join.'

I laugh.

'A bit country yokel for you, don't you think?'

'It might be useful. A bit like Robin Hood, *one for all and all for one*.'

'I thought that was The Three Musketeers,' I laugh.

'Ah, you could be right.'

I collect up the dirty mugs from the removal men and load the dishwasher. My eyes are drawn to the kitchen window and to the boathouse and lake beyond. I pull a notepad from my bag and make a list of things we need. Tomorrow I'll phone round and get quotes from decorators. I'll also make the first plan for our interiors. I feel a tingle of excitement.

'Chinese okay?' says Adam entering the kitchen and patting me on the bum.

'Great.'

'Fabulous to have our own little forest, isn't it?' he grins.

'Has Hunters Moon always had a wood?' I ask.

'No, the history of this place is fascinating. Apparently Marsham Wood belonged to Sir Blandward as part of his estate, Blandward House. We pass the house as we come into Penlyn. It's set back from the road. He got into a gambling debt with the owner of Hunters Moon, Colonel Maldwyn, in 1879 and couldn't afford to pay him, so he handed over part of his land. So we have a forest of our own. The colonel made the lake too by diverting the stream from Ambleside.'

I look at the lake thoughtfully.

'Are we safe here Adam?'

'Absolutely. The perimeter wall was built ten years ago. You can't get in, or out for that matter, unless you go through the gate. You don't have to worry.'

'Okay,' I say, feeling comforted.

'Right,' he says. 'I'll get dinner.'

There is a list of new emails on my phone. I quickly scroll through them and stop on one from an old client.

'I'm feeling excited about work,' I tell him. 'I'm going to start accepting commissions again.'

'Great. This house is going to be lucky for us,' he says, kissing me. He pulls back and I lick my bruised lips.

'That was intense,' I say.

'I feel exhilarated. I'm not sure about that bed upstairs though. I much prefer ours.'

'It's much bigger and just think when I'm pregnant I won't be bumping you out of bed. We can christen that bed after dinner. Make it ours,' I say huskily, kissing his neck.

'That's a date,' he grins.

*

It feels strange going up to a different bedroom and I can't help hankering for our little bedroom in the flat in Oxford. I find myself wondering if the new owners have moved in. Will they be making love tonight, christening their new home?

Adam touches my neck, making me jump.

'You're edgy,' he says. 'You're going to be okay here the next few nights on your own, aren't you?'

I scoff.

'Don't be ridiculous, of course I will be. I'm not a nervous woman, and besides, Laurie is coming over tomorrow night. I said I'd try cooking something on that old Aga.'

He switches off the light. Shadows from the night lamp dance macabrely on the wall.

'I want to fuck you,' he growls into my ear. 'I don't care what your ovaries are doing.'

He pushes me roughly on to the bed and pulls at my shirt. I hear it rip and let out a small gasp.

'Adam,' I say, but his hands are fumbling with the zip on my jeans. His lips crush mine and I fight back a cry as his teeth bite into my lower lip. Excitement overwhelms me and I moan as his lips move to my nipple. I stroke his hair and groan. He pushes my legs apart roughly and enters me forcefully. I gasp with the shock and go to wrap my arms around him but he pins then behind my head. I feel the tension mounting below and can barely control myself. Adam's thrusting is so hard that I can barely stand it.

'Adam,' I whisper, trying to free my arms. With one hand he grasps my breast as he continues to pound into me. He tenses and comes with a loud cry, and I wince as he pinches my nipple.

He finally rolls off me and groans.

'Christ,' he says, 'that was intense.'

My hands are numb where he had held them.

'You got carried away,' I say lightly.

'Sorry Flora, did I hurt you? I don't know what came over me.'

'It's okay,' I smile.

He pulls me into his chest and I listen to the beating of his heart. 'I felt overwhelmingly randy,' he apologises. 'I'm knackered now. I'll see you in the morning.'

He turns over and within seconds is snoring. I lean over to my handbag and pull out the novel I'd been reading. After plumping up the pillows I look around the room and up to the yellowing ceiling. It reminds me to phone the roofer tomorrow. The survey hadn't been that bad but it would be good to get the repairs done sooner than later. I fidget to get in a good position and feel my back twinge where Adam had thrust so forcefully. I look at him. His face is turned away from me but I know he looks boyish and innocent. I'd watched him often when he was asleep. I also know there is determination and strength of character behind the boyishness. The smell of roses takes my attention from the book. I snap my head up, stupidly expecting to see someone, but of course there is no one there. I close the book and open the bedside drawer where I keep the sleeping pills that the doctor had given me after my last miscarriage. It won't hurt to take one for the first few nights here, just until I adjust to the house. I swallow it and click off the lamp. The light from the moon cuts through a gap in the curtains, the rays slicing across the crisp white sheets. I close my eyes and, with the smell of roses around me, I fall asleep.

Chapter Seven

I blow my fringe out of my eyes and make a mental note to phone the hairdressers. I'd spent the morning unpacking and now seem to be in a worse muddle than before. The decorators and my favourite designer Cat Montbault had been booked and I was having great visions for our dream home. I had meant to talk to Adam about gardeners but he'd left so early that all I could muster was a sleepy, *have a good trip*. Perhaps I'll phone the estate agent and ask her about the gardener she mentioned. I may even be lucky enough to talk to Vikki. Where can she be? My back still niggles and I feel a tingle of sexual excitement at the memory of our love making. I lean back in my chair to rest it. The study is bare and the bookshelves empty. Boxes of our books are stacked on the floor. Maybe I'll sort through them after lunch. Feeling the need to stretch, I go to the kitchen where I had left my jacket. The cellar door catches my eye. The handle turns but still the door won't open.

'We'll need a handyman as well as a gardener,' I mutter.

The keys hang on a hook by the front door. I drop them into my handbag. I'll walk to the village. It will be nice to see what is nearby. We'd passed a little shop when we'd driven in yesterday. It will be interesting to see what they sell. Hopefully they will have painkillers for my back, and if I'm lucky some salad vegetables. I need some to go with the lasagne I'm making for Laurie and me later.

It's a warm spring day and I delight in the daffodils that line the driveway and remind myself to pick some on the way back. They will give the house a spring feel. At the gates I turn and look back at Hunters Moon. A little tingle of excitement runs through me when I realise the house is ours. I glance up at the windows and grimace at the heavy drapes that hang there. I'll ask Cat to bring her fabric swatches. The house is going to keep me very busy. I think about my appointment with Doctor Kingsley tomorrow and wonder if I should mention the ache in my back. It's not the first time I've felt it after sex. Something catches my eye, something at the window. I squint against the sun and feel myself turn cold, even though the sun is warm. There's a figure at the window. Someone is in the house. I rub my eyes and look again, but it's gone. There is nobody at the window now and I wonder if I had imagined it. Hurrying back to the house, I forget all about Adam's lectures on security and race upstairs to the bedroom. I fling the door open with my heart racing but no one is there. Could my vision have been a trick of the light? I convince myself that no one is in the house by searching room by room. I even check the door to the cellar, which is still stuck. Finally I unlock the French doors and go outside. The lake is still and the little rowing boat bobs at the side where it has been moored. I shake my head in annoyance. It's impossible for someone to get into the house. All the same, I decide to set the alarm when I go out. Adam did say we have to be security conscious now he is Home Secretary.

The boathouse looks desolate and bare now that everything has been removed. After locking the doors I turn back to the house, my eyes scanning the windows but the only thing reflected back at me are the clouds. I shake my head and go into the house locking the door behind me.

It's then I realise I'm not alone in the house after all.

Chapter Eight

I stare at the stranger in front of me.

'Sorry, the door was open,' he says casually.

'So, you just walk in?' I snap.

It's partly my fault. I shouldn't have left the gate open. He looks uncomfortable and shifts on his feet. He's wearing tatty jeans and a holey fisherman's jumper. His boots are worn and dusty.

'You're right,' he says. 'In my defence I did ring the bell and I called out. I figured as the door was open I could come in. That's village life ... anyway, sorry.'

'What do you want?' I ask, trying not to be too abrupt.

'I've got the van,' he says pointing behind him. 'I usually come round every fortnight with fresh veg, eggs and stuff, all organic. I'm Art Mitchell. I own Greengage farm. It's on the right as you come into the village. I knew the house had been sold and when I saw the sign had gone I thought ...'

'You'd chance your luck.'

'I wouldn't put it quite as mercenary as that.'

'How long have you been here?' I ask, thinking of the figure at the window.

'About five minutes. Anyway, seeing as you don't want anything, I'll be off.'

Realising that I'm being unfriendly, I say quickly, 'What do you have? I do need some salad.'

'Ah,' he says, brushing his hair back. He's good looking in a rugged kind of way. Different to Adam's clean-cut looks. 'I don't have salad. I've got milk, eggs, cream and rhubarb. Nice fresh rhubarb it is too,' he grins. 'You can make a rhubarb crumble. I've got butter. You can make your own custard with my eggs and cream.'

I smile.

'I'll take some.'

'Let me escort you to the van, madam,' he says bowing.

I laugh and follow him down the drive and outside the gates to his van. I turn and look back at the windows but there is no figure this time.

'Did you sell to the people who lived here before?' I ask.

He turns to me.

'Look, I should be honest. I've never sold much here. I was just curious as to who had moved in.'

'So you never met the previous owners?'

He shakes his head.

'I heard about their parties.'

'Parties?'

'Rave ups more like.'

'Oh,' I say surprised. 'Who do you sell to then?'

'The village shop and a couple of people on the outskirts of Penlyn, but don't worry about me. I make a good living. Penlyn is pretty self-sufficient. You'll find the shop has everything you'll need. But you can always give me a call if you need a pint of milk or a dozen eggs. Pop by if you're passing. Both me and the chickens are friendly. Greengage farm, you can't miss it.'

He pulls a creased business card from his pocket and hands it to me.

'Well, I'll need a dessert so I'll have some cream and rhubarb,' I say.

He puts everything into a bag for me and then salutes.

'It was nice meeting you ...' he raises his eyebrows.

'Flora Macintosh.'

He cocks his head.

'Ah, I thought you looked familiar. A bit of advice, I wouldn't go leaving the door open like that if I were you.'

I blush. He's quite right of course. If Adam found out he'd go crazy. *Security is our top priority* he keeps telling me.

'See you then,' he grins and climbs into his van. I watch him drive away and then continue into the village.

*

The April wind is chilly and I regret not bringing a scarf. It's eerily quiet apart from the sound of squawking crows. The smell of burning wood is comforting. I try to remember where I had seen the village shop. I stop to read the plaque on the chapel and find myself wondering how old Hunters Moon is. The village shop is ahead of me. A small group stands outside. They stop talking and part so I can enter the shop.

'Afternoon,' says a man with a pipe.

'Hello,' I smile.

The shop smells of aniseed. Jars of sweets line the shelves behind the counter. I'm pleased to see fresh vegetables in the far corner. A slightly overweight woman, who I guess to be in her sixties, beams at me.

'Good afternoon, what can I get you?'

'I want some salad, tomatoes, lettuce,' I say looking at the vegetable baskets.

'You've just moved into Hunters Moon, haven't you?' she says, her face lighting up.

'Yes, we moved in yesterday.'

'It's very nice for us to have a young couple in the village,' she smiles, 'isn't it Geoff? Our busiest day is pension day,' she laughs.

I turn to see the people from outside have entered the shop and are looking at me.

'We 'eard you'd moved in,' nods the man who I presume to be Geoff. 'Got a lot to do, 'aven't you?'

'Not really, just some decorating,' I say as I pick up a lettuce. I should have known a little village like this would have nosy parkers and not just one it seems.

'Seth can 'elp with the garden. He was doing it for the Meyers,' says one of the women. 'Of course, they 'ad professionals in every so often but Seth can maintain it. It's money for 'im.'

I'm about to ask who Seth is when the shopkeeper says,

'Got someone coming for dinner, have you? It's nice to have company when you're on your own.'

I spin round to face her.

'How do you know I'm on my own?' I say trying to keep my voice steady.

'Oh, I'm sorry love,' she says reaching out a hand to touch me. 'I'm Rhonda Earlswin. My husband Geoff and I own the shop. I saw on the news your husband was off to Brussels.'

I let out a sigh.

'Oh, of course, so you know who we are?'

'You can't miss those burly bodyguards when your husband is around.'

I'm almost wishing they were with me now. I feel edgy and nervous. I'll ask Doctor Kingsley if I ought to have my hormones checked again. That's probably all it is. The thought of Doctor Kingsley reminds me of my miscarriages and I feel myself blush profusely. No doubt they have read about that too in the village.

'But don't worry,' she adds. 'In Penlyn we look after each other. You have any worries you just pick up the phone.'

'Seth can pop round if you like?' says Geoff. 'Do you want us to ask 'im?'

'He doesn't speak,' says Rhonda. 'He knows what needs doing at Hunters Moon though.'

'Why doesn't he speak?' I ask curiously.

'Been that way since birth,' says Geoff.

'Can he write?'

They look at each other.

'He didn't get much schooling due to bullying, so he's not educated really. He's harmless though. You don't need to worry about him.'

'Oh I don't,' I say quickly.

'It would be helpful if he could pop round. I'm sure there are things he can do, especially with the Best Kept Village competition coming up.'

'Best Kept Village?' I say, impressed.

'We've won for the past five years,' boasts Rhonda.

'That's right,' agrees Geoff.

'We're proud of our village. No one lets the village down. Isn't that right Geoff?' says Rhonda.

Geoff nods.

'That's right. No scandal in Penlyn,' he smiles.

'We have a reputation to uphold,' Rhonda says looking closely at me.

'Well, we won't be causing any scandal,' I smile.

'Of course you won't,' says Geoff.

'Leave the girl to choose her veg,' says another woman who introduces herself as Myrtle. 'I live in Meadow Cottage, the thatched one by the church. I'll pop a *Penlyn Pen* into you. We have a lot of things going on in the village.'

'*A Penlyn Pen*?' I query.

'That's our village magazine.'

'That's very kind, thank you.'

Everyone seems to disperse and I'm alone again in the shop. I load my basket and ask for aspirin.

'Are they for you?' asks Rhonda.

I nod.

'My back hurts.'

'You don't want aspirin. That's not good for your insides. I've got a nice tea that will help.'

'That's very kind but I'd like the aspirin.'

'Tell you what, I'll give you both. Promise me you'll try the tea first.'

I smile.

'I promise.'

She hands me a carrier bag.

'Have you registered with the doctor's practice?' she asks.

I shake my head.

'Oh, I expect you have a private ...' she begins.

'No, not at all,' I break in quickly. 'Adam is very supportive of the NHS.'

'That's good. The surgery is only in the next village but Doctor Hemel lives in Penlyn. He's semi-retired now but he's the best. He sees to most of us here in the village.'

'I'll remember,' I say backing towards the door.

'If you need anything, just give us a call. Here's our number. Only me or Geoff answers.'

She jots it down on the side of a paper bag. I smile; I can't remember the last time someone wrote their phone number on a piece of paper for me.

'Don't be afraid to call.'

'We'll ask Seth to pop over. He's handy around the house and doesn't charge anywhere near as much as those professionals,' Geoff says.

'Thanks so much'

I set back to Hunters Moon and as I do I have the strangest sensation that eyes are watching me.

Chapter Nine

'Hello, is it possible to speak to Vikki?'

'Who's calling please?'

'It's Flora Macintosh.' I feel my spirits rise. At last I get to talk to Vikki.

'I'm really sorry Mrs Macintosh but Vikki is no longer with us.'

'Oh, when did she leave you? I've been trying to get hold of her.'

'I'm sorry I really can't give out those details. Is there any way I can help?'

'Apparently Vikki knew quite a lot about the house I bought from you. Do you not have her notes on record?'

'I'm afraid not. What house is it? I'll see if anyone else has the information you need.'

'I've already asked Sienna and she doesn't know. Is there any other way I can contact Vikki. Or could you ask her to contact me? You must have a number for her.'

'I'm really sorry but I'm not allowed to give out personal phone numbers.'

'Could you ask her to call me? I'd be very grateful.'

She hesitates for a moment.

'Yes, of course.'

'Thanks,' I say with a sigh. I decide there is no point asking about the gardener. I'll speak to Adam when he gets home. I click off my phone and go to the kitchen to put the kettle on. I see Rhonda's teabags in the cupboard and pull a face. I know they mean well but camomile and lavender really isn't my thing. I open the French doors and walk out to look at the lake. A flock of crows fly noisily overhead. The chill of the late afternoon gives me goose bumps and I hug my arms around me. The stillness is strangely deafening. It feels odd not to hear the bustle of Oxford or hubbub of London. The little boat, tied to its mooring, bobs on the lake. A shiver runs down my back. I have a strange sensation that someone is watching me. I spin around, but there's no one there. My shoulders tighten with tension as I check the windows, but there's nothing. What's wrong with me? I'm a total wreck. I decide not to tell Adam about the sensations I've been having. The last thing a candidate for Prime Minister needs is a neurotic wife. The house is spectacular from the rear. Its grey stone sparkles in the late afternoon sun. I notice some guttering has come loose and decide to ask Seth if he can fix it. An empty bird feeder swings eerily in the breeze. I must get some bird food, something else to remember when I do the grocery shop. A cloud covers the sun and a chill enters my heart as a terrible feeling of foreboding washes over me. A crow screeches over my head making me jump. I study the tatty garden furniture and find myself wondering if Gerard Meyer's sad wife had sat there in the sunshine, enjoying the view of the lake as I'm doing now. I'll ask Adam to get rid of the whole lot. I'll design a new layout for the patio. The ringing of my phone sends me hurrying back to the house. It's Adam and I have to fight back my excitement and relief when I answer it.

'Hi, it's me. How are things going?'

'Great, I met some of the villagers today.'

'That's good. Is Laurie with you?'

'She's coming over later. There's some lad named Seth who ...'

'Ah yes, I've heard about Seth. He can help out a bit, especially around the garden.'

'Okay, how are things with you?'

'It's okay. Meadows isn't going down too well, all good for me though. He's too bloody stubborn and arrogant and ...'

'Well, don't let him get your blood pressure up,' I warn. 'I'll be glad when you're home.'

'Only a couple more days, and I'll be there. I hope you're planning lots for the house.'

'Oh yes,' I laugh.

'Great, I'd better run darling. I've got loads to get through. I'll try and phone you later tonight, otherwise have a good time with Laurie. I love you.'

'Love you,' I say, stupidly feeling tears prick my eyelids.

I must ask Doctor Kingsley to check my hormones. I hang up reluctantly, wipe my eyes and turn to the kettle to make tea. It's then I see it. I let out a little gasp. The boat is now bobbing in the middle of the lake.

Chapter Ten

'Are you absolutely sure?' Laurie asks.

'Of course I'm sure. The bloody thing has been tied to the mooring from the moment we moved in. It was there when we viewed it and there when I measured up a week ago. It's never moved.'

'The wind must have loosened the rope and blown the boat across the lake,' says Laurie sensibly.

'Okay Columbo, so why has it stopped in the middle?'

'There must be a simple explanation,' she smiles before sipping her wine. 'Shall we go and look?'

I nod. I'd cowardly waited for Laurie to arrive before venturing outside again. She whistles as she admires the landscaped gardens.

'Wow, this is bloody brilliant. You can do wonders with this.'

'So everyone keeps telling me.'

Laurie looks spectacular in white slacks and a two piece emerald top. Her hair is silky smooth and hangs in soft waves about her face. I know I look weary. I'd planned on taking a shower before Laurie arrived but I'd been side-tracked by the boat and had almost forgotten to make the lasagne. I grab my glass of wine and follow her out.

'The housewarming party will be fabulous out here,' she enthuses. 'We could have floating candles on the lake. It will be divine. We must set a date for it tonight.'

I can't take my eyes off the boat.

'How can wind untie knots?' I ask as we get closer.

'If the knot was loose and it's been bouncing around in the lake. I'm all for you having a haunted house but I have to stay rational too,' she laughs as she leans down to study the rope.

'It's still knotted,' she says.

I let out a small gasp.

'But the rope has broken.'

I look down to where she is pointing.

'So that's what happened?' I say relieved.

'No ghost,' smiles Laurie.

'So, you think the feeling of doom I have is all in my head?'

'You have had two miscarriages. I'm not saying it's made you go loopy or anything but it must have upset your hormones. Christ, I feel like the whole world is going to come crashing down when I'm on my period. You haven't been yourself for a while now Flora.'

I feel like a weight has been lifted from my shoulders, although that doesn't explain the figure I saw at the window.

'I'll get dinner,' I say, heading back to the house. 'You enjoy the view.'

Maybe Laurie's right and my hormones are up the creek and my imagination is running riot. All the same, I decide to ask her to stay, just for tonight.

*

I uncork another bottle and fill Laurie's glass. The crystal sparkles in the light from the open fire. The room is warm and I am considering opening a window but am reminded of Adam's security concerns.

'Might as well,' Laurie says, accepting the wine. 'If I'm staying the night I might as well enjoy the good life. Adam sure knows his wine.'

She pulls her laptop from its bag and turns it on. I go to the kitchen and fetch the rhubarb crumble and home-made custard.

'I've got everything for your housewarming. Invitations, guest list, although I'm sure there are some you'll want to scratch off it,' she says taking a bowl from me.

'Wow that looks good. By the way did you get hold of that estate agent? Vikki someone?'

'Apparently she's left and she was the only one who knew the history of Hunters Moon. Can you believe that?'

'I guess they didn't want to step on each other's toes. Haven't you found out anything about it?'

'Only that Meyer's wife died and I'm just presuming it was here.'

She shivers.

'Christ, you kept their bed too didn't you?' she says aghast.

I drag my hair back and tie it with a band.

'Not the actual mattress, just the bedstead,' I laugh. 'Mind you, it brought the animal out in Adam.'

'Ooh, don't tell me any more,' she says, pretending to block up her ears. 'Maybe they had orgies and all kinds on it. Those actor types are known for it aren't they?'

The rhubarb crumble is delicious and I pile more into our dishes.

'They had parties apparently. I met a local farmer today. That's where I got the rhubarb from. His name is Art Mitchell. He heard about their parties but there's something else about the house, Laurie, something strange. I just don't know what it is. I don't believe in ghosts and that stupid stuff but I feel something. Not all the time but I feel it. I smell roses too, just occasionally and especially in our bedroom.'

The wind is building up outside and we listen to its soft wailing.

'Who's your nearest neighbour?' she asks.

'I'm not sure. But they seem a nosy lot here,' I laugh.

Laurie takes her bowl and moves to the fire.

'Let's finish this and then we'll research your Gerard Meyer.'

April 2016
Kerri

She didn't think she could take much more. It was all too much. Sometimes she thought it would be easier to face the truth.

She tried to forget he was there watching them and for a time she did and it was just like old times. The fun, the booze, the sex and for a while she was able to enjoy it the way she always had. And then he spoke.

'Kerri,' he said from above her. 'You like me taking you from behind don't you?'

Her stomach contracted in fear. Please God, not that. She looked up at Gerard; his eyes were vacant from the cocaine. She tried to plead with him but he pushed her head back on to his swollen penis. She wished for the old parties, anything but this. It reminded her constantly of Ben. From behind her she heard him unzip his trousers and had to fight down the nausea that threatened to engulf her. She tightened her muscles and looked up at Gerard.

'Gerard, please.'

'Jesus babe, don't stop,' he groaned.

He was too far gone she realised. He hardly knew what was happening. She tried to relax, tried to prepare herself for what was to come. The loud, pulsating music drowned out her screams.

'Oh yes,' he groaned from behind.

She grabbed Gerard's thighs as she felt herself torn apart. The slaps across her buttocks helped to stop her thinking about the other pain. Then he put his hand around her throat. She gasped and struggled to get her breath. It was too much, oh God, too much.

'Please Gerard,' she pleaded. 'Make him stop.'

Gerard's eyes filled with tears.

'Oh babe,' he whispered. His eyes reflected her pain. She knew he would make it stop if he could but then what would

their life be like? It wouldn't be a life, she knew that. They'd made their pact. One mistake, that's all it was. They had to pay. The alternative was far worse. But she didn't know how long she could live with this terrible guilt or how long she could take the punishment. She bit down hard on her lip until she tasted blood and then thankfully it was over, for this time, at least.

Chapter Eleven

'I recognise her from the photo,' I say.

Kerri Meyer's face smiles at us from the computer screen. She's wearing the hooped earrings I'd seen her wearing in the photograph that had been beside the bed.

'There's not much about her,' says Laurie. 'Kerri Wilson, late wife of the actor Gerard Meyer, well known for his role in Austin Creed's film *The Loner*. Kerri Wilson was an up-and-coming fashion model. It was rumoured that she had previously been a glamour model. It was reported that on May 12th 2016 Kerri Wilson at age 24, suffered a coronary at her home in Oxfordshire. She was alone at the time. A local doctor certified the death. Her husband found her body and described her death as the greatest tragedy of his life. Gerard went super stardom the following year. Rumours of sex parties involving the couple have always been hotly denied by the actor.'

'A local doctor,' I mutter, topping up the wine glasses. 'I wonder if that was Doctor Hemel.'

'No more for me,' protests Laurie putting a hand over her glass. 'I won't be able to see what I'm reading if I have any more.'

'According to Art Mitchell, they certainly had wild parties, but sex parties? That's something else isn't it?' I exclaim.

Laurie laughs.

'Adam obviously picked up the vibes in the bedroom.'

'She was so young,' I say studying her photo. 'Is there nothing else?'

'No, let's try another web page.'

I split open a bag of marshmallows and check my phone. I had hoped to hear from Adam but there are no messages.

'This one says pretty much the same thing,' Laurie says.

'What if you search for *Kerri Meyer and Hunters Moon,* we might find out more that way.'

But all that came up was that Gerard Meyer and his wife had lived in Oxfordshire. A further search of Gerard Meyer just produced hundreds of photos and news of his films. Hunters Moon didn't give any results.

'I wish Vikki would phone me,' I say, feeling exasperated.

'There must be some of the villagers who know the history of the house,' says Laurie. 'Why don't you ask them?'

I nod in agreement and then yawn noisily. The wine was making me sleepy.

'I'll make coffee,' I say.

The wind had got stronger and I could hear the loose guttering knocking against the roof.

'I'm glad you're staying,' I admit. 'I know it's only the guttering but …'

Laurie laughs.

'We'll both do a check of the house before we go to bed.'

I don't think that will reassure me but I don't say anything to Laurie.

*

I'm pulled on to the landing. I feel cold in my nightie.

'Laurie,' I say. 'Where are we going?'

She turns at the top of the stairs and I gasp in surprise. It isn't Laurie at all. The woman's features are blurry but I can see her eyes which are wide and appealing. I try to speak but no sound comes. She looks past me. I should get Adam, but where is Adam? I take a step forward.

'Why are you here?' I try to say but my mouth doesn't move. She stretches out her arm and it is then I see the man in the shadows. The woman looks at me hopefully and her hand reaches out towards me. She stumbles and I try to hurry forward to help her but my legs don't move. Her expression turns to terror as the man steps away from her. I watch helplessly as her body disappears down the stairs.

Terrifying screams echo throughout the house. I want to cover my ears so I don't have to hear them but I can't. Then he sees me. He grabs my arm and shakes me. I scream as he pulls me to the stairs.

'Flora, wake up,' Laurie says shaking my arm. 'You were having a nightmare.'

I'm suddenly thrust into the normality of our bedroom.

'It felt so real,' I say. 'I saw her fall down the stairs here at Hunters Moon. There was a man and ... Oh God, Laurie it was so vivid.'

'Christ, Flora.'

'I couldn't see the man's face. Oh God, Laurie, you don't think it's a premonition do you?'

'I think you have been through a difficult time.'

She lies down next to me and we listen to the wind whistling around the house. I fancy I can hear Laurie's heart pounding.

'When is Adam back?' she asks.

'Saturday.'

'You're staying with me until then. You're a nervous wreck.'

'I'll be fine. I really can't leave the house every time Adam goes away.'

I'm being ridiculous. The house has no more of a history than any other house. I've never believed in ghosts and I'm not going to start now.

'I can smell roses,' says Laurie.

'Finally I'm not the only one,' I say relieved.

She switches on the bedside lamp.

'There, that will help.'

We both laugh at how ridiculous we are. Two women in their mid-thirties too scared to be in the dark.

'We've frightened ourselves,' says Laurie. 'I think you should stop looking into things and focus on getting this place gorgeous. Check out puppies next week.'

I smile and lean over to my phone. It's flashing a message from Adam. *They've cancelled one of our meetings. I'll be home tomorrow.*

Relief washes over me and as Laurie rambles on about puppies I fall asleep.

Chapter Twelve

We stare at the boat from the French doors.

'How did it get back to the mooring?' I ask.

Laurie shrugs.

'I don't know. Maybe the wind blew it back.'

'You've got to admit it's ...'

'I'm sure there's a reasonable explanation,' says Laurie but I hear the doubt in her voice.

'I'll make some bacon butties I say.'

'That sounds brill but I really should get to the office,' she says, glancing at her watch.

'Now I've seen the grounds, I can plan your fab housewarming. You'd better invite the neighbours. It saves them complaining. Not that anyone is going to complain to the Home Secretary. Check out the invites I sent you. It's going to be great,' she says excitedly. 'We'll have candles everywhere and trestle tables by the lake. Have a think about music. I'll be in touch with Adam about security.'

'Thanks for staying,' I say, hugging her.

'No worries, but I'm glad Adam is coming back early. Don't forget to look at puppies,' she orders before kissing me. 'Good luck with Kingsley this afternoon and don't think about that stupid bloody boat. It's nothing.'

I watch her car disappear down the drive and close the front door. My eyes are drawn to the top of the stairs and I shudder at the memory of my dream. It had been so vivid. I close my eyes and try to remember the face of the woman in the dream. Had it been Kerri Wilson? No matter how hard I try I can't seem to get a clear image.

'Damn,' I mutter.

Sunlight streams in through the windows. I look at my reflection in the hall mirror. My face is drawn. Maybe Laurie is right, I need something to distract me. I'll look into getting a puppy as Laurie advised. I take a coffee into the study to check my emails. There's one from Cat offering to pop over on Saturday with her swatches and another from Kathleen James regarding one of my commissions.

Thrilled that you are able to take on a commission I'm free to meet next week if you're available.

I am about to open Laurie's invites when something catches my eye beyond the French doors. The boat is in the middle of the lake again.

*

The gate buzzer sounds, making me jump. A grey-haired man stands at the gate.

'Hello,' I say into the intercom.

'Mrs Macintosh? I'm Henry Dorcas. I live at Claremont Tower, although it's far from being a tower but it's big enough for me.' His voice is croaky like someone who smokes too much. 'I hope you don't mind me popping in. I'm the elder of the village guild.'

I hesitate and then say,

'Oh hello, please come up.'

He walks slowly up the driveway using a silver topped walking stick as an aid. I open the door. He smiles when he reaches me and holds out a hand.

'Hello, I'm Henry. I was hoping to see your husband.'

'He's in Brussels,' I say.

He clicks his tongue.

'Of course, I should have known. I don't keep up with politics too well I'm afraid. I won't bother you. I just wondered if you and your husband would like to come to dinner one evening.'

'I'll check the diary, please come in.'

He nods and steps into the hall. I fetch the diary and check Adam's movements.

'It occurred to me you might both need a little break from the unpacking.'

I smile. Adam hasn't done any unpacking but I don't say anything. We turn at the sound of a key in the lock.

'It's only me,' calls Jan. She nods at Henry Dorcas as she passes on her way to the kitchen.

'Are you free on Sunday?' he asks.

'I'll check with Adam,' I say. 'His diary looks okay but I can never be sure whether he'll be in London. He should be home tonight.'

'Splendid. Here's my number,' he says, handing me a slip of paper. 'I hope you can both make it. House at the top of the hill and shall we say 7.30?'

'Lovely, thank you.'

He lets himself out and I hurry to the kitchen.

'I've collected the shirts from the cleaners,' Jan says, hanging them on the back of the kitchen door.

'Great ...'

'Oh,' she says, looking out of the window, 'That boat's moving.'

I follow her eyes.

'Yes,' I say.

'I'll make a cuppa. Is there anything special for today?' Jan asks.

'I thought we'd sort the study, get those books on to the shelves. Maybe after that we can get the rest of the clothes into the wardrobe.'

'I bought some bird food,' says Jan. 'I'll put that out before we start.'

She opens the back door and steps back in surprise. Standing by the back door is a young lad. He has a card in his hand:

Hello. My name is Seth. I'm dumb. Do you have any jobs for me to do?

An Error of Judgement

He'd struggled to hide the shakes.

'A slight temperature,' he'd told those that had asked. Not that many did, why would they? None of them cared about him. They only cared about the kind words he used. The kind, insincere words in this case. Everyone knew the old bat had been as tight as a duck's arse.

'Molly Fincher was a generous soul,' he lied.

His clothes were sticking to his back. He didn't think he could hold out much longer. He should have taken care of things this morning. He looked up, forced a smile and continued his lies. Molly Fincher had been liked by nobody, least of all her family. He couldn't understand where all these people had come from. Molly's poker friends, no doubt.

'That was lovely,' Stella Fincher told him. 'They were beautiful things you said about mum.'

Insincere and hypocritical words, he thought.

'She deserved them,' he lied.

He felt unsteady on his feet.

'Do you have a virus? You're shaking from head to toe?' she asked.

'It's nothing, just a cold,' he said dismissively.

He thought they'd never go, but finally one by one they drifted off until he was alone. He took a deep breath before reaching into his rucksack. He ought to wait until he got home. He knew that. But he couldn't stand it. He noticed someone had left their jacket. He unzipped his rucksack. He'd be quick. But he wasn't quick enough. He was poised, ready, the hypodermic about to pierce his skin, the drug close to rushing through his bloodstream when he sensed someone behind him. He spun round, dropping the hypodermic but there was no one there. He sighed with relief and leant down to retrieve the needle. He studied it for a moment and then threw it into his rucksack before taking a clean one. Moments later he was in heaven and nothing seemed to matter. He slumped back in his chair and gazed through the open vestry doorway. He didn't notice that the jacket had now gone.

Chapter Thirteen

'Hello,' I say to Seth.

For some reason I had imagined him to be older.

'How did you get in, young man?' demands Jan.

He holds up another card with the gate security numbers on it.

'We have a few jobs you can do, why don't you come in,' I say pleasantly.

Jan's eyes widen.

'Flora,' she warns. 'You shouldn't let people in who sell things at the door.'

She stands between me and Seth. Adam's security lectures have certainly had an effect on her.

'It's okay Jan,' I smile. 'Seth has been helping at Hunters Moon for a while now. Adam knows about him.'

'Is it sensible everyone having the gate key number?'

'Don't worry; I'll speak to Adam about it.'

Seth looks nervously at Jan before stepping into the kitchen.

'Would you like some tea?' I ask.

He shakes his head. I try to gauge his age and figure he must be about twenty.

'I have juice if you'd like.'

He smiles and shakes his head again. I point at the boat.

'The boat has come loose from the mooring, do you think you can take a look at it?'

His watery blue eyes study me curiously. It's unnerving that he doesn't speak but his expression tells me he understands me. He points to some gardening tools he had left by the door.

'Oh yes, it would be great if you could clear the garden a bit,' I say. 'The cellar door is stuck too. Maybe you could have a look at it. I guess the front could do with a tidy if you have time. I want it kept nice for the Best Kept Village competition.'

Jan watches as Seth walks out to the lake.

'I still don't think it's safe to let strangers into the house. Villagers or otherwise,' she says. 'If I were you I'd change the number on the gate.'

'I don't want us to seem stand-offish just because Adam is a politician,' I say firmly and instantly regret my tone.

'Sorry Jan,' I apologise. 'I just don't want the villagers thinking we're uppity.'

She nods.

'Now, how about that cuppa?' I say with a smile. 'I need you to tell me all you know about Gerard Meyer and his wife.'

Jan, realising she is in for a good natter, reaches for the biscuit tin.

'I know he's a good actor,' she smiles.

'What about his private life?' I ask.

'His wife died. Heart attack I think.'

'She didn't fall down the stairs then?'

Jan raises her eyebrows.

'It wasn't big news but I'd have remembered that. I'm sure it must be on the internet.'

'Yes, I checked but there wasn't much.'

Jan looks thoughtful and then says,

'Don't think about it too much.'

'But she was so young to have a heart attack don't you think?'

'These people have too much if you want my opinion. Drugs probably, no doubt they put a strain on her heart.'

'And that's all you know?' I say, disappointed.

'I'm afraid so. Anyway you don't want to get bogged down with the lives of people who lived her before. You've got a future ahead of you. You need to make it your house now.'

I don't tell her that I think Kerri Wilson is haunting the house and for some reason she can't let go of it. I don't want her to tell Adam that I believe in that nonsense.

'Yes, you're right,' I say. 'Let's start by sorting out the study.'

I glance out of the window. The sun glistens on the lake and a sense of peace envelopes me.

'If you hear of anyone with puppies, Jan, let me know.'

'Goodness, you're not serious?'

'I think it will be nice to have a dog here.'

'A lot of mess if you ask me,' she grumbles.

I laugh and go upstairs. Adam will be home later and I'm feeling happy as well as relieved. Hopefully Doctor Kingsley will suggest something to calm down my crazy hormones and I'll stop having these insane thoughts of ghosts and hauntings.

Chapter Fourteen

Doctor Kingsley removes his gloves and beckons me to sit down.

'Thank you, Kim,' he says to the nurse.

She nods and leaves the room.

'You've had two miscarriages haven't you?' he says.

'Yes, the second one I carried for a bit longer.'

'When was your last period?'

'It's a bit confusing,' I say flipping through my diary. 'I had my period exactly twenty-eight days ago but it was very light and then I had another show two weeks ago. They've been a bit all over the place since I had the miscarriage.'

He nods and makes some notes in my file and then types something on to his computer.

'We need to do some blood tests to check what your hormones are doing. Have you considered IVF?'

I shake my head.

'Adam and I have discussed it. It's expensive and there's no guarantee is there?'

He nods in agreement.

'No guarantees, you're quite right. As for the expense, I think after what your husband did for our unit, we can overlook the expenses.'

I try not to look surprised.

'But first,' he continues. 'I need you to keep a temperature chart.'

'I'm doing that. I've done it since the miscarriage.'

He nods in approval.

'How stressed are you? Stress can play a huge part in this.'

I bite my lip.

'I'm a bit stressed,' I admit. 'Adam's job and ... well I find I'm alone a lot more now and I am a bit obsessed with the baby thing.'

He walks to the water dispenser and fills a cup.

'Here,' he says with a smile. 'I think we need to look at relaxation techniques, blood tests to check your hormone levels and I'd like you to have a scan so we can check your ovaries and fallopian tubes. Are you happy with that?'

I nod.

'Yes, thank you.'

'The important thing is to get you pregnant and that's when our work begins. Making sure that baby stays where we want it to stay.'

'I've had backache,' I say, suddenly feeling it's important to mention. 'I sometimes get it after sex.'

Should I also mention Adam's rough love making? I decide not to. It would be embarrassing for Adam.

'I don't think we need to worry too much about that. However, I would like to see you again after the scan and blood tests.'

I fidget uncomfortably in my chair.

'I don't want to ...'

'Jump the queue?' he smiles.

'Yes.'

'I have you registered as my patient. You can attend my Oxford clinic and this is my private mobile number and I want you to call me if you have any concerns.'

This is not being a patient, I find myself thinking. This is priority treatment. I feel qualms but squash them immediately. Surely my baby is worth this? The NHS is wonderful and, as an MP, Adam praises it constantly, but this treatment is something else.

'Thank you,' I say.

'Good. Now, the important thing is that you take it easy. Tell Adam that from me. No stress. Have you registered with a GP since you moved?'

'I have a GP in Oxford.'

'It's good to have a local doctor. Especially with your history and you won't get home visits if you're out of the area.'

'The villagers recommended Doctor Hemel.'

'I don't know him but I'm sure he's good,' he smiles. 'Just remember relaxation is the order of the day.'

'We were going to get a puppy,' I say stupidly.

'Sounds like a great idea,' he grins.

'Could my hormones make me highly sensitive to other things too,' I say, feeling stupid for asking.

'What kind of things?' he says, reclining in his chair.

'I don't know,' I shrug. 'I'm probably being silly. I just sense things in the house sometimes.'

He looks uncomfortable.

'Like what?'

I laugh, 'I'm just being hormonal.'

'Well, don't forget to call me if you have any concerns.'

I take the hand he offers me.

'Thank you so much,' I say, feeling emotional.

'Not a problem,' he smiles.

Chapter Fifteen

Hunters Moon looks glorious in the sunshine. The sun makes everything seem so much better. Adam is right. Hunters Moon is going to be lucky for us. The house is silent, as silent as a graveyard I think and feel a shiver run down my spine. The house smells of polish and disinfectant. Jan, no doubt, had a clean through after I'd left. I walk down the hallway hearing the sound of my footsteps tapping on the flagstones. From the kitchen I glance through the French doors to the boat and feel relief that it is tied to the mooring. The flower beds have been tidied by Seth. On the table is a note from Jan.

That lad was here for two hours. I didn't know what to pay him. I said you would sort things out. He seemed to understand. See you Monday.

I'd completely forgotten about paying Seth. I search in my handbag for Rhonda's number. It rings for ages and I'm just about to hang up when a breathless voice says,

'Hello, Penlyn village shop.'

'Oh, hi, it's Flora Macintosh, I hope I haven't disturbed you.'

'Is everything all right?' she asks anxiously.

'Oh yes, fine. Seth came over today.'

'Yes, I hope that was all right.'

'I don't know how to pay him. Stupid, I know. I had to go out and completely forgot.'

'Not to worry, you can drop it in to us. Its ten pounds an hour. Is that okay?'

'That's fine. Can he come again next week?'

'Of course, I'll speak to him.'

'That's great, thank you.'

'Lovely, you're coming to our little crochet group on Wednesday aren't you? Myrtle said she'd drop the leaflet in. It's a chance for us ladies to get together.'

'Erm ... well ...'

'Lovely, look forward to seeing you. We'll discuss the Best Kept Village competition. It will be lovely having you involved.'

She says goodbye before I can say more. I click off my phone and glance at the leaflet on the table.

Crochet afternoon for the ladies. Bring your hook and yarn and be prepared for a good natter. Village Hall, Wednesday at 2.00 pm.

I shudder at the thought and decide to make an excuse when I drop Seth's money in at the shop. Adam had texted to say he would be home about nine this evening. Tea made, I venture outside, glancing over my shoulder as I make my way to the lake. It's ridiculous. There's nothing odd about the house at all, and even the woods beyond seem less menacing in the late afternoon sunshine. I sit on a bench and enjoy the view.

I look at the opening that leads into the woods and can make out a path. A rabbit catches my eye as it hops among the trees and I decide to explore. I venture through the opening. The sun filters through the leaves and feels warm on my face. I marvel that all this is ours and wonder if Kerri Wilson had been happy here, and whether she liked to walk in the woods like this. A robin cocks his head to study me. I picture Adam and me having picnics here when the weather is warmer. The path forks and I continue, enjoying the feel of the soft ground under my feet and the dense smell of the woodland. My mind chases from one thought to another and I lose sense of time. We should get a puppy, he would love this. Laurie was right when she said the housewarming party would be amazing. We could hang lanterns in the trees. I should get involved in the village, maybe Henry Dorcas can tell me what goes on. There is no reason why I can't get pregnant again. I just need to relax like Doctor Kingsley said. The sun disappears behind a cloud and suddenly the denseness of the wood doesn't seem so inviting now that the sun has gone in. I have been so absorbed in my thoughts that I wasn't aware of how far I had come into the wood. I step on a twig and the snap scares a crow, and he squawks in the treetops. It feels chilly now that the sun has gone in, and dark under the canopy of the wood. I check my phone. I ought to get back and prepare dinner for when Adam gets home. I try to retrace my steps but it's not long before I realise that I don't recognise anything. There's a small flutter of panic in my stomach and I tell myself to stay calm. The house can't be that far away. I'd only walked for ten minutes or so, and I'd been going at a slow pace. I just need to get my bearings. The trees rustle in the wind and I button my cardigan. I must keep calm. Panicking will only make things worse and I have my phone with me. I check it and am comforted by the sight of the half-charged battery symbol but then see there is no signal and feel my stomach churn. I curse myself for being so stupid and coming into the wood alone. It's getting darker as the clouds thicken above me. It's then that I hear a crackling of branches and I spin round. Someone else is in the woods. I'm not alone.

Chapter Sixteen

There shouldn't be anyone in this wood. I strain to hear movement but now I hear nothing. I know I didn't imagine it.

'Hello,' I call.

My voice is carried on the wind. I'm about to call out again when I hear a loud crack. It's quickly followed by another and then someone shouts.

'Leave it Bryn.'

'Hello,' I shout.

I continue along the footpath, which is overgrown with nettles that sting my ankles. It's as I enter a clearing that I see him. He's throwing rabbits into a sack. I let out a small cry. He hears me and turns around, his rifle pointing towards me. His dog barks, its tail wagging excitedly.

I reel back. The man's shirt is stained with blood and I suddenly feel nauseous.

'What the hell are you doing here?' he asks gruffly.

Anger takes over my fear. I nod towards his rifle and say angrily,

'It's none of your business what I'm doing here. You however, are trespassing on my property. I'd appreciate it if you would put that rifle down.'

He pales and lowers the gun.

'Sorry,' he grunts.

'I hope you have a permit for that?' I say, trying not to look at the dead rabbit on the ground. Two ferrets fidget in a cage next to him.

'Rabbits are pests,' he says defiantly. 'Everyone knows that.'

'That doesn't mean you have the right to trespass on private property.'

I look at him and try not to stare at the hair lip that stands out red and disfigured on his face.

'How did you get in?' I ask.

He lets out a short laugh.

'From Chatterpie Lane, I came through the gate. Meyer gave me a key.'

I hold out my hand.

'I'd like that back please.'

He looks angrily at me and finally drops the key into my hand.

'It's only a few rabbits,' he grumbles. 'Meyer liked them kept under control.'

'I'll see you to the gate,' I say, knowing I can easily find my way back to the house from the road.

He grabs his sack and we both look at the dead rabbit on the ground.

'You'd better take that one seeing as you and your ferrets slaughtered it,' I say, fighting to keep the emotion from my voice.

He bags the rabbit and then ties a lead on to his dog. Without a word he marches ahead of me. I have difficulty keeping up and several times stumble on the uneven pathway. We reach the gate and I follow him out, locking it behind me with his key. I recognise where I am and feel relief at knowing that Hunters Moon is just a short distance around the corner.

He dons a cap and says,

'So, you still want me to do the garden?'

There's a smirk on his face and something else. Something I can't quite fathom but it makes me uncomfortable.

'Your 'usband phoned, said you'd still like me to come and keep the gardens right.'

'You're the gardener?' I say, surprised.

He nods.

'Meyer let me into the woods,' he says, 'to keep control. It's a jungle otherwise.'

'I'm not Mr Meyer,' I say firmly. 'I assure you that neither I nor my husband approve of poaching.'

'It ain't poaching when you 'ave a key,' he says. 'We don't call each other names in Penlyn.'

'You don't have a key now, do you?'

He grunts and walks off but not before calling over his shoulder,

'I'll be over on Thursday then, like I told Mr Macintosh.'

Chapter Seventeen

'I'll have a word with him,' says Adam. 'Make sure he doesn't have another key. I'm not happy about someone strolling through our property. I'll get the gate keypad changed. The estate agent should have taken back all the keys. It's annoying. But don't make enemies in the village, after all, that kind of thing goes on all the time in the country. They think nothing of catching a rabbit for a stew.'

'Well, I don't want it going on in our own back garden,' I say forcefully.

'I agree with you, but we don't want to cause any upset.' Adam says, leaning back in his chair.

'I didn't like his attitude. He unnerved me. I'm not sure I want him as our gardener. Why can't Seth do the grounds?'

'Because Seth isn't a gardener, that's why. He'll probably pull up all sorts of things thinking them weeds. He's okay for tidying up and doing the odd job around the place but we need a landscape gardener to keep on top of it. Henry knows him so I'm sure he's okay.'

'Well, I don't want him,' I say stubbornly. 'I don't care if Henry knows him or not.'

Adam pushes his plate away.

'Christ Flora, don't you think I've got enough on my plate without having to come home to this? I thought I could leave the house to you. I had it in my head this would be good for you, something for you to focus on instead of temperature charts and nurseries. I'm not happy about some stranger coming on to the grounds either. At least Earl knows the place.'

His words sting and I stand up to clear the table.

'I'm sorry,' I say feeling hurt. 'I didn't realise I was just the little lady of the house and stupidly I thought having a baby was important to both of us.'

I crash the salad bowl against my plate and storm into the kitchen. I shove the crockery into the dishwasher and slam it shut. Adam follows and hands me a glass of wine.

'I'm sorry,' he says, taking my hand. 'It's been a bugger of a few days and Ralph is being stubborn as usual. There have been murmurs from the cabinet. It's not the best time.'

'Oh,' I say, still feeling small pangs of irritation at his attitude towards the gardener. 'Will it be okay?'

'I don't know. Look, can we just let Earl, the gardener, come and see how you find him. You got off on bad terms. He won't be in the woods again will he? Not now you've taken his key and I'll make sure he doesn't have another.'

'Okay,' I agree reluctantly.

The last thing I want is for us to fight over the gardener. It's far from conducive to my getting pregnant. As though reading my mind, Adam hugs me and says,

'Remember what Simon said. You have to be relaxed. Cultivate a calm attitude.'

I smile.

'Let's have dessert. I've got some home-made crumble left over. I bought the rhubarb from a local farmer.'

'Cool,' he smiles.

'Don't forget our dinner on Sunday with Henry Dorcas,' I remind him.

He grimaces.

'We may have to rearrange. I've got a feeling all this stuff with Ralph is likely to blow up over the weekend. I'll probably be in London.'

'Oh no,' I groan.

'You knew it would be like this, Flora.'

'I know,' I say.

'I could go back to law but I don't think we'll do quite as well.'

'Not so many perks you mean,' I say cynically.

'It has its upside and its downside,' he says.

I take a long sip of wine and say,

'It doesn't seem fair that I'm given priority treatment though, especially when you always talk about how wonderful the NHS is. '

He shakes his head.

'For Christ's sake Flora, I'm doing it for our baby. Simon Kingsley is the best.'

I feel a pang of guilt and put my arms around him.

'I'm sorry,' I say. 'I'm just disappointed you won't be around at the weekend.'

'I'll be home on Monday. Chances are I will be here the weekend but I don't want to cancel at the last minute. I'll phone Henry and arrange another date.'

'I'll make coffee,' I say.

'I'll be in the study,' Adam says, putting his bowl into the dishwasher.

I turn on the radio and start clearing the table. I can smell roses again. It's very faint and around the French doors. I can hear Adam talking on the phone and sigh. I'll phone Laurie, see if she is free to go shopping tomorrow. I'll talk to Adam about the housewarming party tonight and then Laurie and I can get it planned. I pull the curtains and then I see it, a small stain on the wooden doorstep. It looks like something must have got spilt there and dried leaving a stain. Kerri Wilson must have spilt some perfume. A sense of relief envelopes me. That's all it is. There are no ghosts or mysteries in the house. I make tea and take a mug into Adam.

'I've phoned Henry. We've rearranged for Monday. That's okay with you isn't it?'

I fight back my irritation. Adam could have checked with me first.

'Fine,' I say, remembering Simon Kingsley's advice not to get stressed.

'I'm going to do some work on a commission,' I say. 'I'm behind with getting it off to them.'

'Great,' he says, glancing through some papers.

'I found the source of the rose smell,' I say kissing him on the cheek.

'Good,' he says but I can tell he is side-tracked.

'I'm going to work in the kitchen,' I say.

He pulls me on to his lap.

'I love you,' he says. 'Sorry for not being as attentive as I should.'

'I love you too.'

In that moment I felt sure everything was going to be perfect. I couldn't have been more wrong.

Chapter Eighteen

Malcolm came early the next morning to collect Adam for an emergency cabinet meeting. Adam suggested I go to London with him.

'We can go to the opera in the evening,' he'd offered but I knew it wouldn't happen. It never did. As soon as we get to Westminster he'd disappear for his meeting and then something else would come up and he'd cancel our arrangement and I'd be stuck in the London flat feeling alone and fed up. It had happened numerous times in the past and I knew from here on things were only going to get worse.

'I'll stay here,' I'd said. 'Hopefully you'll be back by the evening.'

'Most likely,' he'd said, sorting papers in his briefcase.

'Cat's coming over today anyway. We'll be busy looking at curtain material and whatnot. It's just as well you're going to be in London,' I'd laughed.

But now he'd gone I find myself missing him terribly and although I had convinced myself yesterday there was nothing odd going on I couldn't shake off the feeling that I somehow wasn't alone in the house. I turn on the television and switch to the BBC news channel. The sun is shining and I'm about to open the French doors when I'm stopped by the sound of footsteps on the stairs. My hand freezes on the door handle and my breath catches in my throat. I strain my ears but everything is now silent again. The only sound comes from the television where the newsreader is talking about a flood in the Philippines.

'Adam, is that you?' I ask nervously, walking slowly into the hall. Had Adam forgotten something and rushed in without calling to me? I peek around the living room door.

'Adam?' I repeat.

The front door is closed. I look up to the stairs but there is no one there. A quick glance at the security cameras tells me there is no one outside and Adam's car isn't in the driveway. I have the feeling that someone is behind me, watching me. I spin round with such speed that I almost lose my balance and have to grab the front door for support. There's no one there.

'Adam?' I say quietly, but he isn't here. I know that. With a racing heart I hurry to the kitchen and grab my mobile. Laurie answers on the third ring.

'The house is haunted,' I say without preamble. 'There were footsteps on the stairs. I heard it as clear as anything.'

'Christ,' she mutters. 'Try and calm down Flora, you sound frantic.'

'I am calm,' I say sitting at the kitchen table. 'I heard someone in the house but there's no one here. The front door is closed. All the doors are locked but I heard someone on the stairs, I know I did. I'm not imagining it.'

She's silent for a moment.

'Laurie?' I ask.

'You've been under a lot of pressure Flo,' she says softly. 'A lot happened at once.'

'This isn't stress, I'm sure of it.'

'I can't come over until this evening,' she says apologetically. 'I've got a client in half an hour. She could only do a Saturday. Has Adam left?'

'He's on his way to London. I can't tell him this otherwise he'll think I'm losing my mind. Cat will be here soon. We're going over interiors. I think the spirit of Kerri Wilson is in this house.'

'I'll bring my Ouija board,' she says excitedly.

I shudder.

'Is that safe?'

'Of course it's safe.'

'Okay,' I say doubtfully. 'But only if Adam isn't home. There is no way he'll let me have a séance if he's here.'

'We don't have to tell him,' she argues, 'but okay. Anyway, it's probably a mouse.'

'Big mouse,' I say. 'See you later.'

I click off the phone and slowly walk upstairs. I can't help thinking the footsteps I'd heard were connected to my dream. The house is silent except for the sound of the television. Was the noise from outside and not actually in the house at all? I look out of the window but everything is still. I look down at my little Vauxhall Corsa and see I have a flat tyre.

'Damn,' I mutter. At that moment a red sporty Mercedes pulls up at the gate. I let out a sigh of relief at the sight of Cat. I run down the stairs, push the entry gate button and fling open the front door as her car comes up the driveway.

'God,' says Cat, 'This house is something isn't it? Fancy you living in a film star's house. What with this and moving into Number Ten when Adam is Prime Minister, wow is all I can say.'

'Well, that's unlikely,' I say interrupting her.

'What's the emergency cabinet meeting about then, or aren't you allowed to say?' she asks, handing me a bottle of wine.

'Is it on the news?' I ask.

'Yeah, just now.'

'It's probably nothing,' I say casually.

'Wow, what a great hallway,' she enthuses as she steps inside the house. 'This flagstone floor is fabulous, and I love that chandelier.'

'We have a lake and a wood,' I say. I almost add 'and a resident ghost'.

'I'll put the kettle on.'

She follows me into the kitchen and strokes the Aga.

'Fabulous, can I look around?'

'Sure, feel free.'

She opens the French doors and wanders out.

'Love the lake,' she calls.

I turn to the window to see the boat bobbing in the middle of the lake and my mouth turns dry.

Chapter Nineteen

'You're being ridiculous, Flora. We've only just bought the place. You've got to get used to the noises that's all. They'll be a simple explanation I'm sure. You know damn well there are no such things as ghosts. Get Seth to fix a new mooring. There's probably something loosening it, that's all.'

'I know what I heard, Adam.'

'I don't know what you expect me to do from London,' he says, irritation clear in his voice.

'I think there is something strange about how Kerri Wilson died and …'

'She had a heart attack, you told me.'

'Yes, but …'

'Flora, I thought you were going to stop this.'

'Stop what?'

'Stop poking around the house. There's nothing strange going on. The boat isn't trying to tell you something.'

'Well I'm here and I know what I heard,' I repeat.

'Flora, I can't talk for long, especially about this. Things are really difficult here. I've all kinds breathing down my neck. The backbenchers are calling for a vote of no confidence. We could be close Flora.'

'Close?' I repeat in a whisper.

'I think he might resign. You know what that means.'

'So soon? I thought it was some way off.'

'We need to be ready. I'll phone you ahead of any announcement.'

'But the house, Hunters Moon …' I begin.

'It will be our haven,' he says. 'Please don't get bogged down with stupid ideas of hauntings and silly things like that.

I don't want the press to pick up on stuff like that. You'll be in the public eye, you do realise that don't you?'

'I know. I'm sorry.'

'Anyway, I'll be back tomorrow all being well. If not you can always come up to London.'

'Laurie's coming over,' I say.

'Good, so you won't be alone tonight then?'

'I'm not asking her to stay,' I say firmly. 'I'm not a child.'

'Are you sure you don't want to come to London. We could do something over the next couple of days.'

'I'm fine. I hate London, you know that.'

'Okay, I'll miss you.'

I hang up after telling him I love him. I watch the news until Laurie arrives with her Ouija board. I've lit the candles in readiness and opened a bottle of wine. I expect Doctor Kingsley wouldn't be too impressed with my drinking, but it helps to calm me and if I'm honest the noise on the stairs did unnerve me a bit.

'After an emergency cabinet meeting today there has been silence from ministers. An announcement was expected from the Prime Minister but so far the doors of Number Ten have stayed firmly shut,' the newsreader announces.

I pour the wine into a glass and take a large gulp. I'm not ready to be a Prime Minister's wife. I take the glass and go upstairs to change. I study myself in the wardrobe mirror. I need to gain some weight. I pull up my long blonde hair and fiddle with it, finally tying it back in a hairband. I check my wardrobe to see what I can wear if I have to rush down to London to be with Adam. I know there'll be a photo call and I don't want to let him down. I pull off my jeans and jumper and look critically at my naked body. My small breasts are firm and I cup them in my hand. I fight back the memory of when they were full and the nipples hard a few months ago in the first months of my pregnancy. I take a deep breath and pull a blouse from the wardrobe. Laurie will be here soon with her Ouija board and I feel a small tingle of apprehension. Will we be able to summon up the spirit of Kerri Wilson? I shake my head. How stupid. Of course we won't because the spirit of Kerri Wilson doesn't exist. I pull my jeans over my hips, grab a cardigan and hurry downstairs to prepare a salad. Laurie arrives two hours later and I hurry to answer her buzz at the gate.

'Ta da!' she declares, holding up a box. 'One Ouija board, let's go ghost hunting.'

Chapter Twenty

'Should we do it where I thought I heard her?' I ask nervously.

Laurie sips her wine and looks around the living room.

'Have you sensed her in here?'

I shake my head.

'I guess the boat is where her presence is strongest,' I say with a shiver.

Laurie huffs.

'I'm not having a séance out there in the dark with the woods behind us. Jesus, that's too creepy for words.'

I nod in agreement. The truth is, simply having a séance in Hunters Moon is too creepy for words.

'The hallway or the bedroom then, it was the hallway where I heard the noise and the bedroom where I smell the rose fragrance most.'

'Let's do it in the hallway,' says Laurie, picking up the board and her glass of wine. I follow with the candles and a coffee table for the board.

It feels chilly in the hall. I look at Laurie.

'Do you think this is a bad idea?' I ask.

'It can't do any harm can it? Something's moving that bloody boat and scaring you shitless.'

I nod.

'Right,' she says settling the board on the table.

'Are we supposed to have something belonging to her?' I ask.

'I think it helps but seeing as we don't ...'

'Can you smell the rose fragrance?' I ask.

'No,' she says, after taking a sniff. 'We should have the light off,' she says.

I switch off the light. The hallway is lit by the flickering candles and the moonlight that filters through the small pane in the front door. Eerie shadows move on the walls around us.

'Ready?' asks Laurie.

'I'm so *not* ready,' I say with a nervous laugh.

Laurie takes a deep breath.

'How do you know how to use it?' I whisper, although I'm not sure why I'm whispering.

'YouTube,' she replies.

We burst out laughing and it somehow eases the tension.

'Let's do it,' she says, placing two fingers on the pointer.

Laurie looks up at me. I exhale and place the two fingers of my right hand on it too. My eyes stray to the stairs, although I don't know what I expect to see there.

'Clear your mind,' Laurie instructs.

I close my eyes and attempt to still my thoughts.

'Ouija, are you there?' says Laurie in a spooky voice.

I feel my hand tremble and check it hasn't moved the pointer. She opens one eye and looks at me.

'Are you concentrating?'

'I'm trying to,' I say, my voice hoarse.

'Ouija, are you there?' she asks again, raising her voice slightly.

I feel the pointer move beneath our hands and gasp. Laurie's eyes snap open.

'Don't move your hand,' she instructs.

'We want to communicate with Kerri Wilson. Can you talk to us Kerri?'

The candle flickers and seems about to go out but then the flame continues.

'It's the draught from under the door,' I whisper, feeling it on my bare feet.

Laurie glances at the door and then back to the board.

'Kerri, can you talk to us?' she repeats.

Nothing happens and I'm about to pull my hand from the pointer and call it a night when it suddenly moves beneath our fingers.

'Shit,' mutters Laurie.

'What's happening?' I ask.

'Is that you, Kerri?'

The pointer moves and I watch in amazement. We hold our breath in unison. The pointer is moving slowly towards a letter.

'Can you communicate with us Kerri?' asks Laurie in a trembling voice.

My shoulders ache from where I have hunched them. Suddenly, there is a bang and the front door swings open. I scream and Laurie jumps back knocking the board off the table. The hall is flooded with light and a figure materialises in the doorway. For a second it feels like my heart stops.

'Jesus!' cries Laurie.

'What the hell's going on?' Adam demands.

Chapter Twenty-One

'For Christ's sake Flora, what the hell did you think you were doing?'

'I just ...' I falter. 'I don't know ...'

'Communicating with the dead,' he scoffs, pulling off his shirt. 'Jesus Flora, I thought you had more sense. It doesn't surprise me that Laurie is into that stuff, but you ...'

'Okay Adam, you've made your point.'

He shakes his head and sips from his whisky glass.

'I spoke to Henry about Earl the gardener. He understood you being upset. He doesn't want bad feeling between people in the village though and said he will speak to Earl and make sure he has no other keys.'

I wipe the cleansing milk from my face and turn to him.

'Why are you talking to Henry? What's it got to do with him?'

'He's the elder of the village guild. He maintains harmony in the village. It seemed the best route to take. Keep everything diplomatic Flora. We don't want any shame on the village. It's got a good reputation.'

'It's a bloody country village,' I snap, 'not the bloody House of Commons.'

'Why are you always having a go at me Flora? It's like nothing I do is right any more.'

'It's this bloody house,' I say, pulling back the bedcovers. 'That sodding boat that keeps moving and ...'

'I wish you'd stop talking to Laurie. Her nutcase ideas have rubbed off on to you. There's nothing strange happening in this house and if you mention that bloody boat again I'll chop it up for firewood. There aren't any ghosts, when you're dead you're dead, we both believe that. As for noises, it's an old house.'

I open my mouth to tell him about the figure at the window and then change my mind.

'Okay, whatever you say.'

He drains his whisky glass.

'Flora,' he pleads. 'You're supposed to be taking things calmly. I love you and I don't want to see you in this state. I've got a lot on my plate right now.'

I feel a twinge of guilt.

'I'm sorry,' I say climbing into bed. 'How did it all go this evening?'

'Ralph wormed his way out of it again. He's talking to Brussels in the morning to smooth over his cock-ups. The cabinet are backing him, God only knows why. Everything's a mess.'

'I've not been following things, Adam, I'm sorry.'

'You just focus on yourself okay?' He says, wrapping his arms around me. 'I've arranged for a locksmith to change the locks on Monday and to set a new code for the gates.'

I watch as he removes the St Christopher from around his neck and places it in the jewellery case on the dresser.

'You found it?' I say.

He nods and climbs into bed beside me.

'Our luck will be okay now,' he smiles. 'You have to stop being so anxious.'

'Okay,' I say snuggling up to him. His hand strokes my thigh and I feel an ache well up in my loins.

'God, I'm glad I came home,' he says nuzzling his face into my neck. 'Let's make this bloody baby.'

I wrap my arms around him and force myself to forget Kerri Wilson.

*

The bedroom door slowly opens. I sit up in bed. Adam is sleeping soundly beside me. Then I see her, beckoning to me.

She wants me to go out on to the landing. I hesitate for a second and then step from the bed. I open the door wider and see her at the top of the stairs her hand reaching out to me. Her face is in the shadows. I can smell roses. The fragrance is overpowering me.

'Kerri,' I whisper, 'is that you?'

She strokes her hand over her stomach and longing stabs me in the heart. Oh God, is she pregnant? Then I see him in the shadows. He steps towards her and I open my mouth to scream. I know what is going to happen and can do nothing to stop it. She reaches to him but he steps away from her, his shoulders hunched. I gasp as she stumbles and then watch helplessly as her body bounces down the stairs like a rag doll. He stands still for a moment. I open my mouth to scream but my lips are sealed together. The man begins to turn. He will see me. And then I am at the foot of the stairs. The front door flies open and wind blows through the house. I'm sent reeling back and my mouth finally opens. I begin to scream.

'Flora, for Christ's sake, Flora.'

I wake with a start. My heart is hammering in my chest. Adam leans over me and I push him away, the remnants of the nightmare still in my mind. He grabs my hand.

'You were dreaming.'

I wipe the perspiration from my forehead.

'Sorry,' I say weakly. I throw off the bedcovers and let the cool air flow over my feverish body.

'Go back to sleep,' I say gently. 'You need your rest. I'm going to make some tea.'

He nods and turns over. I step out of bed and cautiously open the bedroom door. The house is silent and I turn on the landing light. I stand at the top of the stairs and wait, as though something may materialise, but nothing does. I walk down them and turn on all the light switches so the house is flooded with light. The house is silent. I take a cup of tea into the study and pull out my laptop. There surely must be something online that will tell me more about Kerri Wilson.

The search brings up the same web pages that Laurie had found. I type in Kerri Wilson, model and scan the results. It's not until I reach page four that the agency she worked for comes up. Surely they will have some information about her. A tingle of excitement runs through me. I'll phone them on Monday.

Chapter Twenty-Two

The decorators arrive on Monday along with Cat and I forget about phoning the agency. Adam left for his constituency clinic and promised to be home that evening unless there was news from Parliament. I spend the day choosing wallpaper with Cat. The house is full of noise and I find myself craving the peace and quiet that is familiar with Hunters Moon. Cat spends much of her time on her mobile ordering curtains and bed linen. At about two in the afternoon we make sandwiches and take them to the boathouse.

'The house is divine Flora,' Cat says. 'I mean, it's just a dream.'

'Do you believe in ghosts?' I ask, pouring juice into glasses.

She laughs.

'You're not going to tell me the house is haunted are you?'

I shrug.

'Laurie came over with her Ouija board on Saturday,' I say slightly shamefaced.

'God, you're joking aren't you? They're bloody dangerous things you know.'

'Do you think I'm mad? It's just that boat keeps coming away from the mooring and drifting to the centre of the lake. It's like it's trying to tell me something. Also, I heard footsteps on the stairs and I keep dreaming someone fell down them.'

'Oh Flora, you must not forget you have had a rough time the past year. There were your miscarriages and then all that's happened to Adam. You're probably hypersensitive,' she says taking my hand.

I sigh.

'That's what Laurie keeps saying.'

'Because it's true.'

'I know. I just wish Adam was at home more.'

'You knew it was going to be difficult when Adam became Home Secretary, Flora.'

She's quite right. I knew from the outset exactly what things would be like if Adam were to realise his dreams. I also want my dream of having a child.

'Have you been in the boat?' she asks, looking out of the window.

'No, I haven't had time,' I say.

'Well lets go in it now, come on, it will be fun,' she enthuses, pulling me outside.

'It doesn't leak,' she laughs stepping into it. 'That's a good start.'

I laugh with her and feel a sense of relief. There is nothing strange or spooky about the boat. As I step in the boat rocks and I grab the side to steady myself.

'Whoops,' she laughs.

She bends and picks something up from the bottom of the boat.

'Here, you dropped your perfume. Oh, what a shame, the top's broken.'

She hands me a beautiful shaped bottle.

'This isn't mine,' I say turning the bottle over in my hand.

'It ought to be. It's gorgeous. What is it?'

My hands smell of roses. The atomiser has come loose and I tighten it. There is a little bit of perfume left in the bottle. I study the label.

'Rose Oud by Kilian, have you heard of it?'

'No, but it's gorgeous. If it's been leaking, that explains why you can smell roses.'

I sniff the bottle. It's the same rose scent that I had smelt in the house.

'If it's not yours, whose is it then?' she asks.

Kerri Wilson's I think, but say,

'I don't know, maybe the woman who lived here before.'

'She's got great taste.'

'The handyman fixed the cellar door. Let's see what we can find in there,' I say, feeling unusually confident being with Cat.

'Sure,' she smiles. 'Why not, seeing as I have my old rags on. Let's see what magic we can work on the cellar. At least you've got the perfect place for storing booze for the party.'

Any remnant of the scent of roses has been replaced by the smell of fresh paint in the house. I place the perfume bottle on the kitchen counter and then check my phone to see there is a text from Adam,

Beautiful day, Henry phoned, said he thought he'd have a barbecue and maybe invite some others from the village as well as us. He wanted to check we were okay with that. I said it would be fine.

I pull a face.

'Everything okay?' asks Cat.

'Yes, just Adam wants to go to a village barbecue tonight.'

'Sounds like fun.'

'This village is a bit too intense if you want my opinion,' I groan,

I turn to see Cat struggling with the cellar door.

'It's a bit bloody stiff isn't it?' Cat says pushing against it.

'It should be okay now. I asked Seth to fix it.'

I try the handle and push but the door still won't budge.

'Perhaps he didn't do it after all,' I say disappointed. 'That's a shame.'

'Oh well,' says Cat wiping her hands. 'Let's sort these drapes out.'

I follow her into the living room glancing back at the cellar door. I was certain I had asked Seth to fix it. I wonder why he didn't.

Chapter Twenty-Three

It's a warm evening. I'd chosen a light blue cotton dress and topped it with a cream cardigan. I'd realised just as we were leaving that I'd forgotten to put perfume on and quickly spray my neck with the remains of the rose perfume that I had found in the boat and left on the kitchen counter.

Tweedledee and Tweedledum follow us in the Range Rover to Henry's house, Claremont Tower. There are a few other cars outside and music drifts over from the back garden. Adam seems relaxed. If he is feeling any pressure from the recent upsets with Ralph, he isn't showing it. I slide my arm through his and he squeezes my hand.

'Has he asked a lot of people?' I ask.

'Only a few from the village I think.'

Tweedledee and Tweedledum station themselves at the front of the house and Adam leads me along the pathway. It isn't a tower at all. In fact, it isn't at all grand like I'd imagined it would be. I'd been expecting a much larger house.

'Excellent, you made it,' Henry exclaims as we reach the door. He shakes Adam's hand warmly. His face widens in a grin on seeing me.

'Hello my dear,' he says, kissing me on the cheek. He smells of stale nicotine and I try not to wrinkle my nose. Adam tips his head to Tweedledee and Tweedledum and apologises.

'I don't have a say in the matter,' he says.

'No worries old chap. It comes with the territory, I understand. Come through. Everyone is here. The steaks are almost done and the wine is flowing.'

Henry looks at me and I find myself shifting under his scrutiny.

'Are you feeling better today?' he asks.

I turn to glare at Adam.

'I said you had a rough day with Earl in the wood and everything.'

'I'm fine,' I say firmly. 'Earl shouldn't have been there.'

Henry shrugs and taps me on the arm.

'Quite right but we all make mistakes. He's handed back the key, that's what counts. No harm meant. We're all on good terms in the village.'

I don't smile back. Earl didn't make a mistake. He was on our land and should never have had a key. I'm not letting it go that easy.

'Most people know not to trespass,' I say firmly.

'Flora,' says Adam with a forced laugh. 'We're here to enjoy ourselves. Henry understands we don't want strangers on the land.'

'Absolutely,' says Henry. However, the smile on his face is tight. He's not being genuine. 'Come through.'

We follow him down the hallway, passing a cluttered oak sideboard as we do. It's full of photos. I try to look at them but Adam pulls me forward. They all seem to be of the same woman. The wallpaper is a dark plum and the lighting is low. I trip over a pair of shoes and Henry mumbles an apology. At the other end of the hall is a door leading outside to the lawn where the guests mingle with wine glasses in their hand. The smell of barbecue smoke reaches my nostrils and I realise I am hungry. I look around to see if Seth is here. I can ask him about the cellar if he is. But I don't spot him. I see Rhonda and Geoff and a few other people that I had seen in the village. Rhonda waves and hurries over with Myrtle at her side.

'Let me get you both a drink,' says Henry.

'This is nice isn't it?' says Adam, but I know he hates barbecues.

'How are you?' Rhonda gushes.

'There's Barry, the roofer,' says Adam. 'I want to talk to him about our roof. I won't be a sec.'

'I'm fine,' I say, accepting a glass of wine from Henry.

'It's wonderful you could come,' says Myrtle. 'We're looking forward to seeing you at our little crochet do on Wednesday.'

'I'm very busy with the house,' I smile, but in truth I'd forgotten all about the crochet group.

'Of course,' says Rhonda. 'You must be up to your eyes. It will be nice for you to get a break. We're so glad Seth could help.'

'Is he here?' I say looking around.

'Seth?' she says surprised. 'Oh no, he's not here.'

'I must pay him,' I say worriedly.

'You can give it to me. I'll pass it on,' says Rhonda. 'You can let me have it on Wednesday at the crochet group.'

I'm truly cornered now. Adam beckons me from the barbecue and I excuse myself to hurry over. A middle-aged balding man stands beside him.

'This is Eric Ambler, our local police sergeant,' says Adam. 'He's going to sort out the security for you when I'm away.'

'But the house is secure,' I protest.

'You've been a little nervous haven't you,' he says softly. 'Eric is going to arrange some extra security.'

'Right,' I say stifling a sigh.

'Nice to meet you,' Eric says shaking my hand with his firm grip. 'Don't you worry about anything.'

'Thanks but I'm not worried.'

'Let's get a burger,' says Adam, pulling me towards the buffet table. 'What's the matter?' he asks once we are out of earshot of the other guests.

'Have you been telling everyone I'm anxious?'

'Of course not,' he says, sounding hurt.

I accept a burger from Geoff and bite into it hungrily.

'Good aren't they?' says Rhonda from behind me. 'How are you settling in? We've seen the comings and goings.'

'Things are coming on well,' I say, taking a sip of wine. 'Did you know the Meyers when they lived there?' I ask.

'Not very well,' she shakes her head. 'They were young. We didn't have much in common with them.'

'They liked their parties,' says Myrtle in a hushed voice.

'Did she fall down the stairs,' I ask before I can stop myself.

'No,' Rhonda says, surprised. 'Why would you think that?'

'I know she died,' I say blushing.

'Drugs,' says Myrtle, glancing over her shoulder. 'They were taking lots of drugs. She had a heart attack didn't she?'

'We don't know anything Myrtle,' admonishes Rhonda. 'Don't start frightening the woman.'

I take another gulp of wine and say boldly,

'I don't get easily frightened. Did you visit the house when they lived there?' I ask.

Rhonda looks uncomfortable and excuses herself to top up her glass.

'They were trouble,' whispers Myrtle. 'They had no respect for the village, parties all the time. But we don't like bad feeling in the village and as long as they didn't bring shame on the village …'

I find myself smiling indulgently.

'What do you mean by shame?' I ask.

Her cheeks redden.

'You know, causing attention, the wrong kind. We've got a reputation here. We have the …'

'The Best Kept Village?' I finish for her.

'Yes,' she says proudly.

'Do you know how Kerri Wilson died? I know the papers said it was a heart attack but …'

'More wine?' interrupts Henry.

'I'll let you circulate,' Myrtle says with a nervous smile

'Can I use your loo?' I ask Henry.

'Up the stairs and to your left, you can't miss it.'

I make my way back along the hallway towards the staircase. I stop and study the photos on the sideboard. They are of the same woman at different periods of her life and I presume her to be Henry's wife. I turn back to the stairs and up the fraying stair carpet. The landing is as dark as the hallway. I turn left as told and open the first door and find myself in a small study. A lamp illuminates the room which is full of books and videos. I pick up one book and see it is written by Professor Dorcas, titled, *Errors of Judgements and their Consequences*. I place it back on the desk and leave the room, closing the door quietly behind me.

'Looking for the loo,' says a voice.

I jump with surprise and turn to the smiling man wearing a dog collar.

'Yes.'

I hold my hand out and he reels back.

'What's that perfume you're wearing?' he asks.

'It's called *Rose Oud*, do you know it?'

He looks flustered and shakes his head.

'No, for a minute I thought it was familiar but I can tell now it isn't. I'm Michael Flynn. I'm the vicar for this parish.'

'Flora Macintosh, we moved into Hunters Moon.'

He has a rounded face and a stomach to match. I try not to look at his paunch. His complexion is red and ruddy. His brown eyes sparkle. There are laughter lines around them. He seems a cheerful man and I warm to him instantly.

'Yes I know. Are you a church goer?' he asks.

I cringe.

'Erm …' I hesitate.

'Ah,' he smiles.

'We only attend for certain events.'

He nods knowingly.

'Yes, I'm sure you would both have to. Anyway,' he smiles, 'the toilet is that one. We won't fight over it.'

I check my reflection in the old ornate mirror in the loo and notice that I'm flushed from the wine. I can hear the music from the garden and the chatter of voices. Did Myrtle and Rhonda seem evasive when I mentioned Kerri Wilson? I push the window open and gaze down at everyone. Adam is chatting to Henry and Rhonda is serving food at the barbecue. Other villagers I don't recognise mill around and I find myself wishing Art Mitchell were here. There was something normal and calming about him. I pull a brush from my handbag and tidy my hair. I decide to visit him at his farm tomorrow. After all, he did say pop by any time. The atmosphere in the garden is jolly and relaxed but there is something about the jolliness that seems false. It almost feels like the barbecue has been put on just for us, like everything is an act. How ridiculous, I tell myself. I've really started thinking in an odd way since we moved into Hunters Moon. I throw my brush back into the handbag and give my reflection a final look.

'Make an effort,' I tell myself. 'It's a nice evening and everyone is being friendly. Do it for Adam if nothing else and for God's sake don't mention anything about Kerri Wilson haunting Hunters Moon. Everyone will think you've lost your marbles.'

Chapter Twenty-Four

The train to London is packed and I have to stand for half of the journey. I'd made a hair appointment and booked myself a facial. The news had been tense and I had an awful feeling that Ralph might resign. I needed to look my best if that happened. I'd also arranged to meet my client to discuss the commission I'd accepted. I'd woken feeling refreshed and positive. I'd abandoned the idea of visiting Art Mitchell. It wouldn't seem right anyway and I had no reason to. We'd come home from the barbecue Monday night slightly drunk and had made passionate love on the floor of the living room. For some weird reason I felt sure we had made the baby we so very much wanted. I feel confident now I have Doctor Kingsley as my gynaecologist.

The busy hair salon and the comforting smell of hair products help me forget Hunters Moon and the strange goings on there. Somehow, being back in London makes everything feel normal again. I relax under the drier as my highlights take and flick through a magazine. I turn the page and I find myself looking at a photo of Adam. He's posing in a dark blue suit. A dazzling white shirt and striped tie can be seen beneath it. He looks deliciously handsome and I smile proudly.

Is this our next Prime Minister? Shouts the headline. My heart is fit to burst with pride when the hairdresser says,

'He's a bit of alright isn't he? We could do with a Prime Minister who looks like him. I certainly wouldn't kick him out of bed.'

'That's my husband,' I say.

Her mouth opens and she blushes profusely.

'Oh, I didn't mean, I didn't ...'

'It's okay,' I laugh.

'Flora, everything okay?' asks Jenna the owner. 'I think those highlights are ready, Karen.'

'I didn't realise this was Mrs Macintosh,' Karen says nervously.

'Ah,' Jenna smiles through the mirror at me. 'Sorry about that.'

'No problem,' I say allowing myself to be led to the sink. 'I just never pictured my husband as a heart-throb.'

I relax as the hot water washes over my scalp and find myself wondering how many other women find Adam attractive. They'll no doubt be more when, and if, he becomes Prime Minister. I push the thoughts from my mind. I'm being ridiculous again. I need to get focused on work. I'm becoming far too introspective.

The meeting with my client goes really well and after my facial I reward myself with some shopping. It's as I'm heading for Tottenham Court Road station that I realise I'm not far from Kerri Wilson's agency. I get directions on my iPhone and then hail a cab to take me there.

The foyer is lined with photos of models. I scan them looking for Kerri Wilson but I can't see any of her.

'Hello, can I help?'

A pretty woman has entered the foyer. She's wearing a vintage boho dress. It's exactly how I imagined Kerri must have looked. I'd visualised her just like this in a flowing dress with a loose bun at the nape of her neck and long dangling earrings hanging from her earlobes.

'Hi,' I say, extending my hand. 'I'm Flora Macintosh.'

'Oh, hi,' she says looking surprised.

'I had hoped to talk to someone about one of your models.'

'Of course, please come through.'

I follow her through a doorway and into a small office. A thick photo album lies on the desk.

'Do you want to book someone?' she asks, pointing to a two-seater leather couch. I sit down and she sits opposite me.

'No, I wanted to ask about a model of yours. I've just bought the house … we've just bought the house where she used to live with her husband.'

She looks uncomfortable.

'We're not allowed to give out personal information about our models,' she says cautiously. 'Or give forwarding addresses. I'm really sorry about that.'

She's uncertain, I can tell. She's wondering if she's allowed to give out information to the wife of the Home Secretary. I fiddle with my newly highlighted hair.

'Her name was Kerri Wilson. She was the wife of Gerard Meyer, the actor.'

Her face gives nothing away.

'I understand she died from a heart attack. She seemed very young. It's kind of playing on my mind.'

She visibly relaxes and says,

'Yes, I knew Kerri.'

I feel a surge of excitement.

'You did? Can you tell me something about her? I sense her in the house do you know what I mean?'

She nods.

'Kerri had a presence.'

She rubs her eyes and then looks up at me.

'Would you like some tea? We have herbal if you prefer?'

'Thank you,' I say.

'I'm Carla James by the way.'

I nod gratefully. She disappears and I flick through the photo album. Carla returns with a tray and pours tea from a pot into two china mugs.

'You've bought Hunters Moon?'

'Yes, we moved in a few weeks back.'

'It's a lovely house,' she says, a wistful note in her voice.

She hands me a cup and says,

'I still miss Kerri dreadfully.'

'How did you know her?'

'Through the agency, we were friends. Kerri was fun loving.'

She looks into her teacup and then back to me.

'Do you really sense her in the house?'

I nod.

'She had a powerful personality,' she smiles.

'She had a heart attack, is that right?'

'I'm chatting as a friend of Kerri's and not for the agency but yes, we heard about it through the media. Not that there was much. It was all low key. Gerard hadn't made it big then. Kerri missed it all. She would have been so proud of him.'

'Did she have a weak heart?'

'Why are you asking these questions?' she asks, looking intensely at me.

I put my teacup down.

'Like I said, I sometimes think I sense her in the house. I'm trying to find out if her spirit is at peace.'

'Poor Kerri,' she sighs. 'I think it all took its toll. The accident and everything, I think it was too much'

'The accident?' I ask, sitting forward in my seat.

'Her friend Ben, he was killed in a car crash. It was six months before her heart attack. She never got over it. She barely came to the agency and when she did she looked drawn and haggard and not her beautiful self.'

'I don't know anything about an accident,' I say.

'It wasn't big news. Ben was an actor, not mega or anything. The car caught fire. He was unrecognisable apparently.'

'Oh God,' I shudder.

'He knocked down a woman from your village. Maybe you know her?'

'It happened in Penlyn?' I say, shocked. No one had ever mentioned an accident that was connected to a friend of Kerri Wilson's. *No scandal in Penlyn*, I find myself thinking.

'I don't think she had a weak heart. Not that she would have said. She changed so dramatically. One day the life and soul of the party and the next she was like the living dead.'

She stands up.

'Would you like to see some photos of her?'

I nod eagerly.

She floats out of the room with her bracelets jangling as she does so. I wonder about the accident and whether I can find anything about it online. Carla returns a minute later with a bulging folder.

'This was Kerri,' she says, pointing to a photo.

I stare at the beautiful features in front of me. She is far more beautiful than I remembered from the bedroom photo. She's wearing large hooped earrings and a long flowing evening gown. Her eyes sparkle with joy.

'We have hundreds,' she says, pulling them out one by one.

I study them closely, looking for something but I'm not sure what. Kerri Wilson is one of the most beautiful women I've ever seen.

Then I remember,

'Do you know what perfume she wore?'

'Perfume, God she wore so many.'

'Did she wear one that smelt of roses?' I say trying to control my excitement.

Carla frowns.

'I'm sorry I really don't recall what perfumes she wore.'

I try not to show my disappointment.

'I remember she loved the boat on their lake. She was always playing around on it.'

Chapter Twenty-Five

'The British Newspaper Archive,' suggests Laurie. 'They have back issues of all newspapers.'

'Is that online?' I say struggling to hear her over Barry, the roofer's, banging.

'Yes, google it and you'll find it.'

'Great, I'll have a look.'

'Has Adam forgiven me?' she asks nervously.

'He doesn't blame you but I've promised to stop looking into all this stuff about Kerri Wilson, so whatever happens don't you dare mention that we had this conversation.'

'Dib dib, dob dob and all that,' she laughs.

'He doesn't know I visited Kerri's old agency, so don't mention that either.'

'Do you want to try another séance, obviously when you're absolutely sure that Adam isn't going to come home and catch us,' she laughs.

'Maybe,' I say dubiously. 'I don't want to conjure up other things though.'

'Okay. Have you had any thoughts on the housewarming? You need to get your invites out.'

'I'll choose the invites today,' I promise.

I click off my phone and make tea for the roofer.

'Great lake,' he says, accepting the mug gratefully.

I turn to look at the lake, a small twinge of anxiety stabbing me, but the boat is safely secured. Is Kerri trying to tell me something? Did something happen in the boat? Did she have her heart attack out here? Was it even a heart attack?

'Been out on it?' asks Barry breaking into my thoughts.

'No, but I'm sure we will soon.'

I return to the house and begin unwrapping the bed linen that had arrived that morning. My eyes are pulled to the laptop and I am tempted to log on to the newspaper archive site, but I resist and instead switch on the radio for Prime Minister's questions. I'll work for a while and then later I'll indulge in the newspaper archive site. Adam won't be home until late so no doubt I'll be eating alone. I try not to think too much about Kerri Wilson. I really should have gone to the crochet group and decide to go to the next one. It might be exactly what I need to relax. Maybe Laurie is right and I need to immerse myself in village life. I open my laptop and get to work on my interior design commission. It is a good project and I'd previously been very excited by it. I email the finished product a few hours later and stretch my aching muscles. Barry is finishing up and I rummage in the freezer for something to eat when I am interrupted by the ringing of the landline. I hurry to the phone in case it is Adam.

'Flora?'

It's Rhonda and I fight back a sigh.

'Hi Rhonda, how are you? It was a lovely barbecue wasn't it?'

'We didn't see you at the crochet group,' she says, disappointment evident in her voice.

'I'm so sorry Rhonda. I had every intention of coming but then I had to go to London this morning and I've not been back long.'

It's a slight exaggeration but I can't possibly admit I didn't bother going. I really didn't think they would miss me.

'Oh, that's okay,' she says seemingly appeased. 'Hopefully you'll come to the next one?'

'Yes, that will be lovely,' I lie.

'Seth called round this morning but he couldn't get in the gate. He's always been able to get in with the pass code.'

I have a strange feeling that I'm being told off and feel resentful. It's like Earl the gardener all over again. I grit my teeth. I don't believe it. Am I being told off for not allowing all and sundry into my house? Maybe Gerard Meyer didn't mind everyone popping round but I certainly do. Poor Kerri if she had to put up with this.

'We have to take security very seriously with Adam being in such a prominent position,' I say trying not to sound defensive. 'As it is people had keys and didn't give them to the estate agent.'

'Yes, of course,' she says seeming to back down. 'I'm sorry. It's just we're so used to people not locking their doors here. But no one told Seth the code had changed. He gets easily upset. He also had something special to give you.'

'I was in London this morning otherwise I could have let him in.'

'The roofer was there,' she says accusingly. I can almost see her turning red under her usual white pallor.

'He came early,' I say and wonder why I'm explaining myself. 'If you give me Seth's address I'll pop round to arrange days with him. I can pay him at the same time.'

There's a moment's silence before she says,

'Seth lives with us. He's my grandson.'

'Oh,' I say taken aback. 'I hadn't realised.'

'Shall he come now?'

Damn it. It's a bit late but I feel to say no would seem a bit unfriendly and there are things that Seth can do around the house. He could fix the cellar door for a start.

'Of course,' I say.

'That's so kind Flora, thank you. It's just he has something to give you.'

'That's great,' I say. 'I can pay him.'

The phone goes dead and I exhale. I really did want to find out about the car accident that Carla had told me about. Hopefully Seth won't be here too long.

Barry's mug is in the sink and he waves from the patio. I sniff the bottle of perfume that sits on the kitchen counter and then make tea for myself. My eyes are drawn again to the laptop but I resist and turn on the radio for the news, listening for the latest political updates but there aren't any. It's not long before the gate buzzer sounds and I see Seth standing there with a box in his hands. I open the gate and wait for him.

'I'm sorry about the key code,' I say. 'We're not giving the new one out. I hope you understand. It's nothing personal. If we arrange the days that you are coming, I'll be here to let you in.'

He nods and steps into the house. He points to a note that is stuck to the box. In bold black letters it reads,

For Flora Macintosh from Seth.

'That's kind, what is it?' I say cautiously.

I then realise asking Seth what it is, is rather pointless and blush at my stupidity. I'm nervous to open the box. I've had one too many surprises since being at Hunters Moon. I barely know Seth, so why would he be buying me gifts? I carefully lift the flap of the box. Something brown and soft wriggles inside. I pull back the other flap and big brown eyes stare longingly at me. It's a golden Labrador puppy. There's a pink ribbon tied loosely around its neck.

'It's so cute,' I say taking it into my arms.

It wriggles excitedly and fights to lick my face. Seth takes an envelope from the box and hands it to me. I cradle the puppy in one hand and slit open the envelope and remove the pink edged notepaper.

Dear Flora Macintosh,

We heard that you were looking for a puppy. Barbara's Labrador from the next village had a litter a few weeks ago and we, in the village, thought you might like one. Please accept her as a housewarming gift from us. We hope she makes you very happy.

Best wishes from Seth and all in the village.

'Hello little one,' I say feeling an outpouring of love for the bubbly bundle in my arms. 'I'm going to call you Kerri.'

Chapter Twenty-Six

'You have a puppy, how adorable,' says Philippa.

I stir the spicy beef and then place the nachos into the oven.

Philippa scoops up Kerri and hugs her close to her chest. There's a pop from the lounge as Adam opens the champagne followed by a whoop from Ken, Philippa's husband.

'Bubbly's ready,' Adam shouts.

'It all seems a bit premature,' I say to Philippa.

'Not in the least. The way things are going I imagine Ralph will be out by the end of the summer,' says Philippa, tickling Kerri under her chin.

'Kerri, what a lovely name,' she coos.

'Don't even go there,' groans Adam, appearing with two champagne glasses. 'She's named after our resident ghost.'

'Adam,' I say surprised.

I hate it when Adam drinks. He's always indiscreet. I'm always telling him but he doesn't seem to listen. He and Ken have already been on the whisky.

'Resident ghost?' says Philippa. 'Do tell us more.'

I glare at Adam.

'There's nothing to tell really,' I say evasively.

One minute Adam tells me not to mention the house and its happenings and the next he is doing it all by himself.

'I'll dish up,' I say, opening the Aga door.

'Flora hears things,' says Adam.

'Adam,' I say, blushing.

'Oh my God, do you really?' asks Philippa.

'I don't believe in that nonsense,' says Ken, making me feel even more stupid. I turn my face from the oven and place the nachos on to the table.

'Have you actually seen something?' asks Philippa.

'No, not exactly,' I say warily, pouring water into glasses.

'She had a séance,' says Adam, rolling his eyes.

I could gladly slap him.

He pushes Kerri away from the table and reaches out for me.

'It's hormones no doubt,' he says softly. He thinks he's making it better but he's just making it a hundred times worse.

'I'll just take a plate out to Tweedledee and Tweedledum,' I say, trying to lighten the atmosphere.

I'd been trying to focus on normal things since coming back from London that day. It is important for me to be calm and relaxed. I'd been determined to get on with the house and to throw myself into work. The house is looking terrific and I feel more hopeful about things. More importantly the strange things I had been experiencing at the house have stopped. I have two commissions to work on and have started redecorating the boathouse. Adam had tied the boat securely and thankfully it hadn't moved since. I'd resisted looking at the newspaper archive site. Getting pregnant was my sole objective now.

'Lovely night,' says Tweedledee.

I find myself wondering what his wife is doing tonight while he is working. I return to the kitchen where the champagne is flowing. Adam has opened another bottle and coaxes me to have a glass.

'This is a night of celebration,' he shouts excitedly. Kerri barks in unison and I seem to be the only one that is not overjoyed.

'You don't know that, Adam,' I say doubtfully.

He turns to me, his expression hurt. His hand tightens around the stem of his champagne flute.

'I thought you'd be happy for me,' he says petulantly.

'I am happy,' I say. 'I just don't want you to get your hopes up.'

'I think it is pretty much a certainty,' says Ken. 'The electorate aren't happy. Ralph seems to be making all the wrong decisions.'

'If Adam doesn't challenge the leadership, someone else will,' agrees Philippa.

'Anyway, to hell with politics,' she says jovially. 'Tell us more about your ghost.'

I grimace at Adam and vow never to mention ghosts to him again.

*

'Kerri Wilson,' I whisper.

She turns her head to me and grabs the arm of the man standing next to her. She has her back to the stairs. I need to do something. In a moment she will fall back and it will be all over. I step forward and suddenly find myself at the bottom of the stairs, looking up.

'No,' I cry. 'This is wrong.'

But it's too late. I see her grasping for something to hold.

'Oh Kerri,' I whimper. 'Wait, please wait.'

She reaches out to him but he steps back and then it happens. Kerri's fragile body bounces down the stairs like a rag doll. She lies in front of me, her dead eyes looking into mine. But these aren't Kerri Wilson's eyes. I watch as her face contorts and changes and I gasp in shock. Then I hear his footsteps on the stairs. He's coming. I need to run. I'm in my nightie and my feet are bare. I lift my hand to the front door when suddenly it opens and standing there with the rain lashing down behind him is Adam.

'What have you done Flora?' he asks.

I look back at the woman. A pool of blood has circled her head. I put my hands to my face and reel back at the wetness of it. I try to wipe the wet away but it won't go and my face gets wetter and wetter.

'What have you done Flora?' repeats Adam.

I gasp and wake with a start.

'Flora,' grunts Adam, 'wake up.'

Kerri has jumped on the bed and is licking my face.

'You've been dreaming,' mumbles Adam, turning over.

I lift Kerri off me and put her on the floor.

'It's okay girl,' I say, wiping my face with a tissue.

My hand reaches down to my abdomen. Have I started my period? I can't feel any cramping but I do feel hot and restless. I take Kerri downstairs and settle her in her basket. It's 2 a.m. Talking about ghosts with Philippa and Ken must have triggered the dream. It's been three weeks since I met Carla at the agency and talked about Kerri Wilson. I'd stuffed the photographs Carla had given me into a bedroom drawer. I don't want Adam to know about them. Relieved to find that my period hasn't started, I climb back into bed and try to get some sleep. Things have been better in the house recently. Everything has calmed down. Even Earl has seemed less menacing when he's come to do the gardening. I am determined to be calm, but I am tense. I know that. My period is due and I've been on edge. I'm overdue and I'm conscious it could come any day but I can't help raising my hopes. I turn over again and try to get comfortable. The villagers are being so kind to us and everyone loves Kerri, our new Labrador pup. But now it feels like Kerri Wilson is calling to me again. I sigh and check the time. It's 2.40 a.m. Adam groans as I move. I remember my nightmare. It was just a dream I tell myself, but what if it wasn't a dream? What if it was a premonition What if?

'Be calm and relaxed,' I tell myself, but I can't seem to stop my mind from buzzing. I can't settle and finally go back downstairs. I reach the bottom and look closely at the flagstone floor. I'm convinced several are stained redder than the others. It's my imagination, surely. I look closer and notice there is a small stain on the corner of one of the flagstones. It could be anything but I can't help thinking it is blood.

The kitchen blinds are drawn and I fight the desire to pull them and check the boat. I take a glass of water into the study where my laptop is open from earlier. There'd be no harm looking at the newspaper archive site, just until I get sleepy. Kerri settles herself on the couch beside me and is soon asleep. It takes no time at all to register with the site and within minutes I'm searching for 'car accident in Oxfordshire'. There are too many results to go through. I feel relieved. I yawn and am about to close the laptop lid when a thought occurs to me. I search for local news and type in 'Penlyn woman knocked down by car'.

The search shows one result. I click the link nervously.

A woman was knocked down in the early hours of Sunday morning on a lonely country road outside the village of Penlyn. She has been named as Margaret Snell and died at the scene. The driver of the car which burst into flames has yet to be named.

I search for news of Margaret Snell and find a short piece that named the driver as Benjamin Miller, an actor and voice-over artist. With trembling hands I google Benjamin Miller and there among the images is a photo of Benjamin Miller with Kerri.

Chapter Twenty-Seven

'That's really looking good,' says Myrtle, inspecting my crochet shawl.

I don't think it is very good at all. In fact I'm still not sure what I'm doing here but they mean well and it's nice to have company. Adam seemed pleased I was joining in.

'It's good to be seen mixing with the public,' he'd said. 'To look like we're in touch with the voters.'

'You can wear that for the Litha celebrations,' says Barbara.

I wouldn't wear it for anything, but I keep silent and smile.

'No, she can't,' corrects Rhonda, 'otherwise we'd all know it's her.'

I look across the table to Lisa. She is new to the village and I'm dying to ask her how she finds it. She and her husband had moved in to The Old Stores on the outskirts. I was surprised because I remembered Sienna telling me that property didn't come up often in the village. She's very pretty and I admire her earrings. Rhonda told me she makes her own jewellery along with pottery bowls and vases.

'What's Litha?' I ask.

'It's the celebration of midsummer. It's like an Italian carnival. Everyone, rich or poor ...' Barbara hesitates and all eyes seem to fall on me. I presume, to everyone in the room, that I come under the 'rich' category.

'Come masked and disguised on to the streets of Penlyn,' she finishes. 'We have a huge bonfire on the village green and our Litha altar is there.'

I look to Lisa who raises her eyebrows.

'We choose the new guild elder during the ceremony. There's a party afterwards. It's held on Midsummer's Day. You'll help, of course,' says Rhonda.

It's not a question. I wonder if I should mention that our housewarming party is also the last week in June. We won't be very popular if we clash with the village traditions. I'd better speak to Adam about it.

'Oh,' I say. 'So has Henry not always been the elder?'

'Pretty much,' smiles Rhonda. 'Geoff was chosen twice and once Jack, you know, the pub landlord, he was picked.'

'Maybe Adam will be chosen this time' I laugh.

They look at me intensely.

'You have to have been in the village for some time,' explains Barbara.

'What will you wear?' asks Lisa.

'You have to be in costume,' says Rhonda. 'There's a prize for the best outfit.'

'We'll have to get together,' I smile at Lisa.

I look down at my crocheted shawl and then back up to the ladies who are diligently working on their pieces. I study them slyly. Barbara concentrates on her soft toy. I smile. She's been stuffing a leg for the whole evening and still can't get the hang of it. Her grey hair is knotted at the neck and her face is far too wrinkled for someone who I guess is in her seventies. Rhonda on the other hand, refusing to grow old gracefully, has dyed her hair red and applies make-up expertly. Myrtle is a mass of nerves and is either biting her nails or chewing her lip. The tutor, Hillary, is lovely and travels from Oxford to be with us. I consider mentioning Margaret Snell and asking if anyone knows what happened the night of the accident but change my mind. Calm and relaxed, I remind myself. My period still hasn't shown and I'm too afraid to even think what that could mean. If this is what calm and relaxed does then I certainly ought to continue with it.

I check my phone and pack up my things. Lisa follows suit and we leave the village hall together.

'Would you like to come back for some tea,' she asks hesitantly. 'I know you're probably very busy with your husband …'

'Adam's always at some meeting or the other. I'm thrilled when he comes home but I never know what time. Tea would be great.'

Her pretty face brightens

'Don't judge me too much. I'm not an interior designer like you.'

She looks at me and says, 'I was surprised you were at the crochet class.'

I pull a face.

'I got pulled in really. It's not my thing.'

'Nor me,' she laughs. 'I got pestered and figured as its creative I'd probably enjoy it but …'

I laugh.

'They're all so old,' she confides.

Her cottage is adorable, despite her words. It's old but quaint and suits Lisa perfectly. It's packed with vintage postcards and lamps draped in colourful scarves. The room smells of jasmine and makes a pleasant change from the rose fragrance in Hunters Moon.

'It's beautiful,' I say accepting a hand-made mug of tea. 'I didn't think there was property available in the village.'

'There wasn't. This has been going through probate for the past two years. The old lady who owned it left a will but it all went to her son who'd died some years before. She never updated it so it was all a bit of a muddle. It finally came on the market and we snapped it up. Of course there's nothing left of Margaret Snell now which is a shame but still …'

'Margaret Snell?' I exclaim.

'Did you know her? I'm really sorry I didn't mean to be disrespectful.'

I put my tea mug down on a rustic table.

'It's just so weird. I've been reading about Margaret Snell and I was going to ask the ladies at the class about her but changed my mind and …'

Lisa looks at me oddly.

'Sorry you must think I'm mad,' I apologise. 'It's just our house … well I sense something happened there. Something to do with the previous owners …'

'The actor?' she says, pouring more tea into my mug. 'What has he got to do with Margaret Snell?'

'Probably nothing,' I say.

I don't want people in the village knowing about my obsession with Hunters Moon's past history.

'She's buried in the church cemetery,' says Lisa, taking a fruit cake from a flowery tin. 'I should have offered you this earlier,' she apologises. 'It's freshly baked.'

She makes me feel inadequate. I never bake, not even so much as a rock cake. I really should make the effort, especially now we're living in the country.

'I don't imagine it will say much about her though,' continues Lisa. 'But the vicar might be able to tell you more.'

'Yes, you're right, he might.' I say, remembering how friendly he was at the barbeque.

'What do you think you'll wear for this Litha thing?' she asks, changing the subject. 'It's all very pagan isn't it?'

I fiddle with my crochet shawl.

'Well, certainly not this,' I smile.

'Absolutely not,' she laughs, 'otherwise we'd all know who you are.'

'Why don't we go around the hire shops together,' enthuses Lisa. 'It will be much more fun than going alone.'

'Sounds great.'

'Text me when you're free.'

She gives me her number and then asks, 'Do you think Adam will go to the celebrations?'

I nod.

‘Oh yes, if he’s able. Adam enjoys networking.’

The excitement of going to the church and possibly finding out more about Margaret Snell is making me fidgety.

‘I should get going,’ I say, ‘Kerri needs her walk.’

Kerri sits patiently by the door her eyes feasting on the fruit cake.

‘Thanks for coming,’ says Lisa, ‘it’s been nice talking to someone who isn’t on their way back from collecting their pension.’

I kiss her on the cheek and leave, grateful to have found a friend in the village.

April 2016
Kerri Wilson

She carefully removed the pad and replaced it with a clean one. The bleeding had eased and she sighed with relief. Carefully she edged her way into bed where Gerard slept soundly. He was completely out of it and wouldn't hear a bomb if it fell on him. She stroked her stomach and allowed the tears to flow, her sobs as silent as she could make them. The room spun around her. She was slowly coming down and the enormity of what had taken place earlier was just beginning to sink in. She wiped away her tears and blew her nose. No one cared what happened to her. Gerard only cared about himself and his glittering future. How did it come to this? How did it all go so horribly wrong? She thought of Ben and shook the image of his broken body from her mind. Oh God, she prayed, please forgive us. If only she could talk to someone, get things out of her head. If she were catholic she could go to confession. Her eyes snapped open. Perhaps she could talk to the village vicar. He wouldn't tell anyone. They take an oath of secrecy, don't they? She relaxed at the thought of unburdening it all. But she couldn't unburden everything, she knew that. She'd be too ashamed to voice everything. But some, she could tell him some. Perhaps she'd write it down, like a letter to God. She closed her eyes but the memory of his hands on her was still fresh in her mind. She shuddered in disgust and shame. She felt violated, dirty. Why was Gerard allowing it? It was debauched and sick and destroying her. Damn them, damn them all. She hoped they all went to hell. If only she didn't love Gerard so much. She slid her hand to his buttocks and felt comforted. It was what they deserved, she knew that. If she could only go back, but like Professor Dorcas says, 'there is no going back. The deed has been done.'

She turned over and laid her arm over Gerard.

'I love you,' she whispered, 'and I forgive you.'

Chapter Twenty-Eight

Kerri bounds through the village chasing leaves that are blown by the wind. I'm enjoying the fresh air and the peacefulness of the country. The path to the church is lined with daffodils and Kerri barks at them as they bend with the breeze.

'Let's see if we can find Margaret?' I say, stroking Kerri.

It then occurs to me that Kerri Wilson may be here too. I stroll around the graves, noticing how well the graves have been kept. I find myself wondering whether Adam and I will see our days out in Penlyn and if we'll be buried here also. A shiver runs down my back at the thought and I tell myself to think of happier things. Kerri and I come full circle. There is no gravestone for Kerri Wilson or Margaret Snell. Didn't Lisa say that Margaret was buried here? Surely she wouldn't have got that wrong. We walk through the cemetery again but can't find Margaret Snell's gravestone. I'm about to go into the church when I spot a small gravestone in the distance. It is alone against the far wall and is covered in weeds. They're so overgrown it's a wonder that I saw it at all. I pull several of the weeds out to see the inscription on the headstone. I study it closely. It's not an old headstone and after brushing off much of the dirt I can see it clearly says 'Margaret Snell 1944 - 2014' I don't know what I expected but it was certainly more than this. There isn't even a RIP inscribed.

A robin lands on the wall and watches me. The church clock chimes, making me jump. Kerri barks, and tries to leap up at the robin. I decide to buy some daffodils and place them on Margaret Snell's grave. It seems wrong for it to be neglected like this. I remember Lisa saying that Margaret Snell's son had died some years before and look around for another tombstone, but Margaret Snell's is the only one by the back wall. Surely they would be together?

'One last time around,' I say to Kerri who wags her tail in eager response. 'If Margaret is here then her son has to be.'

This time I study the inscriptions. Some are difficult to read because of their age but none of these would be Kerri Wilson or Margaret Snell's son. They would look more recent than this. We walk around the cemetery two more times. Maybe Lisa got it wrong about Margaret's son. I glance at the church. It looks cold and desolate and I hesitate about going in. I tentatively push at the door and am almost relieved to find it is locked.

'Well, that's that,' I say, rubbing Kerri's ears.

She scratches the doors impatiently.

'Let's go home,' I say, pulling her away. 'I've got tons of work to do.'

I leave the cemetery and notice the rectory, next door, has its windows open. Surely the vicar would know where Margaret Snell's son is buried and whether Kerri Wilson was here too. Maybe he can tell me more about them. I stroll towards the house, noting the peeling window frames and neglected garden, and wonder why the rector doesn't ask Seth to help out. The front door is partly hidden by overgrown ivy and I struggle to find a doorbell. Kerri sits at the gate and refuses to go any further.

'Come on Kerri,' I coax.

I find the doorbell and push it but hear nothing. Deciding it can't be working I lift the knocker and rap several times. We wait silently but no one comes to the door. The silence is strangely deafening and suddenly all I want is to be back at Hunters Moon. The breeze lifts the curtain at the window and I see Reverend Flynn sitting in a chair in his living room.

'Hello,' I call. 'It's Flora Macintosh.'

There's no response. I move cautiously to the window.

'Reverend Flynn,' I say, peeking in. 'Hello, it's ...'

I trail off and let out a small gasp. Stumbling back from the window my foot gets tangled in Kerri's lead and I cry out as my ankle twists beneath me. I look through the window but Reverend Flynn is still sprawled out in his armchair. I limp back to the cemetery and slump on to a bench. What has happened in this village? If only Margaret Snell could tell me. I glance back at the rectory and a chill runs through me. Do the villagers know that Reverend Flynn is a drug addict? Surely it was something else I saw? But no matter how hard I try to rationalise it, there's no denying that on the coffee table in front of his chair I saw the remnants of some foil and a syringe. Had I looked closer I probably would have seen more. Reverend Flynn wasn't resting as I had at first thought but was in fact completely stoned.

Chapter Twenty-Nine

Instead of heading to Hunters Moon, I find myself walking out of the village towards Greengage farm. My foot throbs and I begin to regret my decision. I should have gone straight home. I'd been tempted to phone Adam but then changed my mind. He'd be cross. Adam was already losing patience with my talking about Kerri Wilson so he isn't going to take kindly to me phoning him about the vicar. But I need to talk to someone and Laurie hadn't picked up her phone.

Greengage farm is set back from the road but a wooden sign makes it easy to find. I sigh with relief at the sight of Art Mitchell's van in the driveway. Art seemed a sensible, rational person. Surely he will make me see how crazy I am being. There has to be a reasonable explanation for what I saw.

The gate creaks as I open it and Art Mitchell strolls around the corner of the farmhouse, his wellingtons covered in mud. Beside him a black Labrador barks in excitement and Kerri pulls me forward. I wince in pain.

'Hello there,' smiles Art.

The dogs sniff each other excitedly.

'You've got a puppy?' he says smiling.

'Yes, she's called Kerri. The village gave her to me.'

'Generous of them,' he says, a hint of cynicism in his voice. 'I hope she's had all her jabs.'

'Oh yes.'

'I think she's made a friend in Rosie,' he adds, patting Kerri.

'Is there somewhere I can sit down?' I ask, the throbbing in my foot becoming unbearable.

'That's swollen, what have you done?' He says, looking at my foot. 'Come into the house. It's not as tidy as usual I fear,' he smiles. 'You can let Kerri off the lead. She won't go far.'

I release Kerri and she runs off with Rosie. Art pulls off his wellingtons revealing holey socks. I smile and follow him into a homely, but messy, kitchen.

'I did warn you,' he grins, throwing clothes off a kitchen chair so I can sit down. I remove my sandal and grimace at my swollen foot.

'I twisted it somehow. I went to the vicarage,' I say.

He turns from filling the kettle.

'That's what religion does to you.'

'I'm not religious,' I say.

'I didn't have you down as the religious type.'

'We're not. Adam has to attend sometimes, you know, it's kind of political.'

He nods.

'How are you settling in at Hunters Moon? Left any doors open recently?'

'We've got new security locks now,' I smile.

He rummages in a cupboard for teabags and several boxes fall from the shelves.

'I don't normally have people for tea,' he explains.

'I'm sure that's not true,' I laugh.

'Well, not many politicians' wives anyway.'

'Oh we're just like normal people,' I say, accepting a ginger biscuit.

He rattles a tin and Rosie bounds in, followed by Kerri.

'Dog treats. Rosie will do anything for them.'

Kerri jumps up at him almost knocking him over.

'She's boisterous,' he says patting her.

'Do you know Reverend Flynn?' I ask.

He runs his hands through his hair. His nails are grubby and I try to imagine Adam on a farm with wellies and grubby fingernails. I smile. Adam is so particular about his appearance, and he wouldn't be seen dead in holey socks.

Art pulls a face.

'Can't say I do. No such thing as a Sunday in farming. I certainly wouldn't spend my rest day in a church in any case.'

I nod. I search in my head for the right words.

'Are there rumours about him?'

He raises his eyebrows.

'Rumours? Not that I've heard of, but I'm not really in the village.'

'I went there to ask him about Margaret Snell and I couldn't make him answer. The living room window was open and I saw him through there. He was completely out of it. I think he was on drugs. Is it possible the vicar could be taking drugs?'

'Crikey,' he says, widening his eyes. 'I'd be surprised. This village is obsessed with its image. *Nobody brings shame on the village*, they say.'

'No scandal,' I add.

He nods and laughs.

'Yep, so a junkie vicar wouldn't really fit in would he?'

I sip my tea and look around the messy kitchen. There's no sign of a woman's touch.

'Do you live alone?' I ask.

'I do now. My wife left a year ago.'

'Oh I'm so sorry.'

He grabs an apple from a bowl on the table.

'It's okay. It was a bit of a mess anyway. Turned out farming wasn't her thing after all. It took her six years to realise, but anyway …'

'If you need some help, Jan, that's my housekeeper, she could do with some extra work …'

'We don't all earn politician's salaries,' he grins.

I feel my face grow hot.

'I'm sorry. She's not that expensive though, and could help with ironing and …'

He looks down at his creased shirt.

'Ah, right.'

I push myself up from the table.

'I'm sorry. I'm just putting my foot in it. I really ought to get back.'

'No, you're not leaving until you've had a scone with my own clotted cream,' he says pointing to the chair. 'Besides, I'll take you back. I don't think it's sensible to walk too much on that foot.'

A sharp ache shoots through my ankle and I sit back down again. I watch as he expertly prepares the scones.

'Did you know Margaret Snell?'

He hands me a scone piled with cream.

'Yeah, I knew her. She was a lonely old thing. She lived at The Old Stores. She had a bit of a drink problem. Talking of drinks, can I offer you more tea?'

I strain to see Kerri from the window.

'She'll be fine,' he smiles.

'Okay, another cup would be nice. Did you know about Margaret Snell's accident?'

He runs his hand through his hair and looks thoughtful.

'It was about two years ago I think. It was a friend of the couple that lived at your place, knocked her down with his car. I don't think anyone knew what actually happened. The car caught fire.'

'She's buried at the back of the cemetery. It seems strange. It's like she's been isolated. And Lisa said the house took a long time to go through probate because Margaret hadn't changed her will after her son died and everything was left to him. The strange thing is that there's no sign of another Snell in the cemetery.'

'I can't help you there,' he says handing me the tea. 'I only know Margaret wasn't popular in the village but I couldn't tell you why. I never knew she had a son.'

'It's all odd,' I mutter. 'Don't laugh at me but I can't help thinking something odd happened at Hunters Moon but I just don't know what. Adam thinks I'm getting too preoccupied with the house so I'm getting more involved with the village.'

'I imagine there's a lot you can do in that house. You're an interior designer aren't you?'

'Yes, how did you know?'

'I googled you.'

'Oh,' I say surprised.

'I thought I'd check out the politics of my local politician. I can't say they're mine.'

My phone bleeps and I pull it from my jeans pocket. It's a text from Laurie.

Adam texted me, said he would be home tonight to discuss the housewarming. He said about eight. See you both then. I promise not to bring my Ouija board.

I feel annoyed that Adam and Laurie had made plans behind my back and then reprimand myself for being so stupid. I'm here with Art aren't I, having a cream tea? I won't be mentioning that to Adam.

'I ought to go. My friend will be over later to discuss our housewarming party.'

'Sure, I'll drop you off.'

'I hope you'll come to the housewarming?'

'Sure, why not. I'll discuss politics with your other friends.'

I feel he's mocking me and suddenly feel stupid for having come to see him. Maybe Adam is right and I should stop all these stupid thoughts about the village and get on with my life. But the vicar, surely it isn't right for a vicar to be on drugs?

Chapter Thirty

I arrive back at Hunters Moon and decide to take a hot bath before Adam gets home. I've got three hours before Laurie arrives. Kerri flops into her basket and promptly falls asleep, her exertions of the day catching up with her. I read the note Jan has left and then take the freshly laundered shirts upstairs. My foot throbs more than it did earlier and I rest on the bed for a while until the pain eases. I can smell the faint scent of roses and study the carpet for any perfume stains. I'm about to bend to check under the bed when there's a knock from downstairs. I'd made sure the gates were shut after Art had driven off and the front door was locked. Jan would have bolted the back doors and there are no windows open so it couldn't have been the wind. Kerri was sleeping soundly when I came upstairs. Could she have woken up? I listen, but all is quiet again.

'Kerri,' I call.

I'm supposed to be getting a grip. Focusing on work, not on silly noises I hear in the house. They will have reasonable explanations, I tell myself. But I'm not in the least convinced. I slip my feet back into my sandals and open the bedroom door. I limp down the stairs and the memory of my dream comes flooding into my mind. I'm almost at the bottom step when there's another knock. I stop in my tracks and grip the banister.

'Kerri, what are you doing?' I call.

I walk slowly to the source of the sound and stop when I reach the cellar door. It's coming from there. The hallway is dark and I can see through the kitchen doorway that leaden clouds are covering the sky. The wind has come up and an empty flowerpot rattles about on the patio. Kerri still sleeps soundly in her basket. The last time I had tried the cellar door it was still jammed. I creep towards it, trying to be as quiet as I can, although I've no idea why.

'Kerri,' I whisper, 'wake up girl.'

But Kerri continues to sleep. Her play date with Rosie has totally wiped her out. The cellar door handle turns easily and I'm so surprised when the door opens that I close it again quickly. Seth must have fixed the lock. It's dark inside and I fumble for a light switch. A cold, gritty draught greets me. I push the door back and secure it by placing one of the ornate chairs from the hallway, against it. My foot has swollen again and I sit on the chair for a few moments to rest it and look down into the cellar. The chair is strong and sturdy. The door won't move with that against it. Adam and I had bought them a month after we'd married. We'd seen them in a little antique shop in Stratford upon Avon. They had always looked out of place in our flat but Hunters Moon is perfect for them. At last we have the home we had always dreamt of and I'm scared to go into my own cellar. As a precaution I hobble to the kitchen where I pull a carving knife from the cutlery drawer. I'm not sure what I'm expecting to find in the cellar but I want to be prepared for whatever it is.

Chapter Thirty-One

Wielding the knife in my left hand I grab the banister with the other and cautiously step down to the cellar. Its musty smell travels up to meet me. The cellar is brightly lit and even before I'm halfway down I can see there is no one here. I look back to check the chair is still firmly in place. It's when I reach the bottom that I see a window flapping in the wind but it's too high for me to reach and there isn't a stepladder.

'Bugger,' I mutter.

I really don't want the window left open, especially with no bolt on the outside of the cellar door, but there's nothing to stand on, aside from a few boxes. None of them look sturdy enough to take my weight. I lift the lid off one and curiously look inside to find an assortment of Christmas decorations. On the shelves above the boxes are used paintbrushes and old tins of paint. I should phone the estate agent and ask them to take the boxes away. I strain my ears and for a second I feel sure I hear a light patter above me. I lift the knife and sigh in irritation. What on earth am I doing? Adam would have a fit if he could see me. I hobble back to the steps. I grab the banister and pull myself up, listening for any sound as I do so. The hallway is dark and I limp to the light switch. I see an image of myself in the hall mirror, a pale-faced woman with pinched cheeks and wild hair. It doesn't look like me. A strange woman is in my house wielding a carving knife like a crazed lunatic. I stare in shock, my eyes wide and disbelieving and then from the corner of my eye I see it, a movement.

*

My eyes dart to the front door and then back to the mirror. I don't know what it was that I saw but I know I saw something. I can't decide whether to run to the front door or face the intruder. At that moment Kerri barks and I find the nerve to confront whoever it is in the house. I limp towards the kitchen archway with my heart thumping in my chest.

'Who's there?' I call.

There's no reply except Kerri's barking. She runs to greet me but I ignore her and lift the knife higher before peeking around the door.

'Who is it?' I yell angrily.

The kitchen is empty. Jan's note is on the table where I'd left it. Kerri jumps up behind me and I turn to pat her. What did I see in the mirror? Am I going mad? For a second I don't notice anything different. I'm not looking for it so it eludes me but then I realise. The perfume bottle has gone. I turn to put the knife on the table and scream. Earl is looking at me through the glass panel of the back door, his eyes menacing.

Chapter Thirty-Two

I open the back door and meet Earl's eyes. I struggle not to look at the hair lip which seems redder than usual.

'How long have you been here?' I ask.

He looks at the knife in my hand and then his eyes roam to my breasts. I follow his gaze and realise the top buttons of my shirt have popped undone. I pull it together and look at the mug in his hand.

'Just came to bring me cup back,' he says with a smirk. 'No need to pull a knife on me. Ain't never had that before.'

I should put the knife down, I know, but I somehow feel safer with it in my hand. A loud bang from the hallway makes me jump and I almost drop the knife. The wind must have blown the cellar door shut.

'Flora, what the fuck?'

I spin around to face Adam. Seeing him in his smart suit seems surreal. One of us is out of place here and I can't help thinking it's me.

'I ...'

I try to imagine what I look like. Hair wild, eyes wide and frightened and what's worse, I'm brandishing a carving knife.

'I was bringing my mug back,' says Earl innocently. 'And she came at me with a knife.'

I glare at him. There was nothing innocent about him before Adam appeared and it wasn't true that I came at him with a knife.

'Jesus, put that down Flora,' demands Adam.

I drop the knife on to the table.

'The cellar window was knocking,' I say hoarsely. 'I ... I went to investigate and when I came back I saw a figure in the kitchen through the mirror.'

'And you got a knife?' he asks, disbelief written across his face.

'I thought ... I suppose I thought.'

'What did you think Flora?' asks Adam.

'I must have seen Earl's reflection in the window,' I say, feeling stupid.

'Didn't you know Earl was here?'

'No, I've been out. I got back about an hour ago. There was no one here when I arrived home.'

'Earl?' asks Adam.

Earl shrugs.

'The housekeeper let me in. I been doing the garden like you said. I cut back in the woods like you asked me and the housekeeper woman made me some tea. I just brought me cup back like I said.'

Adam's eyes bore into mine. He's telling me not to say any more.

'The perfume has gone,' I whisper.

Adam turns to Earl.

'Thanks Earl. We've kept you late. Be sure to put the overtime on your bill.'

'Sure thing Mr Macintosh, thank you,' he says touching his cap.

'I want to pay you for your time and obviously we don't want this getting out and all around the village. Flora's not been herself for a bit and ...'

'Adam,' I protest.

'Oh sure, no worries, I don't talk to no one,' says Earl.

I feel sure he sneers at me. He puts the cup into the kitchen sink and with a last look at me he leaves.

'Jesus Christ, Flora, what the hell were you doing?' Adam sighs.

'I thought someone had broken in,' I say, feeling hurt and angry. 'I'm going to change. Laurie will be here soon.'

'Flo, I'm worried about you.'

His arms come around me and I fight back the urge to cry.

'I'm okay.'

He bites his lip.

'Do you think you should see a doctor, Flora?'

'What?' I say.

'You've not been right since the last miscarriage and maybe ...'

I take a step back from him.

'He was acting weird,' I say realising I sound silly. 'The perfume bottle has gone too.'

Adam sighs.

'Yes, I'm sure that's Earl's type,' he scoffs.

'I'm going to have a bath. Laurie will be here soon,' I snap and hobble up the stairs.

'Let me help you,' he says reaching out his arm.

I slap at his hand. 'I don't need any help.'

*

I try to relax in the warm water and close my eyes. The tears trickle down my cheek and I'm not sure if they are tears of self-pity or anger. Is Adam right, am I putting myself under too much stress? Is the strain of wanting a baby taking its toll on me? Maybe I should phone Doctor Kingsley in the morning. I wipe the tears from my cheek and reach out for the sponge. The smell of lavender oil helps to soothe me and when Adam taps softly on the door I'm feeling calmer than earlier. He's changed into jeans and a sweatshirt and carries a mug of tea.

'I thought you might want a cuppa,' he smiles.

'Thanks.'

He sits on the side of the bath.

'What happened to your foot?' he asks, reaching down and touching it gently.

'I twisted it when I was out walking today.'

I decide not to tell him about the cemetery.

'Adam, I'm not losing my mind.'

He strokes my hair.

'I'm not for one minute saying you are, but wielding kitchen knives is not your usual behaviour is it?'

'I just ...'

'I've closed the cellar window. I don't know how that got open. Can you ask Seth? Maybe he opened it when he fixed the cellar door. I don't want you leaving the house with windows open or doors unlocked. I'm not saying it is you but security is important. Can you be sure to check whenever you go out?'

'I do check.'

'I know you do.'

'Did you move the perfume?'

'I don't even remember seeing any perfume.'

'It was on the kitchen counter, Cat found ...' I say, but am interrupted by the gate buzzer.

'Maybe Jan threw it away,' he says getting up. 'Are you sure you didn't put it back in the bedroom?'

'No ... I ... It's that rose smell. Don't you remember?'

'Flo, you're getting anxious again.'

'Sorry.'

'That'll be Laurie. See you in a bit,' he says hurrying out of the bathroom.

I climb carefully from the bath and study my foot. The swelling has gone down a bit but the last thing I'm in the mood for is company.

May 2016
Kerri Wilson

She carefully climbed into the boat and reached behind her to untie the mooring. The boat drifted lazily on the water and she sighed. The notepad lay in her lap. She looked down at it and finally opened it to a blank page.

'Gerard, please forgive me. I just can't do this,' she said softly.

She'd write it. Then she'd talk to Gerard. Maybe she wouldn't have to post it, maybe he will agree with her. A little voice in her head said, 'don't be a fool. Everything is happening for him, why would he give all that up?'

But Margaret Snell, she argued, that's why. She didn't deserve this and nor did Ben. It was wrong. She couldn't keep doing this to him, to his memory.

She began writing.

The effort wearied her and when she'd finished she dropped the pen in her lap as though the effort to hold it any longer was too much. A sense of freedom enveloped her. She had unburdened at last. She won't send it yet. She'll talk to Gerard later. Surely she'd be able to convince him. If she couldn't ... She forced her mind away from that thought and using the oars manoeuvred the boat back to the bank. Perhaps she'd take a nap. She ripped the note from the pad and went upstairs, her body heavy and tired.

She felt for the small lever that opened the secret drawer in the dressing table. There was a tiny click and then it popped open and she slid the note inside. The front door slammed at that moment making her jump.

'Guess what I've got,' Gerard shouted. 'We'll be high on this shit for months.'

She closed the drawer and turned as he burst into the room waving a plastic bag.

'Gerard, I want to talk to you,' she said.

'Sure baby,' he said taking her into his arms. 'Let's make the most of some of this first.'

She nodded. She could do with getting out of it. Get away from these haunting thoughts. Then she'd talk to him.

Chapter Thirty-Three

'I'm so sorry,' says Jan, 'I should have asked Earl to leave when I did. I thought as you hired him it would be okay.'

Adam's voice reaches us from the television set. It's *Today in Parliament* and Adam is firing a question at the leader of the opposition. I switch it off and tap Jan on the arm.

'It's okay. Did *you* move the perfume from the kitchen counter?'

'No, I didn't,' she says glancing over to where the perfume had been.

'Do you remember when you last saw it?'

She shakes her head. I look out the window. Seth is repotting flowers as I had asked him to do.

'Will you be okay if I pop out for a bit?' I ask Jan.

'I've got loads to do. I just feel so low after what happened. I can't bear the thought of you being frightened and here all alone with that gardener. He gives me the creeps too.'

'I don't think we'll be having him much longer,' I say decisively.

Jan looks at me oddly.

'I hope you're not going to do anything silly,' she warns.

'No, I'm in enough trouble with Adam as it is,' I smile.

Seth gives me a wide grin as I open the French doors.

'Did you see Earl yesterday?' I ask.

His face clouds over and he nods.

'Did you fix the cellar door?'

He nods again.

'The window was left open. I know it was warm yesterday. Did you open it while you were working in the cellar?'

Seth bites his lip. He doesn't want to get into trouble. He nods slowly.

'Okay Seth. It's okay. You haven't seen the perfume bottle that was in the kitchen have you?'

He looks puzzled.

'Never mind,' I smile, not wanting to worry him. He looks relieved and begins to play with Kerri.

*

I decide not to phone Henry Dorcas before visiting. After all, it's a village, where everyone knows everyone and nobody minds you dropping in unannounced. A small bubble of anger had been building up in me ever since my confrontation with Earl. I'd be very interested to know how many of Hunters Moon keys Henry Dorcas has.

A red Golf is parked in the driveway and for a moment I feel butterflies in my stomach. I ignore them, push open the gate and stride to the front door. It's a while before I hear footsteps in the hallway. I pull my shoulders back and smile when he opens the door. He looks flustered and seems slightly breathless.

'Hello,' I say before he can speak. 'I wonder if you have a few minutes.'

He struggles to hide his surprise.

'Oh, of course, how are you my dear?'

I pull an envelope from my bag and hand it over.

'We're having a little housewarming. It's fancy dress. I do hope you can make it.'

He opens the envelope and looks at the date.

'It's the night of the Litha,' he says surprised.

'Yes unfortunately, but we'd like to host the party at Hunters Moon if you're okay with that?'

'Oh,' he says taken aback. 'That's very kind of you both.'

'We thought it would be a good way to get to know the villagers.'

That is, Adam thought it would be a good way. To gloss over any bad feeling I've caused is what he meant.

'Lovely,' he smiles. 'I'll announce it at the next guild meeting. Perhaps one of you would like to attend?'

'I'll speak to Adam. I was wondering,' I say hesitantly, 'if you had any back copies of the Penlyn Pen?'

'I'm sure I have. Won't you come in and I'll find them.'

I follow him into the gloomy hallway. He leads the way to the kitchen and I glance at the photographs on the sideboard as we pass.

'Are these photos of your wife?' I ask.

He stops in his stride and turns to face me.

'Yes, that's Rachel. She's in Bluefields Nursing Home.'

The name rings a bell and I try to recall where I had heard it before. He picks up a leaflet from the sideboard and hands it to me.

'I'm giving a lecture in Oxford next week. Perhaps you'd like to come?'

I look at the leaflet.

'Morality in the twentieth century,' I say, reading the title.

'Yes, not an easy one.'

I raise my eyebrows but say nothing.

'The magazines are in my study. I won't be a moment,' he says.

I watch him go upstairs. I hover outside the living room and then venture in. The room is messy with newspapers and magazines scattered all over the floor. It doesn't look like the carpet has been vacuumed in a while. There's a humming sound from the TV. I can hear Henry moving around upstairs. My foot throbs and I look around for somewhere to sit that isn't covered in newspapers. I move a cushion back and sit on the old tatty couch. I have to move to the side to lift my foot. It's swollen again and it occurs to me I may have to make a visit to the doctor. My hip hits something as I sit back and the television bursts into life. For a moment I can't understand what I'm watching and then I realise and my body grows hot.

My eyes are glued to the naked couple on the screen. I can't pull my eyes from the sight of the woman as she takes the man's penis into her mouth again and again, his hand on her head, pushing her until she chokes. A thud comes from upstairs and I fumble for the remote. I frantically push the buttons to turn it off but accidentally turn up the sound instead. The moans of both the man and woman surround the room. I hit the off button and all is silent. I then see the DVD machine is still working.

'Shit,' I curse.

I look around for another remote and then realise the DVD must have still been running when Henry opened the door. He'd only switched off the television. I take a few deep breaths to calm my racing heart and then quickly stand up and go back to the hall.

'I've found a few. The study needs tidying,' he calls.

I remember all the videos I'd seen in there on the night of the barbecue and feel sick. Henry comes down the stairs, his breathing heavy. I struggle to meet his eyes.

'They go back about ten years,' he smiles. 'That should be interesting for you.'

I take them from him. They have a musty nicotine smell about them.

'Do you remember the accident that killed Margaret Snell?' I say bluntly.

I take him by surprise and he visibly starts at my question.

'Margaret Snell?' he repeats.

'She lived at The Old Stores, where Lisa now lives.'

'Lisa?' he says trying to recover.

'Have you not met them? They moved in a little while ago.'

He smiles in acknowledgement.

'Ah yes, I know who you mean.'

'Margaret Snell used to live there, with her son.'

His lips tighten and his blue eyes harden. I force myself to meet his hostile stare.

'Why would you be interested in Margaret Snell?' he asks.

'She was killed in a car accident wasn't she?'

'I believe she was. I'm not sure why you're upsetting yourselves with stories like that. Adam told me that you were taking things calmly these days.'

I clench my fists. Adam has been talking about me to Henry Dorcas? How dare he discuss our private life with someone we barely know?

'I'm looking into the history of Hunters Moon,' I lie. 'It's strange she has such a small tombstone and that her grave is at the back of the cemetery, by the wall. It's almost like someone didn't want her close to other graves.'

He laughs but I can tell it's forced.

'Oh dear, you do have a vivid imagination. I believe it was more a matter of finance. The Snell's were quite a poor family if I recall, and they didn't prepare for things like that. I'm not sure how the Snell family are connected to Hunters Moon though.'

'Oh,' I say turning to the door, 'Benjamin Miller, the man who knocked her down was a friend of Gerard Meyer and his wife Kerri. They lived at Hunters Moon. You must remember?'

He nods.

'Ah yes, I seem to recall that now.'

I struggle with the front door and he leans in from behind me to lift the latch. The smell of nicotine washes over me.

'Do you know if anyone else has keys to our house?' I ask bluntly.

'No one has a key to your house as far as I know,' he says firmly.

'That's good. They should all have been handed back to the estate agent. We can't be too careful.'

'In your husband's position, yes,' he agrees.

'What happened to Margaret Snell's son?' I ask, the fresh air a welcome relief to my nostrils. 'He doesn't seem to be in the cemetery?'

He looks at his watch.

'I'm expecting a phone call, will you excuse me. Thanks for the invitation. Enjoy the magazines,' he says as he shuts the door.

Chapter Thirty-Four

'Margaret Snell?' Rhonda repeats.

'Did you know her well?' I say, picking up my bunch of daffodils.

There's a grunt from Geoff as he fills up the vegetable baskets.

'We barely knew the Snells,' he says.

'No one did,' adds a lady who had been glancing through the magazines.

'But she lived in the village didn't she?'

'There's a new crochet magazine out. I put one by for you,' Rhonda says as she pulls a magazine from under the counter.

'Do you know why her son isn't buried in the cemetery?'

'Is that the new one?' says the lady pointing to the magazine in my hand. 'I haven't seen that one.'

'I can order you a copy,' says Rhonda. 'Have you met Flora Macintosh? She and her husband moved into Hunters Moon.'

'I heard,' says the woman. 'I'm Courtney Willis. I run the Women's Institute. You're far too young for that I know.'

'Did Margaret Snell go the Women's Institute?' I ask, refusing to be ignored.

Rhonda tries to hide her sigh.

'Flora, why are you worrying about people in the village who are dead?'

'I'm just curious,' I smile. 'It's such a close-knit community. I can't understand why Margaret's son isn't in the cemetery and why Margaret's grave is so far from everyone else.'

'Not far enough,' mutters Geoff.

Rhonda shoots him a look.

'Sorry?' I ask.

'Nothing,' he mumbles.

'Did Margaret Snell's son die very young?'

Rhonda sighs.

I turn to Courtney Willis.

'Did you know Kerri Wilson when she lived at Hunters Moon?' I ask.

'Not very well, they kept themselves to themselves.'

'But you all know it was Kerri Wilson's friend Ben who killed Margaret Snell with his car?' I realise there is an accusatory tone in my voice. Why won't anyone be honest with me? What are they trying to hide?

'That's right,' says Geoff. 'It was an unfortunate accident.'

'Where is her son buried?'

Rhonda's face clouds over and she shifts uncomfortably.

'I think I hear the phone ringing,' she says, her voice breaking as she rushes out the back.

'Anything else we can get you?' Geoff asks, his face stern.

'No, thanks.'

I close the door of the shop and walk slowly to the cemetery. My foot is less swollen today but it's still painful. I place the daffodils in a small pot I'd found by the water trough and arrange them below Margaret Snell's tombstone before making my way back to Hunters Moon. The people of Penlyn are hiding something and I feel certain it has something to do with our house.

*

'Do you know the date you're looking for?' asks the blonde-haired library assistant. She smells of Chanel Chance perfume.

'I'm not sure exactly. It was about eighteen months ago.'

'Okay, I'll bring up the folders for late 2014 and early 2015. Hopefully you'll find the article in one of those newspapers. We don't close until eight tonight so you have plenty of time.'

I check the time on my phone. It's two o'clock. I'd phoned Jan who had agreed to take Kerri for her afternoon walk.

'I'll double-check all the locks when I leave,' she had assured me.

I sip from the bottled water I had brought with me and begin leafing through the folders. By three o'clock my eyes are watery and I sit back for a break. The assistant smiles at me and I realise that she has recognised who I am. I drag another folder towards me. No matter how many newspapers I go through there is no mention of Margaret Snell's accident. I can't even find an obituary for her in the local paper. At four o'clock, I close the folder I've been looking through and rub my eyes. I ought to get back. I go to stand up and as I do my head spins and nausea rises up in my stomach. I grip the table and take a deep breath.

'Are you okay?' asks the assistant, standing over me.

'I just got a bit dizzy,' I say, sipping my water.

'It's a bit hot in here,' she says.

I nod in agreement and remove my cardigan. I'm disappointed at not finding anything about the Snells. My head throbs and I really ought to call it a day. There are two more folders left. It won't take long to go through those I decide. It's at the end of the first one that I find a short piece on Margaret Snell.

Local Woman Killed in Horrific Accident: Margaret Snell, aged seventy, was knocked down in a horrific car accident on Saturday 14th November. Mrs Snell and the driver of the vehicle were both found dead at the scene of the accident by the emergency services. Mrs Snell was a resident of Penlyn. She had lived alone since the suicide of her son, Peter Snell, in 1997. Peter Snell was found hanged a week after being cleared of the rape of Kate Earlswin.'

I let out a gasp. Kate Earlswin. There can't be many people with that name in the village. I check my phone again. It's almost five-thirty. I stand up and walk to the desk.

'Would it be possible to see the newspapers from 1997?' I ask.

'Of course, I'll bring up what we have.'

Unfortunately, Peter Snell isn't mentioned until October 1997. It's just after seven o'clock when I find the article and my stomach flutters in excitement.

Local man Peter Snell, aged 25, found hanged in Marsham Woods.

I take a sharp breath. Marsham Woods are the woods at the back of our house. Did Peter Snell hang himself in our woods? I shiver at the thought. I continue reading.

Peter Snell, a local handyman, was found hanged in Marsham Woods on Saturday October 15th. Just a few days earlier Snell had been found not guilty at Oxford Crown court of the rape of 17-year-old Kate Earlswin in June of this year. Police have confirmed Snell's death was suicide but said they would not be releasing the suicide note. The family of Kate Earlswin made no comment on Snell's death. One villager is reported to have said 'The guilt was too much for him.' The village of Penlyn hit the news in June when 17-year-old Kate Earlswin collapsed into the village hall during a village committee meeting. She was reported to have been bleeding and in severe shock. Hours later Snell was arrested on a charge of rape. In court he claimed that Earlswin had consented to sex and that they had arranged the meeting the day before. Earlswin's story was sketchy and the court found Snell not guilty through lack of evidence. There was uproar in the court room following the verdict. Snell is survived by his mother Margaret Snell.

I check the time and hurry to the desk again.

'Is it possible to photocopy this?' I ask.

She points to a photocopier machine in the corner.

'It's 5p a page.'

'Great.'

'We're closing in fifteen minutes.'

I look in surprise at my phone. There are two messages from Adam.

'Thanks.'

I rush back and flick through the issues until I get to June. I find the report of the rape and photocopy that too. I then search the papers for the court case. There is a photo of Kate Earlswin and I find myself staring at a younger version of Rhonda. My phone bleeps again but I ignore it until I have photocopied all the pages I need. I fold them neatly and slip them into my handbag. It's now a few minutes to eight and the library assistant and her colleague are smiling at me.

'Sorry to rush you,' says the assistant.

I hand back the folders reluctantly, and thank her. Once outside I pull my phone from my bag and read Adam's messages.

'Be home late.'

'Everything okay, not heard back from you?'

'Leaving now, hope you're okay.'

I'm about to tap in a reply when it rings and Adam's name pops up on to the screen.

'Hi,' I say.

'Everything okay?' he asks concern in his voice. 'It's not like you not to reply to my messages.'

'Sorry, I'm in Oxford, shopping. I got carried away.'

'Great. I'm in the car on the way back from London. I'll be home in about fifteen minutes. Have you eaten?'

'No, I haven't,' I say. It's no wonder that I came over faint in the library.

'I'll grab a pizza if you like?'

'Great thanks.'

I hang up. I decide not to mention my library visit to Adam. He'll get irritated again. I am, after all, supposed to be taking things calmly. On the way home I find myself wondering what happened to Kate Earlswin.

Chapter Thirty-Five

I stand at the edge of the woods with Kerri at my side. The sun dapples playfully on the leaves of the trees. It's a calm and peaceful sight but twenty years earlier Peter Snell had hung himself in these very woods. Someone from the next village had found his body. They hadn't wanted to be named in the newspapers. Rhonda and Geoff's daughter had been raped by him, shame in the village, I think. Is that why they don't want to talk about it, and why everyone is so evasive when I ask about the Snells? But why would Peter Snell wait until after the court case to commit suicide? If his guilt was all-consuming surely he would have confessed to the rape in court. I chew my lip as I walk back to the house. Where was Kate Earlswin now? She didn't live in the village, not as far as I knew anyway, and it was no use asking the locals. The only Earlswin tombstone I had seen in the cemetery was presumably that of Geoff's parents, both having been born in the 1920s. It had been a big story. The newspapers had made much of it. There was talk of devil worship but that had later been dismissed. Kate Earlswin's tear-stained face was splashed across the papers as were Peter Snell's and his mother's as they came out of court. The verdict was a shock and there had been an unprecedented outcry in the courtroom with the parents avenging the decision. Penlyn had been quiet ever since. Not a hint or whiff of scandal. I'd gone back to the library to search but there was nothing. The villagers had obviously made sure that Penlyn would not be under the spotlight again.

Laurie answers on the first ring.

'I was just about to call you,' she says. 'I've arranged security for the party. When can they come and check out everything?'

'Oh, I guess anytime.'

'Fabulous and I have some great costume ideas to show you. We also need to go through your guest list. Is Adam inviting any foreign dignitaries? Our security guys need to be aware of any high-profile guests.'

'I'll ask him. He's doing a television debate today. I'm not sure when he'll be home.'

'Okay, but don't forget.'

'Okay,' I say, my mind still on Peter Snell.

'You okay?' she asks. 'You're not having more problems with your resident ghost are you?'

'No, I just ... Are you free to meet for lunch?'

I hear her flicking through her diary.

'I've got an hour at two. Is that any good?'

I let out a little sigh.

'That's brilliant,' I say. 'Can you come here?'

*

'Do you still know that judge?' I ask, handing her a plate of salmon sandwiches.

'Ooh that good-looking stud, Julian, do you mean? Yes I do, but we're just friends now, unfortunately.'

'Could you ask him how I get a court transcript?'

Her eyes widen.

'What do you want a court transcript for?'

'Twenty years ago there was a rape in the village. The rapist hung himself in those woods.'

I point to the window.

'Christ, really?' Laurie shivers

I pull the photocopied sheets from my handbag and hand them to her.

'It's all here. The thing is no one in the village will talk about it but you can find it in back issues of the local paper. It was the daughter of the village shop owners. He got off but a few days after the court case he hung himself.'

She reads through the sheets while I sip my tea.

'Is that your ghost then?'

I shake my head.

'No, but Kerri Wilson's friend Ben, had a fatal car crash. It was just outside the village and he knocked down Margaret Snell, Peter Snell's mother, and killed her.'

Laurie frowns.

'So, what's odd about all this? Accidents happen don't they?'

I shrug. The truth is, even I don't know what is odd about everything but something doesn't seem right.

'And then there's Earl the gardener and the DVD at Henry's ...'

'Slow down. I'm getting lost.'

'I think something odd happened here with Kerri Wilson but I don't know what. I can't help thinking that maybe Kerri didn't have a heart attack but was murdered.'

Laurie looks at me oddly.

'Flora, seriously, where is this all coming from?'

'I have this recurrent dream. I told you about it. You were here when I had it and then all these things ... Earl looks at me strangely when he's here. It's like he's undressing me. It really unnerves me. I keep wondering if he was involved somehow. No one in the village has ever mentioned Peter Snell but they know he hung himself in the wood and ...'

'It may not have been your part of the wood, Flora.'

'And Henry is weird. I got there yesterday to ask about Margaret Snell and he was all breathless and flushed. He'd clearly been watching a porn movie because I accidently turned on the remote when he was upstairs.'

She shakes her head.

'How did you accidentally turn on a porn movie?'

I sigh.

'Does it matter Laurie? I sat on the remote, okay?'

'We've all watched a bit of porn. Look, I'm not taking sides or anything. I'm just trying to get things in perspective for you. You can't blame the villagers for not wanting to talk about their daughter being raped. I expect everyone is protecting the family. As for Earl, maybe he is a bit of a perv. He can't get in now can he and just tell Adam you want another gardener? As for the accident with that guy, what was his name?'

'Ben,' I say feeling suddenly deflated.

'I don't understand what that has got to do with Kerri Wilson. Do you still think she is haunting the house?'

It all sounds so normal hearing it from Laurie and I'm relieved I didn't share any of this with Adam after all. I'm being totally ridiculous.

'You're quite right,' I say. 'I'm getting everything out of proportion. I just can't help thinking something strange happened to Kerri Wilson but I don't know what.'

Laurie puts down her plate and takes my hand.

'Even if it did, does it matter?'

'I suppose not. But that perfume went missing, the bottle that Cat found in the boat.'

'You haven't just forgotten where you put it?'

'I don't know,' I say, feeling confused.

'You look really pale Flora and you're not eating your lunch. I really think you should stop all this and focus on the party, and on your commissions.'

I nod.

'Are you and Adam still trying for the baby?'

'Of course.'

'That should be the most important thing. Take the puppy for regular walks. Can't you change its name,' she says pulling a face. 'Calling it bloody *Kerri* of all things.'

'Perhaps you're right.'

She squeezes my hand and says, 'How about if we look at the costume ideas?'

'Okay but Lisa and I were going to the hire shops together this week.'

'Oh right,' says Laurie, trying not to look hurt.

‘It’s my way of getting involved in the village,’ I explain. ‘I’ve got my crochet group tomorrow although somehow I don’t think Rhonda will be too pleased to see me after my cross-examination of her.’

‘Let’s go over all the arrangements then,’ she smiles. ‘We’ve had responses. You’ll have at least seventy-five here. Shall I send out the second wave of invites?’

I glance out at the lake and the boat that bobs gently at its mooring. Maybe I’ll make an appointment with the doctor. It’s true I haven’t been feeling myself just lately. I’ll try and get an appointment with Doctor Hemel as Rhonda had suggested.

‘Yes, okay,’ I say.

The more the merrier Adam would say.

Chapter Thirty-Six

After Laurie leaves I take a mug of tea to the bedroom and turn on the television to watch the recording of Adam's TV debate. He looks smart and gloriously handsome. I smile at the thought of him arriving home with the studio make-up still on. He was right when he said he was going grey. He looks distinguished. An urge to make love with him overcomes me and I check my phone to see what time he had left. I've just enough time to take a bath.

I check the doors and windows and then run a bath. Kerri is sprawled out on the bed. She's made it her own and I know it doesn't please Adam.

'You'll be kicked off when daddy gets home,' I say rubbing her ears. She thinks it's a signal to play and jumps down from the bed. The smell of roses wafts over and it reminds me that I still haven't checked under the bed to see if some perfume had been spilt there. I bend down and peek under only to have Kerri follow and try to turn it into a game.

There's nothing under the bed that I can see and after throwing lavender bath salts into the tub I climb in and lie back, allowing the warm water to flow over me. My body begins to relax and I think about what Laurie had said. She's quite right. All my fancies from earlier seem silly now that I had talked them over with her. I was making a mystery out of things that were quite ordinary. Of course the villagers didn't want Kate Earlswin's rape dragged up again. Kate probably left the village for that very reason. Peter Snell most likely had, as was reported, a severe bout of guilt and hanged himself. It probably wasn't in our part of the woods at all. It was only natural in an old house like this that I might believe odd things happened. But they didn't and that's what I need to remember and, even if they did, like Laurie said, what does it matter? As for Earl, he's just some perv. There are plenty of them around. Henry is another one in my opinion, but I can't judge. After all, Adam and I have watched porn in the past. It's really none of my business why Margaret Snell is buried at the back of the cemetery. Perhaps that's what the village requested. I imagine the vicar couldn't say no. I relax in the bath and think about the party. We'll make it the best party Penlyn has ever seen.

The front door slams and Adam calls up the stairs.

'Where are you?'

'In the bath, you're home sooner than I thought.'

I hear him throw his case on to the bedroom chair. A few seconds later he walks in. He looks just as gorgeous as he did on the television earlier.

'I've been thinking about you,' I say sexily. 'You looked gorgeous tonight.'

'Did you watch it?'

'I did and you were great.'

He sits on the side of the bath and I take his hand, putting it on my breast.

'Is it ovulation time?' he asks.

'We can do it other times,' I say.

'Oh good,' he smiles leaning down to kiss me. 'If you say so then that's okay with me.'

I climb from the bath and put my arms around his neck. I feel his hardness through his trousers and cover it with my hand.

'Let's go into the bedroom,' he says huskily.

Kerri dives off the bed as we fall on to it and starts barking when she thinks we want to play.

'That bloody dog, Flora,' laughs Adam. 'She's taking my place these days.'

'Well, if you will spend so much time away.'

He fumbles with his trousers and I giggle.

'Sorry Flora, I know you put up with a lot and ...'

I pull him back down and silence him with a kiss.

'Jesus Flo,' he moans, turning me so I'm lying at the bottom of the bed. Kerri tries to lick my hand and I giggle even more. Adam enters me and I arch my back. I wind my arms around his neck and look ahead of me to the window, when I feel myself tense.

'Flo,' he whispers.

The bed creaks beneath us but all I can see is Henry's porn film. The woman's whimpers seem to echo in my head and then I realise. There had been something familiar about the film and now I know what it was. I look at the window behind Adam's head. It was the small stained-glass fanlight window in the bedroom. It's identical to the one in here. The porn movie had been made at Hunters Moon.

Chapter Thirty-Seven

Adam waves from the car and I wait until the gates have locked before hurrying back into the house where the decorators are finishing off in the boathouse. I put the flipchart up in the study and then stare at it not sure where to begin. I'm conscious there are still boxes to unpack. Putting off my list I go into the kitchen to make tea for the decorators. Seth is coming after lunch. I'll ask him to put the boxes in the cellar. I see my temperature chart and realise I haven't taken it the past two days. I curse and check when my next period is due and then realise that I'm well overdue. My stomach does a little flip and my heart races. Could I be pregnant? Was Laurie right about the puppy?

I scoop Kerri up and hug her and she returns my affection with her own and soon my face is wet from her kisses. Once the decorators have their tea I take my cup into the study and begin writing on the flipchart.

Did Kerri Wilson die in a sex game that went tragically wrong? Did the village cover it up?

Was someone filming Kerri having sex and why?
If it was manslaughter how did they cover it up and how did the media get the heart attack story?

Even if I have got everything wrong, why does Henry have a porn film that was made at Hunters Moon?

Oh God. Is there a secret camera in our bedroom? Did Kerri Wilson not know she was being filmed? Has Henry Dorcas filmed us? My mind rushes back to the first time Adam and I had made love in the bedroom and how Adam had held me down and my face colours at the memory. Oh God, how many times had I been naked in my bedroom. Anger surges through me and I rush up the stairs. I scan the bedroom ceiling and walls. There is nothing that resembles a camera. Our new fitted wardrobe covers most of the wall and I try to remember what was there when we had viewed. Did we keep the house details?

'Bugger,' I mutter.

Maybe the video had been filmed somewhere else. It's possible there are other houses with similar stained-glass windows. I can't be a hundred per cent certain it was ours. The only way I will ever know if that video was taken here was to go back into Henry's house and steal it. The thought of it makes me feel physically sick. I remember the Penlyn Pen magazines he had given me and try to work out how I could use those as an excuse to go back to his house and somehow get the DVD. But supposing he has taken it out of the recorder. It could be any one of those he had on the shelf in the study upstairs. I sip my tea and lay my hand on my stomach. If I am pregnant then surely I should focus on that. It is possible that it could have been any bedroom.

Did Peter Snell kill himself, or was it murder? I add to my flipchart.

What happened to Kate Earlswin? Did she leave the village?

A thought enters my head and I add underneath,
Did Kate Earlswin get pregnant?

My heart thuds in my chest. The child would be about twenty years old now. Could Seth be Kate Earlswin's child? My head spins and I sit back down until the dizzy spell passes. I should make an appointment with Doctor Kingsley.

I tear the sheet from the flipchart. I can't tell Adam any of this. The time seems to drag as I wait for Seth. I potter around the house emptying boxes. Finally he arrives. He has a toy for Kerri and I let him play with her for a while before making him a drink and asking if he'll help me sort through some boxes. He's surprised and looks out to the garden.

'There's not much needs doing outside,' I say. 'But I really need to get some of these boxes unpacked and stuff that we don't need I want to put in the cellar. Can you help with that?'

He scratches his chin and then nods. I go through the boxes systematically in the hope of finding the original house details. It's painstaking and boring. Seth takes several boxes down to the cellar and I open the French doors to let in some air. We finally reach a box with family photos and I seize upon the chance to question Seth about his mother. He glances through a couple of my parents and I point to them saying,

'That's my mum. She used to teach the piano. She died when I was a teenager. This is my dad; he moved to Australia and has a new wife.'

He studies the photos and then points to the cellar.

'No, I think I'll keep these ones. Do you have photos of your mum?'

He's taken aback, shakes his head and then begins to use his hands in what seems to be sign language. He stops when he realises what he's doing.

'Can you sign?' I ask.

He looks around and grabs an envelope from one of the boxes. With the pen I'd been using to write notes he scribbles something on the paper and hands it to me.

Not good.

It reads. He looks at me and then scribbles some more.

Mother left.

'Left the village, you mean?'

He nods.

'What about your father?'

He fidgets and averts his eyes. I wait for him to write more but he doesn't.

'Is he alive?'

He seems to hesitate and then shakes his head. Can I ask him if his father is Peter Snell, I wonder? I decide against it and say simply, 'I'm sorry Seth.'

I don't need Seth to tell me any more. It's clear that Seth is Kate Earlswin's son and that his father Peter Snell died in the woods.

Chapter Thirty-Eight

I watch Seth walk through the main gates and then make my way back to the kitchen to make a sandwich. Adam had texted to say he would be home at nine.

I'm taking tomorrow off. I'll be able to help with some of the unpacking.

'That's lovely, isn't it?' I say stroking Kerri. 'Adam will be home with us.'

I pop two slices of bread into the toaster and search around the kitchen for the bottle of Rose Oud. How could it disappear like that? It had been sitting on the kitchen counter for days. Who could have taken it? Jan hadn't moved it. I try to remember who had been in the house. Would Earl have taken it? Surely not. The toaster pops just as I decide to check the recycling box out the back. It's a waste of time. The perfume bottle isn't there. Kerri rummages through the rubbish with her nose and I pull her away.

The toast now looks decidedly unappealing and I make tea instead and take it with Kerri to the cellar. Sitting cross-legged I pull out several boxes and search for the house details. When I do find them I'm disappointed to find they don't help me at all. The photos of the bedrooms are small and I can't see clearly whether there was anything on the walls.

'Damn it,' I mumble.

The details are no longer on the internet so I can't check them on the computer. I put the house details to one side and make a mental note to scan them. I may then be able to zoom in on the photo. Kerri finds a piece of string and begins to play.

'Come on Kerri,' I say. 'Let's go back up.'

In the study I scan the house details and then zoom into the wall where I imagined the camera may have been. There is nothing there. I let out a small sigh of relief. It's an hour before Adam will be home. I decide to have a lie down. I'm feeling more tired than usual. I lie on the bed and look around the room. There doesn't seem to be any signs on the wall that anything had been fitted there. I turn over and try to nap but I'm too restless. I study my reflection in the dressing table mirror. The earrings I'm wearing are big and clumsy and I take them off. I'll wear the pearls Adam bought me last Christmas. As I'm searching for them it occurs to me that the perfume bottle may have been put away in the dresser. Maybe Jan did it without thinking. But a search of the drawers reveals only underwear, socks and sweaters. I sigh and roughly shove the jewellery case back into the drawer. How can the bloody bottle have just disappeared like that? I hear a click and a little drawer springs out at me. I stare at in astonishment. The dresser has a secret drawer. Lying in it is a scrap of paper and several photographs. I lift them out. They're photos of Kerri with Ben. Carefully I unfold the piece of paper. It's a note written in bold black ink. It's a confession by Kerri Wilson.

To whom it may concern, May 12th 2016
I, Kerri Wilson, wish to confess to an incident that happened on the 14th November 2015. Three of us were driving back from Oxford in a vintage car owned by Ben. My husband Gerard was driving. We lied about that. Henry Dorcas, a neighbour from our village, with Geoff Earlswin, came to our assistance after my husband phoned him. It was he who suggested that we make it look like Ben was driving the car. It was my husband, Gerard Meyer, who knocked down Margaret Snell. I know we should have told the truth at the time but my husband feared for his career. We're sorry for our deceit. Please take this into consideration. We were

mistakenly guided by Henry Dorcas. I'm not putting the blame on anyone other than ourselves but would hope leniency would be considered when hearing of our plight. We were high on drugs and made a terrible mistake, the consequences of which we will live with forever.
Kerri Wilson (Meyer)

Gerard Meyer had been driving the car. Why hadn't I guessed that?

I look at the date and then go downstairs. I find the web page and discover that May 12th 2016 was the day Kerri Wilson died. Had Kerri fought with Gerard that day? Did Henry come round to discuss her note? Did she fall down the stairs during an argument?

I feel overcome with dizziness and close my eyes as a strong wave of nausea overtakes me. As soon as I feel able to stand I walk slowly to the kitchen and phone Doctor Kingsley.

'I think I may be pregnant,' I tell him.

*

'I would say around four weeks,' Doctor Kingsley tells Adam. 'But it is difficult to be sure with Flora's spasmodic cycles.'

Adam holds my hand.

'I told you that you would get pregnant,' he smiles.

'The important thing now is for us to do everything we can to make sure Flora holds on to this baby,' says Doctor Kingsley. 'Her scan was normal and the blood test showed that her hormones were fluctuating but were steady enough. My advice is to register with the local GP. He needs to be aware. I'm giving Flora a prescription for ...'

'Would it best if she were in hospital?' Adam asks.

'I wish you wouldn't talk about me like I'm not here,' I say.

'Sorry darling.'

Doctor Kingsley nods.

'Quite right,' he smiles. 'What's concerning me is your blood pressure. It's higher than I would like. Is there something bothering you?'

Kerri Wilson's letter is in the pocket of my jeans. 'I've got a bit anxious lately,' I admit.

Adam nods.

'Flora has been anxious about the new house. There's a lot to do and ...'

'I got it in my head that the place was haunted,' I say making light of it.

'I don't want you having high blood pressure,' says Doctor Kingsley. 'That would concern me.'

'We have the housewarming party to organise and ...'

'Should we cancel that?' asks Adam.

I turn pleading eyes on to Doctor Kingsley. I want a baby desperately but I can't be cooped up here day in and day out.

'I need something to do,' I say.

'As long as it's not séances and whatnot,' says Adam sternly.

'Séances?' retorts Doctor Kingsley.

'I promise to be calm.'

Adam hugs me.

'We're going to have this baby,' he says. 'Simon will take good care of you.'

'But I am banning all talk of ghosts and hauntings,' warns Doctor Kingsley. 'Otherwise you'll have to spend the duration of the pregnancy in a rest home so I can be sure there is no undue strain on you or the baby.'

'I promise,' I say.

I have no idea if I can keep the promise but I'm determined to try.

Chapter Thirty-Nine

I'd been determined to keep my promise. I'd pushed from my mind thoughts of Kerri Wilson and Margaret Snell but my recurring nightmare comes to haunt me every few days, and I always wake up feeling panicky. The nightmares are so vivid that I am getting nervous of being near the stairs. I don't mention any of this to Adam. He's preoccupied with the goings on at Westminster.

Lisa and I went shopping for costumes for the Litha. My bump was beginning to show and I wore it with pride. I felt well and would not allow myself to think of anything but happy thoughts. If I felt anything strange in the house I ignored it. If Earl looked at me oddly I pretended not to notice. When the villagers rallied round to help after hearing my pregnancy news I welcomed it. I contacted House of Fraser and ordered a bottle of Rose Oud. I told myself it was my treat for getting pregnant again. I had none of the symptoms I had with my previous two pregnancies and felt happy and serene. I am going over the food menu with the caterer when my mobile rings.

'I need to speak with you,' Felicity says without preamble.

Something tells me to be cautious.

'I'm not getting out too much,' I say cautiously. 'I'm taking things carefully.'

'On the phone is fine. I don't want anyone to overhear though, are you alone?'

I turn to look at Jan.

'Hang on, I'll take it in the lounge,' I say. I close the door of the living room and relax on the couch. My feet are slightly swollen and it occurs to me I should phone Doctor Kingsley and mention it.

'I'm alone,' I tell Felicity.

'We can't make your party. Ralph's in trouble,' she says bluntly.

'What kind of trouble?'

'If it comes out, he'll be finished. Not only will he have to resign but his reputation will be in tatters.'

I find myself wondering why Adam hadn't mentioned anything. He's probably concerned that it might upset me and in turn affect the pregnancy. I wish he would stop treating me with kid gloves.

'What's happened?' I ask.

There's a little sob at the other end of the phone and my heart goes out to her.

'He's been an idiot, Flora. It's was just a one off. But she's a sex worker.'

'Sex worker?' I repeat stupidly.

'A prostitute,' she says and I hear her blow her nose.

'Oh Felicity, are you okay?'

'Of course,' she snaps. 'He was stressed, it happens doesn't it?'

Not to Prime Ministers I think, but keep quiet.

'The bitch is threatening to go to the press.'

A little voice in my head tells me this could be it. This could be Adam's opportunity and a little pang of dread runs through me.

'Perhaps she won't,' I say.

'I need you to talk to Adam. He's always stood by Ralph. Once the news gets out the bastards will gang up on him, I know it. Not that any of them are whiter than white. They're all probably at it.'

She trails off and my mind wanders to Adam and the words of the hairdresser all those weeks ago. *I wouldn't kick him out of bed.*

'Flora, I know Adam is under pressure but he's always been Ralph's ally. Will you speak to him? I know if he comes out publicly on Ralph's side it will make all the difference. I know they're all pushing him to challenge the leadership. It was an error of judgement, Flora. We've all made them haven't we?'

Henry Dorcas's words come back to me. I'd gone to his lecture a few weeks ago. Doctor Kingsley had suggested I do things to take my mind off the pregnancy so I didn't get worried about every little twinge. *Know your weaknesses,* Henry had warned. *Errors of judgements are products of our human weakness. We know what the consequences might be but we still take the risk.*

Ralph would have known the consequences. I can't encourage Adam to be party to that? Ralph will pull Adam down with him.

'Oh Felicity, I don't know what to say? How much do the media know?'

'Nothing yet but it's just a matter of time isn't it? Will you talk to Adam?'

'I'll tell him you called me. I can't guarantee anything Felicity.'

There's a few seconds of silence.

'What do I do?' she asks, her voice cracking.

'Oh Felicity,' I say feeling tears well up in my eyes.

'Everyone is going to pity me.'

My mobile bleeps with another call. I glance at the screen and see it is Adam. A few moments later I hear the land line phone ringing and then a gentle tap at the door. Jan peeks round holding the phone.

'Adam,' she mouths. 'He says it's urgent.'

I nod.

'Felicity, I have to go. Adam is on the other line. I promise to speak to him.'

'Thank you, Flora, you're a sweetheart,' she says and hangs up.

I place a protective hand over my stomach and take a breath. I knew this day would come and that one day Adam would realise his ambitions but I really don't relish the media glare on us.

'Flora, it's me,' says Adam. 'How are you?'

'I'm fine, honestly I'm fine.'

'Good. I may be late. There's been ...'

'Felicity just phoned. She's really upset.'

'Damn it, where's her consideration. She knows you're taking it easy because of the pregnancy.'

'It's okay,' I assure him. 'I've got the caterers here. The tables, chairs, everything has been delivered.'

'Great. I won't be too late I promise. I've got to attend a crisis meeting.'

'Felicity begged me to ask you to support Ralph.'

He sighs.

'I don't want you fretting about it. Promise me?'

My heart swells with love for him.

'I promise.'

'It will be okay.'

'What if Ralph resigns?' I ask.

'There is pressure on me to challenge the leadership,' he admits. 'But I want to see if Ralph can ride the wave. You focus on the party preparations. Who knows we might have more to celebrate.'

Chapter Forty

It's Midsummer's Day, the day of the Litha celebrations. I'd been feeling nauseous since breakfast. Adam had insisted I take things easy until the festival began. Bottles of champagne sit in buckets on the patio ready for our party after the Litha celebrations. It had been a rough week for Adam. He'd carried the knowledge of Ralph's indiscretion around with him. Ralph was continuing as though everything was normal but it was only a matter of time before the shit hit the fan. Felicity hadn't contacted me again. We knew that once the scandal hit the papers Adam would have to tell Ralph to resign. I couldn't begin to imagine what Felicity was going through. I tried to phone her a few times but she had refused to take my call. She, no doubt, believes I didn't encourage Adam to support Ralph.

'This is my disguise,' Laurie says revealing a hand-held Venetian mask.

I've still to change. My head is throbbing and I wonder if it will be okay to take a paracetamol.

'You look fabulous,' I say.

There is a hive of activity on the patio. It's a warm day and Kerri is basking in the attention she is getting from everyone.

I call Doctor Kingsley and ask about the paracetamol.

'Take the lowest dose possible,' he advises. 'I'll see you both later.'

'I think I'll lie down for a bit,' I say. 'I'll take a paracetamol and rest my head. I've got time haven't I?'

'Don't worry, everything is in hand. Leave the party organisation to me,' she smiles. 'Let me help you upstairs.'

'I'm pregnant, Laurie, not ill.'

'Sorry,' she apologises.

All the activity leading up to the party had tired me. I lie on the bed and listen to the party preparations and within seconds I am asleep.

*

She beckons to me. I try to tell her I can't come this time. I have to rest. But she continues to beckon until I follow her out on to the landing. I don't want to watch her fall. I need to be calm for the baby. I open my mouth to tell her this but she is no longer there. I look down to see her lying on the hallway floor and fight back a gasp. I seem to float down the stairs and there standing in the doorway the rain pelting down behind him is Adam.

'What have you done?' he asks.

'I didn't …' I begin but a voice behind me says,

'She fell, I tried to catch her.'

I swing round.

'You didn't try to catch her, I saw you,' I scream.

His hands reach out to me and I fall backwards. There's a loud crash as I hit something. My feet slide on the woman's blood and I scream again. There is crashing all around me. I don't know where to run.

My eyes open and I sit up with a start. It takes me a moment to register what the noise is and then I remember the party. My eyes focus on my Demelza costume, hanging next to Adam's, Ross Poldark cloak.

'How are you feeling? I didn't want to disturb you,' Adam says.

'How long have you been there?' I ask.

'A while,' he says. 'The carnival has started. We should get ready.'

My headache has eased but I still feel nauseous. I slip into my costume and fix the wig to my head. The red hair suits me. Adam looks like a real-life Ross Poldark, except he's far more handsome. I take a selfie of us together before we leave.

'How far would you have gone to cover for Ralph?' I ask.

He looks at me, puzzlement written across his face.

'I've always been loyal to him, you know that.'

'I know, but why have you been?'

'He was good to me at the start of my political career. He opened doors that may never have opened. I'm grateful.'

'You don't condone what he's done though?'

He bites his lip.

'It was a big mistake.'

'An error of judgement,' I say thoughtfully.

There's a rapping at the door.

'Everyone is wondering where we are,' says Adam.

Cat pops her head around.

'We're all going now. Are you two ready?'

'I'll be ready in two minutes,' I say. I decide to enjoy the party as much as possible. In a few weeks our lives will change forever.

'Adam,' I say as he opens the door for us to leave. 'You'd never make a big mistake would you?'

He pulls me to him and runs his fingers through the wig hair.

'Don't be daft. I'm not an idiot.'

His warm lips meet mine and I feel comforted.

'Let's go. I want to show off my beautiful wife.'

Chapter Forty-One

I have so many memories of the night of the Litha celebrations. There was the sea of masks dancing through the streets, a fire dancer performing to lively Celtic music, a parade of life-sized puppets, exotic costumes and colourful displays. The atmosphere on the street was electric. It was wonderful to be able to welcome the villagers to Hunters Moon. Adam and I greeted everyone in our hallway. A woman in a pink ostrich outfit waltzed around with trays of champagne and waiters in smart white shirts and black bow ties stood with trays of crackers and caviar. There were black-hooded men and white-feathered women. Our bedrooms were cluttered with boas and coats. The strong fragrance of perfume permeated the patio and gardens.

Henry moved among the guests like the host, seeing to their needs, but something about his behaviour made me feel uneasy. At midnight the church bell tolled and a volley of fireworks from the other side of the lake lit up the sky. I looked over to the vicar. He looked normal. Not how I imagined a drug addict might look. The champagne had been flowing and it felt odd being the only sober person among many merry alcohol-fuelled guests.

'How are you feeling?' Doctor Kingsley asked.

'Very sober,' I laugh, sipping my flavoured water.

'Adam tells me you had a nap today.'

'Yes, I'm feeling tired a lot.'

'I think I'd like to take some bloods next week. Can you pop to my consulting room?'

I nod.

'Wonderful party,' says the vicar, joining us. 'I'm sorry I didn't dress up.'

'You look every inch the vicar,' I smile.

'Hello,' says a voice behind me. I turn to see Art Mitchell. He's dressed in a Poldark outfit and looks very handsome.

'Wow, for a second I thought you were Adam. I can't believe there are two Ross Poldark's in this village tonight,' I say smiling.

'Adam's got pulled into a conga line. I managed to get away before it got me too', he laughs. 'Thanks for the invite.'

'I'm glad you could make it.'

'How could I not. I haven't seen you for a bit,' he says shyly.

'I've been a bit cautious,' I say, stroking my stomach.

'Congratulations. Are you up to a Litha dance?' he asks as the music changes. 'I think Ross Poldark should dance with Demelza at least once this evening don't you?'

'I don't see why not,' I say taking his hand.

I'm surprised at what an accomplished dancer Art Mitchell is. He glides me around to The Blue Danube expertly.

'The vicar's looking pretty normal tonight. Did you explore that any further?' he asks.

'I've been exploring a lot actually and, well I have to think of the baby. Everyone keeps telling me not to get anxious.'

'Ah, right …'

I pull back and look at him.

'What?'

'I asked around about Margaret Snell. I have a friend who works on the local rag and he remembered her funeral.'

I feel a flutter of excitement in my stomach.

'What did he tell you?'

'He went along to cover it. Not that there was much to cover. There was only the vicar and old Henry Dorcas there. But when he asked some questions about the funeral, the accident and so on, they got quite nasty. Threw him out of the church and threatened to sue the paper if he mentioned the funeral.'

'I put flowers on her grave but someone destroyed them,' I say remembering the broken daffodils scattered around the graveside. 'Did you know that Rhonda and Geoff's daughter was raped by Margaret Snell's son?'

He grins.

'Ah, that was the next thing I was going to tell you.'

'You've gone to a lot of trouble.'

'I've got nothing else to do except look after my girls,' he smiles.

'Your girls?' I ask surprised.

'The hens. By the way, Rosie wouldn't mind seeing Kerri again.'

'We'll drop round for coffee and treats,' I smile.

The music stops and there is a drum roll from the band. Geoff has climbed up on to the bandstand by the lake and without thinking he pulls the mike from its stand. A screeching echoes around us.

'Sorry,' he apologises tapping the mike. 'It's gone midnight. It's time to announce the new elder.'

Rhonda steps forward. She's dressed as a corn maiden and looks much younger with her wig of long hair. I want to ask her about her daughter. Seth looks on proudly, his cheeks rosy from the champagne. I find myself stupidly hoping that Adam has been chosen as the new elder even though I know that isn't possible. Sienna waves to me and walks over to join us.

'It's all very antiquated this isn't it?' she grins. 'By the way, your dress looks terrific.'

'I've got Lisa to thank for that. She convinced me the dress looked good. Do you know Lisa? She bought The Old Stores?'

'Yes, I showed her around actually. You've done wonders with Hunters Moon.'

'Have you seen the boathouse?' I ask.

She shakes her head. There's another drum roll and we all look at Geoff.

'The votes are in,' he says. 'I hereby declare the new guild elder is …'

There is a moment of silence. Everyone holds their breath in anticipation. Could it be Adam I wonder? Will he accept if he is chosen?

'Henry Dorcas,' Geoff says gleefully.

I look over at Henry. He looks menacing in his black cloak and mask. He removes it and steps up triumphantly to the platform.

'Well, that's a surprise,' says Art.

'He's certainly popular in the village isn't he?' says Lisa, joining us.

'We hope Adam Macintosh will accept the honour of handing over the certificate and crown,' says Geoff, nodding to Adam.

There are loud cheers as Adam steps forward. Henry makes a brief acceptance speech and then the band strikes up again. I look over to Seth. His face is expressionless. He isn't smiling like everyone else. I look back to Henry who is gleefully accepting everyone's congratulatory words and I feel anger rising within me.

'Will you excuse me,' I say to Sienna and Art. 'I'm feeling a bit hot.'

'Shall I get you some water?' Sienna asks.

'I'm fine, thanks.'

I turn to Art.

'We'll pop over next week.'

'Look forward to it.'

I walk into the house, through the hallway and out the front door. There was never a better time to check that DVD of Henry's than now and I decide not to waste it.

*

I can only blame hormones on what I did next. Using the light from my phone I hurry to Henry's house. I remember Rhonda's words no one locks their doors in Penlyn. The music from Hunters Moon follows me to Claremont Tower. There are still revellers in the village and I pass without too much notice. A man wearing an eye patch offers me a swig from his vodka bottle.

'Happy Litha,' he yells.

I decline pleasantly and continue to Claremont Tower. I look behind me and when I'm assured that I'm alone, I walk round to the back door. The handle turns and the door opens. I gasp in surprise. Did Kerri leave the doors of Hunters Moon unlocked when she was there? I pray that the DVD is still in the TV player and that I don't have to search through Henry's study. It's difficult to see from the torch on my phone but eventually I find the remote. It takes me some time to get into the channel for the player. Finally I'm in and I sit mesmerised watching Kerri Wilson having oral sex with Gerard Meyer. Then the camera is moved and I feel dizzy as my own bedroom spins around in front of me. Oh God, I was right, it was filmed in our bedroom. Then I see a figure behind Kerri. Kerri says something but I can't make out what it is. She lets out a sob and I hold my breath in shock as the man enters her from behind. I feel the nausea rise up as I watch him rip into her anus and in that moment I want to kill him. I want to kill Henry Dorcas.

Chapter Forty-Two

I don't know how long I sat there staring at the television screen. I can't imagine how I looked in my eighteenth-century Demelza Poldark costume watching a blue movie. I click it off and force myself from the couch. Had Kerri been forced against her will? I eject the DVD from the machine and leave the house with it in my hand. My mind reels and I find myself walking in the wrong direction. How can he possibly be the guild elder? Surely if the people of Penlyn knew about this they wouldn't want him? Was he responsible for Kerri Wilson's death? Was it a sex game that went wrong? Was she trying to escape and then fell down the stairs? Had Henry been blackmailing them? He'd obviously helped them cover everything up and then made them pay for their mistakes. Kerri Wilson was overcome with remorse. That was why she looked so terrible. Henry took advantage of her weakness. The party is in full swing when I return and no one seems to have missed me. I clutch my stomach as a sharp pain shoots through it. I'm not supposed to be getting stressed. I slide the DVD inside the pocket of my dress. I'll hide it in the boathouse.

Lisa meets me at the French doors.

'There you are. I've been looking for you.'

She looks closely at me.

'Are you okay?' she asks worriedly. 'You're very pale.'

'I've got a pain,' I say.

'Let me fetch Adam,' she says turning.

I grab her arm.

'No. Can I talk to you?'

I take some deep breaths in the hope the pain will ease.

'Let me get you some water,' she says.

'I think Kerri Wilson died after a sex game went wrong. I believe Henry Dorcas is involved. I think Henry Dorcas is covering up all kinds of things that happened in the village.'

A hand touches my shoulder and I shiver.

'Flora, I've been looking for you. Are you okay?'

It's Adam. He's worried. It's written all over his face. He can see the pain in mine.

'I'm okay,' I say.

'I'll take her to the boathouse,' says Lisa, 'It's quieter there.'

I lay my hand over the DVD in my pocket.

'Shall I get Simon?' he asks anxiously.

'I'll be fine,' I tell Adam. 'Please don't worry.'

'Promise me. Simon is here. It's not a problem to speak to him if we're concerned.'

'I'm just hot.'

'Perhaps if we sit in the boat,' suggests Lisa. 'You'll feel the breeze on the lake and we can get away from the crowd.'

Lisa pushes the boat away from the mooring. It's cool on the lake and I realise my fear of it had been totally irrational. The lake looks beautiful with the floating candles. Lanterns hang in the bushes and shrubs. The grounds are awash with light. Everywhere including the woods beyond look romantic with the soft lights Laurie had arranged everywhere. I try to relax but it is difficult.

The band plays on and couples spin around the garden like tops. I hear the pop of a champagne cork and the cheers that accompany it. Philippa is patting Adam on the back. All his political cronies are here. They're all trying to get in on the act, I find myself thinking cynically. Suddenly everyone wants to be Adam's friend. I find myself wondering what Ralph and Felicity are doing. Did they hate us for having the party? I can smell the faint scent of the rose perfume in the boat and my mind travels back to Kerri Wilson.

'I don't like Henry,' Lisa says, 'but he's well respected. You need to be sure before you accuse him of anything.'

I nod. She's quite right, I know that.

'You don't have any proof, do you? As far as everyone is concerned she had a heart attack.'

'She was pronounced dead by a local doctor,' I say scathingly.

'Maybe you shouldn't think about it. Not with the baby on the way.'

I know she's right but I can't help thinking that Kerri Wilson is owed something.

'He helped cover up the accident that killed Margaret Snell and he was blackmailing Kerri Wilson somehow. He … he was having debauched sex with her. I've got a video recording of it in my pocket.'

Lisa gasps.

'He recorded it,' I say angrily.

Lisa gapes at me.

'Oh my God,' she says.

'I think I should tell Adam,' I say.

'How would you explain having a DVD belonging to Henry? You'd have to admit you went into his house and took it. It might all backfire on you Flora. You can't be sure she didn't consent. She was …'

'Was what?' I ask.

'Known to be a bit flighty. After all, weren't there rumours of parties at their house? You don't know who was at their parties. Also why would Henry cover things up?'

'They don't want Penlyn on the map. There is a big taboo about scandal in the village. It sounds ridiculous I know but they had a big scandal here about twenty years ago. I think they kind of closed ranks.'

At that moment a firework explodes above us, making me jump. The boat rocks and I grab the side. If only everyone would leave. I can't think straight with all this noise.

'Why don't you wait until the morning? Things will be clearer then. There's no point telling Adam now. He's been drinking and won't be able to make sense of what you're saying.'

'Do you believe me?' I ask anxiously.

She nods.

'Yes, I think Dorcas is a slimy toad.'

I drop my hand into the water and ease my feet from the narrow heels I'd been wearing. My bare foot lands on something soft and I look down to see a hair scrunch on the bottom of the boat.

I'm about to ask Lisa if it is hers when I see the blackened stains on it. This time I'm not imagining things. The scrunch has dried blood on it.

'Oh Flora,' cries Lisa as I throw up into the lake.

I pull my hand roughly from the water. How did the perfume bottle and scrunch get into the boat?

Chapter Forty-Three

'Dance with me,' Adam says.

His words are slurred. He's had far too much champagne. I'm tired and grateful that the guests are slowly leaving.

'Thanks for a fabulous night,' says Philippa as she staggers towards us. 'It's been brilliant.'

She steps on to a discarded trifle and bursts out laughing.

'You're welcome,' I say.

Adam leads me on to the deserted patio and we begin to dance. From the corner of my eye I see Rhonda and Geoff laughing with Henry in the kitchen.

'How are you feeling?' Adam asks.

'I'm okay,' I lie.

The truth is I'm seething with anger. How dare they laugh and joke in my kitchen and eat our food and drink our champagne. I tell myself to stay calm. I have to think of the baby.

'I'm making coffee,' says Laurie, tapping me on the arm. 'Do you want a cup?'

I nod. It's getting chilly now and I shiver. Adam wraps my shawl around me.

'It's been a great night, Flo, thanks for all you've done.'

'I didn't do anything. Shall we go in? It's getting chilly.'

We walk into the kitchen where the final few guests have congregated. I don't see Seth. Kerri is being fussed over by Sienna.

'Thank you for holding the party,' says Rhonda. 'It's been lovely and what you've done to the house is amazing.'

'Thank you,' I say, forcing a smile.

'It's certainly very different,' says Henry.

I shoot him a look.

'Is it? In what way?'

I realise my voice is hostile and Adam looks at me warily.

'It's different,' Henry says, his eyes meeting mine. 'It's more tasteful.'

I swallow down the acidic taste in my mouth.

'Tasteful?' I say with a cynical laugh. 'You know all about taste don't you Henry.'

'Flora,' warns Adam.

I ignore him and say viciously,

'Is the bedroom to your taste, Henry?'

Rhonda tries to hide her gasp but I hear it.

'Flora,' whispers Lisa. 'Is this the right time. Think of the baby.'

'I don't understand,' says Henry.

'Oh, I think you do,' I say boldly.

Adam grabs me by the arm.

'Flora, what the hell is going on?' he hisses into my ear. 'There's a time and place and this isn't it?'

Philippa is standing by the kitchen door in her fur boa. She's looks at me oddly.

'Is everything okay, Adam?' she asks.

'Everything is great, Phil. Thanks so much for coming. I'll see you out.'

'Great night,' says Ken, kissing me on the cheek.

'So pleased you could make it,' I say, not taking my eyes off Henry.

Adam shoots me a warning glance and then follows Philippa and Ken to the front door.

'Here's your tea,' says Laurie.

She pulls a kitchen chair out for me. I look around the room. All of Adam's cronies have gone. The kitchen is a tip with empty glasses and discarded plates everywhere. Henry is avoiding my eyes. Adam returns and Henry says,

'I should be going too.'

'So soon?' says Adam, who is clearly unaware of the time.

'Ask him Adam,' I say loudly. 'Ask him what happened in our house. Ask him what happened to Kerri Wilson and Margaret Snell, come to that.'

I feel a huge sense of relief now that I've brought it out into the open. It's like something has been freed within me.

'Flo, let's go upstairs. You're not feeling well,' Laurie says, taking my arm.

'Laurie,' I say. 'Whose side are you on?'

'It's not about sides Flo,' she responds looking hurt.

'We should leave,' Rhonda says to Geoff.

'You all covered up the accident that killed Margaret Snell didn't you?'

Rhonda gasps and Geoff's face colours.

'That's in the past,' says Geoff.

'It was immoral,' I cry. 'If it had been any one other than Margaret Snell would you have done the same? You destroyed the daffodils I laid at her grave, didn't you? What's wrong with you people?'

'Flora for Christ's sake, stop it!' says Adam firmly, standing in front of me. 'You'll make yourself ill. We don't need this right now, you know that.'

'I don't know what you're talking about,' says Henry.

'Don't you? I know about Kate. I know what happened.'

I turn to Rhonda who sways on her feet. Laurie quickly pulls out a chair for her.

'I'm really sorry Rhonda. I can't imagine what you all went through. The media and everything, but Margaret Snell didn't do anything wrong.'

'Flora, this isn't our business,' snaps Adam.

He turns to Henry.

'I'm sorry about this.'

'Adam,' I say indignantly.

'I should get going,' says Sienna.

'Of course,' says Adam, 'I'm so sorry.'

How dare he apologise on my behalf.

'Let me see you out,' he says, glaring at me.

'It's fine. Thanks for a lovely evening.'

The front door slams behind her. There's silence and then Henry says,

'She's right; we did cover up the accident.'

'Henry,' warns Geoff.

'It's okay,' says Henry.

He meets my eyes.

'You came to my lecture,' he says. 'Errors of judgement carry consequences. Maybe this is the consequence for us. I don't believe it was an error of judgement on our part though.'

'But Kerri Wilson,' I interrupt.

'Knew what she was doing. She could have gone to the police any time she wanted. They phoned me. They didn't want his glittering career to come to a tragic end and do you blame them? I remember it as if it were yesterday. They were a tragedy in waiting.'

November 2015
An Error of Judgement

It took less than five minutes for Henry to get there. Thankfully there was no one else around. He tried not to look at them with disgust. They'd done nothing but bring shame on the village since they arrived. Fortunately they'd managed to keep it under wraps. He should have known it would come to something like this. They were a tragedy waiting to happen.

It was utter carnage. He sighed. Why did they have to drag him into this?

'Oh God, Henry, you've got to help me. I don't know what to do. She came out of bloody nowhere and the next thing I knew the car was out of control. I didn't mean to hit her and …'

Henry slapped him hard around the face and Kerri screamed.

'For pity's sake, act like a man, and you …' he turned to Kerri. 'Shut up or the whole bloody village will be here.'

The sharp beam of headlights silenced them all.

'It's Geoff,' said Henry.

'What are we going to do? Shall we call the police?' asked Gerard, his eyes wild.

'You're stoned. You're nothing but a spoilt little shit. You've just killed two people because of your irresponsibility and you're going to put Penlyn on the map in a way we don't need,' Henry said scathingly.

Geoff was leaning over the woman on the road.

'It's Margaret Snell,' he said.

There was a sharp intake of breath from Henry.

'Great. This could dredge everything back up.'

Kerri stumbled forward. Her legs were like jelly. She was nauseous and her head felt fit to burst.

'You must phone the police,' she said earnestly, gripping Gerard's arm. 'You must.'

She looked at Ben's bloodied face. His neck had been slashed open by the windscreen and tears burst from her eyes like a dam.

'Oh Ben, oh God, Ben,' she moaned.

Henry grabbed her by the arm. The smell of alcohol and marijuana knocked him back.

'Keep it down,' he snapped.

She pulled her arm back.

'Let go of me. There's something wrong with you. Why the fuck did you phone him Gerard?' she sobbed. 'This is horrific, you can't just make out it never happened.'

Gerard looked around, his eyes vacant.

'I'm on the cusp of my career Kerri. How can I give it up now? Ben asked me to drive, he knew the risk.'

Henry fought back a sigh. The idiot was trying to blame it on someone else. Her hands lashed out to Gerard, her nails clawing at his face.

'You bastard, you weak, stupid bastard, how dare you blame Ben. Call the fucking police.'

He grabbed her hands roughly.

'Kerri, for Christ's sake keep your voice down.'

'We don't want the media crawling over the village. Not again,' said Henry.

'Gerard, how can you live with yourself?' she hissed, tears running down her face. Her hair clung to her neck. She felt she would go mad if she had to look at the mangled wreck of the car much longer.

'What kind of life will we have, Kerri, if we call the police?'

She watched mesmerised as Henry and Geoff carefully pulled Ben's head from the smashed windscreen and slowly edged him across to the driver's seat.

'What about the woman?' she cried hysterically. 'You can't cover that up.'

'She's just an old drunk,' mumbled Henry.

'Margaret Snell finally got her comeuppance,' said Geoff. He looked at the body on the road and grimaced.

'Join your evil son, Peter,' he spat.

'Enough,' said Henry. 'We've got work to do.'

Kerri tried to shut out what was happening. She told herself it would be so much worse if they called the police. Gerard would be done for murder, or at the very least manslaughter. His career would be over. Their celebrity lifestyle would end. If only they could go back. If only Gerard had said no to driving the car. If only ...

The heat from the burning car made her feel dizzy and she fought the nausea that threatened to engulf her.

'Ben was driving the car,' Henry told her. 'He was coming to visit you from a party he'd been to.'

Gerard was nodding.

'Margaret Snell came out of nowhere. No one will know exactly what happened. But everyone knew she was a lush. The car burst into flames. Kerri, are you listening to me?'

She gave a little nod of her head.

'Go home both of you,' he ordered. 'Everything is going to be all right.'

Kerri stared at him.

'You're mad. You're all mad. These are decent people. You can't cover this up.'

'Huh,' scoffed Geoff. 'Margaret Snell never had a decent bone in her body.'

'If you cared so much about your decent friends, why were you driving over the limit and high on drugs,' demanded Henry. 'Leave it to us and go home. You've made the mistake, you can't undo it.'

But Kerri knew this mistake would have its price and she didn't dare think what that might be.

Chapter Forty-Four

'They were high on drugs, all three of them. Can you imagine if the police had been called? It would have thrown Penlyn into the spotlight. The mystery surrounding Peter Snell would be dredged up and Rhonda and Geoff would have to go through all that agony again and all because of three irresponsible people,' says Henry.

'But it's immoral. You covered up manslaughter,' I say angrily.

Adam rests a hand on my shoulder.

'Flo, it has nothing to do with us.'

I reel around to face him.

'Are you serious, they broke the law?'

'What would you suggest we do? Blow the whistle on Gerard Meyer? Bring a glittering career to a shameful end. It won't bring them back will it?' says Rhonda.

'What about Margaret Snell? Didn't she deserve a decent burial?'

'She had a decent burial,' says a voice from the French doors. I turn to see the vicar standing there.

'I conducted the funeral. She had the funeral that she could afford. There was no money. The villagers paid for the headstone.'

'We're not as callous as you think,' says Henry. 'I rather think your imagination has run a little riot.'

I open my mouth to reply and then remember Lisa's words. How do I know that what I saw on the video wasn't with Kerri's consent? I can't admit to stealing the DVD. But there is the bloodied scrunch and the stains on the flagstones.

'What about Ben? Did he deserve that?'

'Deserve what?' asks Henry. 'He wanted Gerard to drive the car back here. No one put a gun to his head. He killed himself. He made the decision to get in that car. It was an error of judgement.'

I grit my teeth.

'I don't believe Kerri had a heart attack.'

As I say the words I realise how ridiculous I sound. I've got nothing to back up my claims apart from a few bad dreams and a bloodied scrunch. I can't be certain that the stain on the flagstones is even blood.

'You're right,' says Henry, 'she didn't.'

Chapter Forty-Five

'I was right,' I say.

'I think Flora has had enough excitement. As you know we're expecting a baby and I don't want her getting upset.' Adam says, getting up.

'Absolutely,' agrees Rhonda.

I see Laurie and Doctor Kingsley nodding in agreement.

'What happened to her?' I ask, 'What happened to Kerri Wilson?'

'She took an overdose,' says the vicar.

I scoff.

'I don't believe you,' I say. 'I know about you. I know you're a drug addict. Why should I believe anything you say?'

'Christ Flora,' gasps Adam. 'What are you saying?'

'I saw him. He'd been shooting up. He was totally out of it.'

Rhonda falls into a chair.

'Oh my Lord,' she mutters. 'What a thing to say.'

'On insulin,' says Henry softly. 'If you saw Michael shooting up anything, it was insulin. I rather think you're turning Penlyn and its villagers into a novel, my dear.'

He's struggling to compose himself. He's angry I can see it in his eyes.

'Michael's diabetic. I'm sure he won't mind me saying that he's not very good at taking care of himself. He doesn't medicate as well as he ought to.'

I struggle to remember what I'd seen that day. Could I have been mistaken?

'But ... I ...'

'I apologise. You caught me on a bad day,' says Reverend Flynn. 'We all have our crosses to bear and for me it's my health.'

I feel suddenly tired and flop into a chair.

'If we've committed any sin it was to protect the innocent. Rhonda and Geoff didn't deserve more heartache. Margaret Snell? Well, she testified under oath for her son when she knew damn well he raped Kate,' says Henry.

Rhonda lets out a tiny sob.

'Do you blame us? We gave her a better funeral than she would have had,' says Geoff. 'Our Katie tried to kill herself when she discovered she was pregnant. That's why Seth was born with his impediment. Penlyn is a decent village. We didn't need that kind of riff-raff.'

'Okay Geoff,' warns Henry.

'The daffodils I put on the grave, you destroyed them,' I say accusingly.

'Why would we do that?' asks Rhonda, looking hurt.

'Someone did,' I say.

'You don't think we've got better things to do than visit Maggie Snell's grave to see who has left flowers,' scoffs Geoff. 'The cemetery is exposed to the elements. It was most likely the wind.'

I look at everyone around me, each giving me a pitying look.

'I think there's a body in the lake,' I say. There are murmurs and I realise I'm sounding completely mad.

'I think the police should drain the lake.'

'Flora,' says Laurie. 'Let me get you some water.'

I wave the glass away.

'I found this in the boat,' I say showing them the scrunch. 'I believe Kerri fell down the stairs trying to escape someone.'

I look directly at Henry.

'Her death was covered up. I don't know what happened but I think she is in the lake. I don't believe you when you say she killed herself.'

I hold up the bloodied scrunch. Adam looks shocked and turns to Henry.

Henry laughs and I want to slap him.

'Do you know how deep that lake is?' he asks. 'It's three foot deep if that. Don't you think your body would have been seen by now? Kerri Wilson took an overdose. She and her husband took drugs the day she died. Kerri took one too many. Gerard thinks she never got over the accident. She wanted to own up, confess to the police, but he didn't. We didn't call the police when she died, Meyer didn't want that. Doctor Hemel certified the death. He pronounced her dead due to cardiac arrest. It wasn't far from the truth. She died from a cardiac arrest caused by the overdose. There's no body in your shallow lake. I think my dear you have got yourself overstressed and have been imagining all kinds.'

'But the boat...' I say turning to Adam. 'It's always coming off the mooring and ...'

I point to the French doors.

'Flora, there are no such thing as ghosts,' says Adam, placing his hands on my shoulders.

Doctor Kingsley wraps something around my arm and Rhonda and Geoff discreetly leave.

'It's too high for my liking,' Simon says.

I look down at the blood pressure gauge.

'Oh Flo,' says Laurie. 'Everything is going to be okay.'

Reverend Flynn takes my hand gently.

'I'm so sorry for giving you a fright.'

'The foil,' I whisper.

He looks puzzled.

'Foil?' he questions.

'But ...'

Did I imagine it?

'You need to rest,' says Henry. 'We'll leave you to ...'

People seem to float out of the kitchen until it is just me, Adam and Doctor Kingsley.

'You're really stressed Flo. I should have seen it coming. The last miscarriage and my ambition, it's all been too much. I blame myself. I shouldn't have left you alone so much,' says Adam stroking my hand. 'Simon said he thought you were on the verge of a breakdown but I didn't want to believe it.'

'What!' I say shocked.

'Nothing happened in this house Flo. Kerri Wilson committed suicide. There's no body in the lake. Henry is right, it's not possible. This is all in your head and in your dreams. You've become obsessed with Kerri Wilson.'

'But I've seen things, I've seen …'

'What have you seen Flora?' asks Doctor Kingsley.

I stop when I see their faces. Everyone thinks I'm crazy. Oh God, am I? Did I see figures at the window or did I imagine them? I was stressed when we came here. The two miscarriages had taken their toll. The rose smell was simply spilt perfume. Have I got my dreams and reality confused?

'I think a short stay in hospital won't do any harm. We need to get this blood pressure down. You can get some well-earned rest,' says Doctor Kingsley.

'He's right,' says Adam.

'Your hormones and the stress have taken their toll. We want to have this baby don't we?'

'Oh God,' I groan.

The baby is the most important thing. How could I have lost the plot so easily? I look up at Adam and into his pain-filled eyes. The anguish on his face tears me apart. How can I do this to him? He has given me everything.

'I'm sorry,' I whisper. 'It just felt like …'

'It's okay,' he whispers, kissing me. 'Let's just get you well.'

I nod.

'I'll have a private ambulance here first thing. Let her get some sleep and then we'll admit her to St Lukes,' says Simon.

'St Lukes Care Home?' I repeat. 'But that's so extravagant Adam.'

'I want you to get the best care. You'll get some respite there and when you come home you'll be back to your old self.'

Tears trickle down my cheeks.

'I'm sorry Adam. You've got so much to cope with. I feel like I've let you down.'

'Just get better so you can be by my side.'

I nod. I'm going to get better, I tell myself. I'm not going to think about Kerri Wilson any more.

Chapter Forty-Six

Two weeks later

'Everything is ready for you,' says Jan. 'The house is looking nice. The gardens are blooming beautifully with the lovely weather.'

I smile. Everyone had been exceptionally kind since my breakdown. Jan had even said that she had seen it coming but didn't think as housekeeper it was her place to say anything. Laurie said she felt guilty for bringing the Ouija board.

'I feel like I exacerbated everything,' she'd said miserably. 'Adam gave me a right ticking off.'

'It wasn't anyone's fault,' I assured her.

I put my half-eaten sandwich back on to the plate.

'Mrs Macintosh, the programme you wanted to see is starting,' says a nurse coming up behind me.

'Ok great. I'll come in.'

She turns to fetch a wheelchair but I shake my head. It's ridiculous. I'm pregnant, not an invalid.

'It's okay,' I say.

Doctor Kingsley said I could go home tomorrow and I can't wait. My bloods were normal and providing I take things easy and don't get stressed, he said there is no reason at all why I can't hold on to this baby. I think back to the party and how I had ruined things. I can't forget the sad look in Adam's eyes when he'd led me to the bedroom.

'Just rest,' he'd said. 'Everything is going to be fine.'

'I'm so sorry,' I'd whispered tearfully.

'It's fine. You are going to be fine.'

He was kind but there was weariness in his voice. I'd become a liability and I hated myself for it. I walk slowly to my room and stop at the sight of a stranger standing by my bed. He's studying my notes.

'Hello,' I say.

He turns guiltily.

'Oh, Mrs Macintosh, sorry, I've been caught red-handed.'

He offers his hand.

'Let me help you. I'm Doctor Hemel. Your husband asked me to pop by. You're coming home tomorrow he said.'

'Yes, I am,' I say cautiously and then tell myself not to be so stupid. It was all in my mind. Kerri Wilson hadn't been murdered in the house. No one had been murdered in the house. Most certainly no one had been dumped in the lake. It was far too shallow. How I hadn't realised that, I don't know. But Doctor Hemel was the doctor who certified Kerri's death. He hadn't been honest. If reported, surely he would be struck off.

'I'll be registering with a doctor,' I say more forcefully than I meant.

'Oh right, well that's fine then,' he says hiding his surprise at my words.

'Thank you very much though,' I add.

'It's not a problem. Adam asked me to introduce myself but that's fine.'

I want to ask him about Kerri Wilson but I daren't. I'm sure if I so much as mention Kerri's name I will subject myself to another week here, and I really want to go home. Instead Doctor Hemel saves me the trouble and says,

'I'd like to put things straight with you about Kerri Wilson.'

I don't speak.

'Kerri was a drug addict. She came to me a few times. She wanted to get off them. It isn't easy to do that when everyone around you is taking them. She took more in the last few months. I prescribed methadone to help her withdraw but I don't think she really tried. She'd been dead some hours by the time her husband realised. What we found at her bedside indicated that she had taken well over the amount that she knew would have been safe. I believe she committed suicide. She did suffer a heart attack, caused by the overdose. Her husband couldn't face the publicity of an inquest. It was easier this way. He didn't want people to know that she killed herself.'

I avoid his eyes.

'Thank you for telling me.'

'Everyone in the village wants you to get better.'

'Thank you.'

'I'm happy to be able to help. Your husband feels that being in hospital is one thing but coming out and being back home might be more difficult. I'm aware you're not allowed any medication but there are relaxation ...'

'Thank you,' I interrupt. 'I'll look into it. Doctor Kingsley has given me some classes to attend.'

He nods and slips the chart back on to the end of the bed.

'If you need me when you get home please don't hesitate to give me a call. Adam has my number.'

I wait until he leaves before turning on the television. Adam is doing a live interview and I don't want to miss it. Ralph's liaison had hit the front papers this morning. He still hasn't made a statement. The backbenchers have been calling for his resignation. All eyes are on Adam's performance this morning and I'm nervous as to how Adam will respond to questions.

The television presenter introduces him and my heart flutters at the sight of Adam in his white shirt and suit. His hair is perfectly styled and he looks so handsome. I smile at the signs of make-up on his face. I know how much he hates that.

'Thank you for coming on the show Mr Macintosh. We've many things to ask you. Not least, of course, Bluefields

Nursing Home. But first we have to talk about the Prime Minister and these allegations.'

Bluefields, the name echoes in my head. Where had I heard that before? I struggle to remember.

'Home Secretary, are you able to confirm or deny reports that Ralph Meadows is about to resign? Clearly this would have a profound effect on your future. Are you able to discuss with us the revelations that were splashed across the newspapers today? We don't seem to be getting a statement from the Prime Minister himself.'

Adam shifts slightly in his seat. I see his jaw twitch and know that's he uncomfortable with the question. He pulls his shoulders back and says,

'It would be imprudent of me to do so. That's very much for the Prime Minister and I can assure you there will be a statement within the next twenty-four hours and ...'

'Will the Prime Minister be resigning?' breaks in the presenter.

'A statement will be issued by lunchtime today.'

I clap my hands. Adam knows exactly what to say and how to say it.

'Can we expect a new Prime Minister quite soon?' smiles the presenter.

'You'll have to wait and see,' grins Adam turning his handsome face to the camera.

'But surely Mr Macintosh, the Prime Minister can't continue. Not after this.'

'Like I said, there will be a statement from Number Ten shortly. I can't comment on what Ralph Meadows intends to say.'

'Will you take over the leadership?'

Adam smiles again.

'At the moment we have a Prime Minister.'

'Okay, you're clearly not going to give anything away. Perhaps we'll come back to this in a bit,' smiles the presenter.

'You've taken under your wing the fight to keep Bluefields Nursing Home open. Obviously it is in your constituency but isn't there a need for housing? Isn't that one of the things you say you stand for, affordable housing for the young? And yet here we have a developer happy to build that affordable housing but you're supporting the fight to prevent that.'

'We also need care homes for our elderly,' smiles Adam.

'But isn't it a fact that this particular home needs extensive renovation and that residents could be moved to a much more desirable residency?'

'It's also important that elderly residents stay close to their families. My party believes in the family, and I am sure you agree, we owe so much to the elderly in this country.'

I stare lovingly at him. Then I remember where I had heard about Bluefields. It's the home where Henry's wife lives.

Chapter Forty-Seven

We turn the corner from the tree-lined road and up the windy lane into Penlyn. I remove my sunglasses to get a clear view of the house as we approach. The sun appears from behind a cloud as we drive through the gates and along the gravel driveway of Hunters Moon, bathing the house in its warmth.

Earl is up a ladder cutting back the ivy from the walls. I rather liked the ivy trailing up the house. I decide not to say anything. Earl touches his cap in acknowledgement of us and I marvel at how normal everything seems. I fumble with the door handle and Adam leans over to help me.

'Thanks Malcolm,' Adam says, slipping my arm into his. 'I don't think we'll need you now until tomorrow.'

My little car still sits on the drive. I notice it has a flat tyre again. I remember getting it pumped up to go to the library. I try to recall when that was and then dismiss it. I don't want to think of anything that will take my mind back to thoughts of Kerri Wilson or the Litha celebrations.

Jan rushes down the steps and hugs me.

'I'm so glad you're home,' she says. 'I've got the kettle on and I've made a carrot cake.'

'Sounds wonderful,' I say.

'I'm okay,' I say to Adam as he goes to help me up the steps. 'I'm pregnant, not ill. You don't need to mollycoddle me.'

'Sorry,' he says dropping his arm.

He looks up at Earl.

'It's looking good,' he says cheerfully.

I glance up and mourn the loss of the ivy. The house looks less inviting without it. The ivy had always made it seem cosy.

The house is spotless and I can see the new patio furniture laid out. My eyes then stray to the boat which is bobbing innocently at its mooring.

'They look nice,' I say nodding to the furniture.

'Don't they just,' says Jan, smiling. 'I'll take our tea and cake out there. It's a beautiful day.'

Ralph had managed to stay in power and had fought off the calls for his resignation, for now at least, but there was unease from within his own party. The media hadn't eased up on him. His public apology a few days before hadn't eased any of the pressure. I'm finding it hard to understand Adam's loyalty, but loyal he is. I can hear him now on the phone. He has barely been off it since collecting me from the hospital. Ralph's indiscretion had been splashed over the newspapers continually since the story first broke. Felicity sent me a card which simply read *Good luck. If Adam takes this on you'll need it.*

Adam had torn it up angrily.

'Inconsiderate bitch,' he'd snarled.

'She's probably upset,' I'd said, but I had to agree it was a bit over the top.

I gratefully take the tea that Jan offers.

'Oh yes,' Adam says, as though just remembering. 'You had a visitor. Art Mitchell, do you know him?'

I see his jaw twitch.

'Yes, he's the farmer I told you about.'

'Ah right. I couldn't place him.'

His phone bleeps again and he sighs.

'I have to take these calls,' he apologises before disappearing into the kitchen. Jan follows him with her eyes.

'It's all happening isn't it? Do you think he will be Prime Minister?'

'I think it's a possibility.'

'Will you be happy living at Number Ten?'

'It's a case of having to be, Jan. Besides we're not moving in yet. Who knows what will happen. Doctor Kingsley wants to be sure I'm okay before moving to London and Adam says we'll be here at Hunters Moon most weekends if it does happen. We will still need you,' I say, seeing her worried expression.

'As long as you do,' she says her face relaxing.

'Of course we will,' I say, patting her hand.

'I'll get the teapot,' she says.

I look out to the lake and hear Henry's words again,

'It's three foot deep if that. Don't you think your body would have been seen by now?'

I shudder and lean across to the pile of post that has been waiting for me.

There's a small package and I turn it around in my hands trying to remember what I had ordered and then it comes to me. The perfume, of course; I'd totally forgotten about it. I remove the top from the antique shaped bottle and lift it to my nose. The perfume smells much fresher and more floral. The old bottle was obviously going stale. I push it back into the box as Jan returns.

'Did you find that perfume bottle?' I ask.

She shakes her head.

'No, sorry, I didn't.'

I flick through the letters and stretch back in my chair. The rest had been good but it has left me strangely tired. Sitting on the patio reminds me of the party and I try to push it from my mind. God, I'd made such a fool of myself. I must stop by the estate agents and apologise to Sienna. She had sent a beautiful bouquet to the hospital. The least I can do is say thank you and apologise for my crazy behaviour. Adam finally joins us. He looks distracted and spends much of the time tapping away on his laptop. Finally he says,

'I really should go to London. I don't want to leave you alone though. I can phone Laurie, see if she can stay, or maybe Lisa?'

'Laurie is in London on business,' I smile. 'I'll be fine, you go.'

'I should be back by this evening but I'll phone Lisa. It's your first night home. I don't want you to be alone.'

He kisses me on the cheek.

'Adam,' I ask, 'isn't Bluefields the care home where Henry's wife is?'

He wrinkles his brow.

'It might be. She has dementia doesn't she?'

His phone rings and he pulls a face.

'I'd better take this.'

I flip through the rest of the post and stop on a large brown envelope. I rip it open and feel a flutter of excitement. It's the ground plan for Hunters Moon. I'd completely forgotten about that. I'd ordered it from the Land Registry so that I could see how much of the woods belong to the property. I shove the plan back into the envelope without looking at it. Adam will be cross if he finds out.

'Lisa's popping over in a bit,' he calls.

'Great.'

He comes out and wraps his arms around me.

'Ralph has called a meeting.'

My heart beats a little faster.

'Do you think you'll be okay to come to London tomorrow with me, just in case?'

I nod. I need to think what I'm going to wear. Laurie had suggested my red Chanel suit.

'Very Jackie Kennedy,' she'd said. 'It's perfect for the first photos of the new Prime Minister and his wife.'

I can't believe it. It looks like Adam is finally going to be Prime Minister. His dreams have finally come true. I think of Felicity and the words of the hairdresser and then quickly push them from my mind. We have a charmed life and it is going to stay that way. I'll make sure of that.

Chapter Forty-Eight

I sip my tea and relax back into the warmth of the bath. Lisa had visited earlier but I'd sent her home. I'd really had enough of everyone running around me and I was desperate for some time alone.

Kerri was sitting contentedly on the floor of the bathroom, guarding her new toy. The radio was on softly. My ears were pricked for news about Ralph but the news was dominated by a story regarding the health service. Adam once told me this was a common tactic to distract the public when there were more serious issues at stake. Adam had phoned when he'd arrived in London and said he would be in the crisis meeting for the next few hours. It was nine o'clock and I didn't expect a statement from Ralph now. Maybe I wouldn't have to go to London tomorrow and stand with Adam as he addressed the nation as the new Prime Minister, but I knew if it wasn't tomorrow then it would be the next day. It was only a matter of time before Ralph did resign and then Adam would become PM. He was the popular choice with both the public and the house. I lay my hands on my stomach and think about the brown envelope on the kitchen table. I was itching to have a good look at the Land Registry plan but knew it was not a good idea. It would trigger memories of the party. My phone vibrates and I glance over to it. It's Adam.

'Hi, how are you feeling? Is Lisa with you?'

'Yes,' I lie 'and I'm feeling fine. I'm having a bath.'

'Great,' he says, relief evident in his voice. 'Ralph is going to resign in a week's time. The department are in overdrive to keep the media off topic. There is a hell of a lot that has to be done but we did it, Flora, I am going to be the next Prime Minister. Can you believe it?'

I feel my heart sink.

'Oh Adam,' I say.

'I'll be back tonight. Don't wait up though. It will be a while before we finish here.'

'Okay,' I say.

'We've done it Flora. We made it. We can't go any higher and now what with the baby coming ... It's all ...'

His voice breaks with emotion.

'I love you,' I say.

'I love you too. I'll see you soon.'

I hang up and climb from the bath.

'Life is going to be very different, Kerri,' I say, patting her head.

She jumps up, wagging her tail excitedly. After feeding her, I take the rest of my unopened post, along with the brown envelope, up to bed. The rose scent is much fainter in the bedroom now and after kicking of my slippers I bend down to look under the bed, using my phone torch so that I can get a better look. I drag out the shoe boxes I had shoved under there and shine the torch, but I can't see anything. I'll ask Jan to give the carpet a good wash. That should surely shift it. Maybe I'll also ask her to wash the flagstones in the hall with some bleach.

I sniff from the new bottle of Rose Oud that I had ordered and close my eyes. Kerri Wilson committed suicide I tell myself. There is nothing odd or unusual in what happened to her. Her death had been registered. I'd checked. What on earth made me think she was in the lake? Maybe everyone is right, I'd lost the plot. Things had finally become too much for me. It had been hard coping with the first miscarriage and then the second one had been a shock. I'd been five months pregnant, we'd even decided on his name, Matthew. It was a difficult time. But I'm going to get better I tell myself. I'd not had the dream for a while now and forced myself to think of something else. It was a bad idea to brood on things before I went to sleep. Tomorrow I'll go and visit Sienna and then perhaps Art Mitchell. I smile at the memory of Adam's face when he'd told me about Art's visit. He'd been jealous. Kerri jumps on to the bed as I pull back the bedcovers, knocking off my overstuffed tote bag.

'Kerri,' I groan, leaning over to pick things up.

My eyes land on the DVD and I stare at it. No, I tell myself. Don't even think it. Kerri Wilson no doubt knew what she was doing. Hadn't Lisa said that Kerri had been a bit flighty? Who knows who she'd had sex with? But Henry Dorcas … I shudder at the thought. Why would she? Had Gerard forced her? Did she do it for him? I shove the DVD and Kerri's letter into the false drawer of the dresser.

'Focus on other things,' I tell myself, throwing the rest of the stuff back into the bag. 'It's past, over. You have to think about your life, Adam's future and the baby.'

I spot Art's business card and glance at the time. It's not too late to phone and it would seem rude not to thank him for coming round. It rings once and he answers.

'Hello Art, it's Flora Macintosh.'

'Flora,' he says surprised. 'Hi, how are you?'

'I'm fine, thanks for coming round. I'm sorry I wasn't here.'

'No worries. I came on my round after the party but … Lisa at The Old Stores told me … well, that you'd been taken ill.'

'I had a breakdown,' I say bluntly. 'I got all kinds of ideas in my head.'

'That's what Lisa said. I've got to admit I was a bit surprised. I didn't have you down as the breakdown type somehow.'

I feel a small tremor of gratitude. I didn't have me down as the breakdown type either.

'I got a bit carried away with my imagination and what I thought had happened at Hunters Moon and …'

'You don't have to explain anything to me. I'm not a big fan of Dorcas or anyone else in the village for that matter. They're all too two-faced for my liking.'

I smile. I like how forthright he is. I remember Adam's jealousy and realise why. Art is a good-looking man. He has a very appealing nature too. It would be easy to fall for him. There is nothing complicated about him. He seems content, unlike Adam who seems to be forever striving forward with his ambition.

'It looks like we ... I will not be at Hunters Moon as much as before. Adam looks set to be the Prime Minister.'

'I did wonder.'

I'm silent. I want to offer to visit with Kerri. To feel some kind of normality before going to Number Ten but it seems presumptuous, so I'm pleased when he says,

'So, when are you going to pop around with Kerri? Rosie is keen to see her again. She gets lonely with only me for company.'

'We'd love to. How about tomorrow?'

'Great, come for lunch.'

'Okay, we'll see you about twelve.'

I lean back on the pillows before opening the brown envelope and removing the plans. I study the map of the woods and the man-made lake. Henry was right the lake is only three foot deep. I lift the plans closer and study the map. For a minute I can't make sense of what I'm looking at, and then my heart races when I realise. The lake is three foot deep, Henry wasn't wrong about that, but marked in the middle of the lake is a small circle. It reads *site of old well*. The lake may be three foot deep but a well can be forty foot deep, deep enough to hide a body.

Chapter Forty-Nine

Adam's face is splashed all over the front pages of the newspapers. *'A heart-throb PM for Britain?'* reads the headline. Adam's handsome features stare back at me and I realise how much of a heart-throb he has become. I'd always been aware of his appeal but I hadn't fully realised the extent.

Adam pushes them to one side and pours coffee into our mugs.

'It's insane,' he says. 'It's more about my looks than the job.'

I can't help wondering how Ralph and Felicity are feeling. The papers, as always, print sensation. Adam is in line for the position but it's by no means a done deal.

'Is Ralph okay with you?' I ask.

'It's politics. Ralph won't last after that debacle. She's just accepted a good whack from *The Mirror* to tell her story. He knows he'd be a fool to continue. He's best to go now before the shit really hits the fan.'

The gate buzzer sounds and he jumps up.

'That'll be Luke.'

Luke was Adam's PA. A young, energetic, ambitious young man, who was no doubt very excited at the prospect of being PA to the Prime Minister.

'We've a lot to go over today. I need to be ready for Ralph's resignation.'

'I've got my Chanel red suit,' I say hugging him. 'I thought I'd wear that for the first photo call.'

'As long as it shows you're pregnant,' he smiles. 'What are your plans for today?'

'I'm going to see Sienna. I should apologise for my behaviour at the party. It must have been very embarrassing.'

'Don't think about it.'

'Could you pump up my tyre?'

'Malcolm can take you into town. I'd prefer that, just in case the press are around. I don't want you hassled.'

I sigh.

'Okay. Have lunch without me. I'm going to meet a friend.'

I don't mention Art by name. I decide it is probably best. Luke waves from the hallway and then he and Adam disappear into the study. After taking a quick shower, I spray with Rose Oud and then Kerri and I climb into the car.

'That's a nice perfume,' compliments Malcolm.

'Thanks, it's new.'

We pull up at the estate agents just as my phone rings. It's Jan and she's fighting back tears.

'There something wrong with Molly.'

Molly is her cat and she and Fred think the world of her.

'He's going to the vet today. He's had some bleeding and …'

'It's okay Jan, don't worry about us. Take your time.'

'I may not be in tomorrow but I'll be there Friday. It's just the laundry, Adam's suits are ready and I put all the shirts in. I'm so sorry …'

'Oh for goodness' sake, don't worry about that. I'm in town. I can collect them. I'll phone you later for an update.'

'Thank you, Flora.'

I hang up and fight back my tears. My hormones are so erratic that the smallest thing sets me off. I dab at my eyes with a tissue. I can't now imagine life without Kerri who now sits next to me, her head lolling in my lap.

'Poor Jan,' I mumble.

Malcolm drops me at the estate agents. A notice board lines the wall behind the receptionist. It reads *'Our staff, we are here to help.'*

'Hi, I was hoping to see Sienna,' I say.

The pretty brunette behind the desk sits up straight.

'She's out the back. I'll go and get her for you Mrs Macintosh.'

'Thanks.'

'What a gorgeous puppy,' she says, leaning down to fuss Kerri.

I look at the newspaper on her desk and wonder if there is a photo of me inside. Is that how she knew me? I glance at the photos displayed on the notice board. I don't hear Sienna come through from the back. I only hear her gasp of surprise. I turn around. Her face is ashen.

'Oh God,' she says.

'Are you okay?' I ask stepping forward.

'God, you gave me a shock. As I walked through the door I smelt your perfume and for a second I thought Vikki was here.'

Tears spring to her eyes and she brushes them away with her hand.

'Vikki?' I ask.

'Vikki Merchant, she used to work here.'

'Oh yes.'

'You're wearing her perfume.'

My legs turn to jelly.

'Would you like a chair,' Sienna asks, pulling one forward.

I sit down and take a breath.

'Vikki wore this perfume?' I ask.

'Rose Oud isn't it? She always wore it. God, you've spun me back a few months.'

'Where is she working now?' I ask.

'Don't you know?' she looks at me oddly. 'It was all over the news.'

'Know what?' A tingle of apprehension runs through me.

'Vikki went missing. It was a few days before I showed you around Hunters Moon. At that time we just thought she was ill. She hadn't called in sick though, which wasn't like her. We phoned and got no reply and eventually contacted her sister who went to her flat in Cowley. There was no sign of anything amiss and we all presumed she'd gone off somewhere. She was a bit pissed with a bloke she was seeing, not that she talked much about him. Her sister decided to call the police. She's down as a missing person now.'

My head spins and my hands begin to shake.

'When was she last seen, do they know?'

'She had a viewing in Ambleside, the village next to Penlyn, the day before your viewing. She arrived but no one saw her after that.'

I look at the staff photos on the notice board.

'We should take her off. I keep saying it,' says Sienna.

My eyes are drawn to the woman with a white scrunch in her hair.

'That's Vikki,' says Sienna pointing to the photo.

'Yes,' I say. 'I know,'

I grab Sienna's arm as I come over faint.

Chapter Fifty

'I'm okay,' I say. 'It's just my hormones.'

I sip the water from the glass Sienna hands me.

'A lot has been happening for you with the move and your husband's political career,' she says gently.

'Yes,' I say but I'm distracted. My mind is on Vikki Merchant.

'Did Vikki have keys to Hunters Moon?'

'Not personally, she would take them from here when she had a viewing.'

I'm about to tell her about the bottle of Rose Oud that I had found in the boat but stop myself. I'd come here to apologise for my mad ramblings on the day of the party. I don't want to start rambling again. The next thing I know Adam will call Simon and then I'll be whisked back to St Lukes.

'I won't keep you,' I say. 'I just wanted to apologise for my behaviour at the party. You must have thought me crazy.'

'No, not at all,' she says looking uncomfortable. 'You've been under a lot of strain I imagine. I don't think I could cope with a politician for a husband.'

'You're very kind,' I smile, pulling gently at Kerri's lead. 'Please come over for tea sometime and see what changes we've made to the house.'

I climb back into the car with Sienna watching from the doorway. My hands are still shaking as I try to make sense of what she had just told me. Did the perfume in the boat belong to Vikki Merchant and not Kerri after all? Stop it, I tell myself angrily. Stop it right now. There is nothing odd about an old bottle of perfume. Maybe it was Vikki Merchant's although I can't imagine how she dropped it in the boat. But the scrunch, was that hers too?

'Loads of women wear white scrunches for goodness' sake,' I mumble.

'Sorry, what was that?' asks Malcolm.

'Just me thinking aloud,' I say.

We park outside the laundrette and I go in to collect Adam's shirts.

'No Jan today?' asks a guy behind the counter. His name tag reads *Len* and I vaguely remember Jan mentioning him.

'Her cat is sick so she's going to be at the vets today.'

'Aw, that's a shame. Here is your laundry.'

He hands me the shirts and suits on a hanger.

'Give Jan our best,' he smiles.

'I will thank you.'

'Oh yes, we found this in one of the suit's pockets.'

He hands me a large pearl drop earring. It's vaguely familiar.

'It isn't mine,' I say. 'But it looks familiar.'

'Maybe Jan's,' he smiles. 'Perhaps it got caught up in the laundry. She's always loaded up with stuff when she comes. We can barely see her face under it,' he laughs.

'I'll ask her. It's the kind of earring she wears. Thanks Len.'

I pay the bill and Kerri and I climb back into the waiting car.

'Back home?' asks Malcolm.

'You can drop us at the church actually, and then Kerri and I can call in to see a friend. Kerri needs a walk. Perhaps you could take the laundry back for me.'

Maybe I'll change my mind when I get to the church, I tell myself. Maybe I will realise how crazy I am being again and go straight on to Art's farm.

But I don't. Reverend Flynn's car is in the driveway and I make my way to the front door. I'm hesitant; I don't want someone telling Adam that I was here. The last thing I need is to go back into St Lukes just as Adam becomes Prime Minister.

There is no reply when I ring the doorbell. I hear sounds from the back garden and cautiously open the gate. It's unlocked. Reverent Flynn is kneeling on a pad, planting seeds into pots. There is a mug at his side. He turns at the sound of the gate and smiles.

'Mrs Macintosh,' he says, clearly surprised.

His expression changes for a moment and he reels back on his kneeling pad. He can smell my perfume, just as I had hoped he would.

'I hope I'm not disturbing you,' I say.

'Of course not, it's lovely to see you. How are you feeling?'

'I'm much better thank you.'

'I'm pleased to hear it. Can I get you a cup of tea? I was just about to get myself a top up.'

'That sounds great thank you.'

He stands up and fetches a chair from the patio.

'You rest your feet, while I make the tea.'

Kerri begins to play with his watering hose and I have to tug her away from it. Reverend Flynn returns with two mugs and pulls up a chair beside me.

'I came to apologise for my behaviour on the night of the party.'

'Oh,' he says, waving a hand. 'It's all forgotten.'

'You recognise my perfume, don't you?' I say taking him by surprise.

'I …'

'Did you know Vikki Merchant?'

He swallows.

'I didn't know her very well.'

I sip my tea.

'She used to wear this perfume didn't she? You recognised it at Henry's barbecue.'

He sighs.

'Please don't make a mystery of this …'

'I'm not,' I interrupt. 'I just wondered if you knew what happened to her.'

He places his mug of tea on to a table.

'She disappeared. I presume that is what you're talking about. The police are aware she came to see me but I couldn't reveal what we discussed.'

'Was she religious?'

'Mrs Macintosh ...'

'Okay, I just wondered. It's just I found a bottle of her perfume in the house and ...'

'She had a faith yes, and something had happened and she was having difficulty making a decision so ...'

'She was pregnant wasn't she,' I say, remembering my dream. From his reaction I know I am right. It wasn't Kerri Wilson's spirit I had been sensing in the house but Vikki Merchant's. Someone had murdered Vikki Merchant in our house.

Chapter Fifty-One

'Thanks for the tea,' I say as I stand up to leave. Kerri runs to me with a packet of seeds in her mouth.

'Oh no, I'm so sorry,' I say pulling the packet off her.

He laughs.

'Not to worry.'

I glance through the living room doorway as he leads me through the house. I remember the day I had seen him lying on the chair. That wasn't insulin; I'd swear my life on it. I look at his hand and notice that he is shaking.

'Well, you'd best be getting on,' he says.

I see a bead of sweat on his forehead.

'Was Vikki unsure about keeping the baby?' I ask.

'I really can't say what we discussed. I'm sorry.'

'Do you know who the father was?'

'Mrs Macintosh, I really can't discuss this with you.'

He mops his forehead with a handkerchief.

'Of course, I'm sorry. It isn't any of my business.'

He gives me a curious look.

'I wish I could tell you more.'

I smile. I think the Reverend Flynn knows a lot more than he is telling me.

'Thanks, I'll erm … let you get on.'

I feel sure the moment the door is closed he will shoot up. If I was right about Reverend Flynn then how many other things was I right about? Were Henry and Rhonda telling me the truth?

*

It's a relief to see Art. All my fancies seem to disappear when I enter his messy kitchen. Rosie is delighted to see Kerri and after sniffing each other they run off together.

'You won't see her for a while,' he grins.

I feel really happy to see him. He's the one person in the village who seems centred and normal.

'I made a cake,' he says proudly, holding up a burnt offering.

'It's not as bad as it looks. Icing covers a multitude of sins.'

After tea he takes me outside to collect the eggs from the coop.

'Can I say you're looking terrific,' he says, handing me a basket. 'Ever collected eggs before?'

'Only from the supermarket,' I laugh.

Kerri and Rosie dash around outside the chicken coop and Art sends them packing with some dog biscuits.

'She gets spoilt here,' I say, carefully holding an egg.

'I'll put some in a carton for you. Eggs that is, not dog biscuits,' he grins.

I bend to get another egg and feel dizzy. He steadies me by the arm.

'Sorry, I get a bit woozy at times.'

He helps me out of the coop and leads me to a bench.

'Sit down and I'll get you some water.'

I wait while he goes into the farmhouse. I find myself wondering if Art had ever met Vikki Merchant. It's unlikely and he didn't seem to be aware of the perfume. He returns with a jug of water and two glasses.

'It is warm today,' he says.

'Thanks. I've not done much but I'm still tired from sitting doing nothing in that stupid respite place. Honestly, I'm beginning to feel like an invalid instead of pregnant.'

'Why did you go in there?' he asks, puzzled.

'I had a breakdown.'

He turns to look at me.

'Do you believe that?'

I look towards the coop and mull over his words.

'I don't know,' I say honestly. 'It seemed easier to go along with it. Adam was worried and I'd got myself all worked up about things that happened in the village and …'

'Like the vicar being on drugs and Margaret Snell's accident being covered up?'

'Yes,' I say nodding. 'I wasn't wrong. They did cover it up. Gerard Meyer was driving, not his friend. They said it would have been wrong for Gerard's career to be over before it had even begun.'

'What did your husband say?' he asked.

'He didn't want me to get involved. He's got his career to think about, don't forget. The last thing he needs is for his neurotic wife to turn into Miss Marple. You can't blame him.'

'I did some investigating too,' Art admits. 'But when I came round to see you to share what I'd discovered your husband told me you'd had a breakdown and were in hospital. It's just when I saw you at the party you didn't look like you were about to have a breakdown so I found it a bit hard to believe.'

I recount my run in with Henry and Geoff at the party. Their honest disclosures and how stupid I'd felt when Henry had told me that a body couldn't possibly be in the lake. I didn't tell him about the DVD I'd found at Henry's though. It just felt too intimate to share.

'I think I misunderstood everything though. Kerri committed suicide. I can believe that. I think the guilt was too much and she took an overdose.'

'All the same, they covered up things they shouldn't have, so you're right. I reckon they covered up Peter Snell's death,' he says.

'My mate on the paper said there were rumours for a while that the villagers tried to get Snell to leave. That they hung the noose around his neck and threatened to hang him if he didn't agree. Some said he had a heart arrhythmia and that caused a heart attack. Of course, it's all hearsay, and from a long time ago, but I can't help thinking it may well be true.'

I nod.

'It was a long time ago but Gerard Meyer's accident wasn't a long time ago.'

I turn to face him.

'Did you know Vikki Merchant?'

'Only that she is the estate agent from Oxford that went missing.'

'I smell her perfume in the house.'

'How do you know it's her perfume?' he says as he opens a packet of Custard Creams.

I explain how I didn't know it was Vikki's perfume until this morning and how I had always presumed it to be Kerri Wilson's.

I lay a hand on my stomach.

'We found the perfume bottle in the boat and ...'

I hesitate before taking the scrunch from my bag and handing it to him.

'And this, I found this in the boat and I'm now starting to think that ...'

'Something happened to Vikki Merchant in your house?' he says, reading my mind.

'I know, it's crazy and the scrunch could be anyone's, right? I have to think of the baby and Adam's high profile.'

'Have a Custard Cream,' he smiles.

'I shouldn't be here. Adam gets jealous. I sensed he was jealous when he told me that you had visited.'

He laughs.

'Married women aren't my scene.'

I find myself feeling slightly disappointed and try not to let it show.

'At least not as a rule,' he adds and I feel myself blush.

'You know,' he says changing the subject, 'I don't believe you are imagining things. You're really not the type to have flights of fancy. I don't know you well but I'm pretty convinced you're level-headed. Why don't I ask my friend at the newspapers if he knows anyone in forensics? He seems to know just about everyone. We could check if this is blood.'

'Thank you. That would be great. I should be getting back, thanks so much for the tea and the chat.'

'Let me just put some eggs in a carton.'

Armed with eggs and treats for Kerri, I reluctantly leave.

'Don't forget,' he calls. 'If you ever want to chat, or think things aren't all they should be, just give me a ring.'

'Thanks, Art, I will.'

*

Adam is still holed up with Luke when I get back. Kerri is exhausted and flops on to the bed. I hang the laundry on the back of the door and then sit on the bed beside her with my laptop. It takes me less than two minutes to find the news story about Vikki Merchant. I can't imagine how I didn't see it before.

Estate Agent Goes Missing ran the headline. No wonder I haven't been able to get hold of her. My mind begins to race and I fight to keep it under control.

'Flora,' calls Adam.

I walk out on to the landing. 'Everything okay?' he asks, looking up at me.

'Yes, fine.'

'Great, just another few hours and I'll be finished here. I thought we could all go out to eat later. Are you up to that?'

'Sounds great,' I smile.

He nods and goes back to the study. I take the shirts and suits from the back of the door and then remember the earring. I take it from my purse and drop it into a little glass dish on the dressing table. I make a mental note to mention it to Jan and as I do so my mobile rings. I look down at it and see by a weird coincidence it is her.

'You must have sensed me thinking about you. How's Molly?' I ask.

'She's still at the vets. We're hoping to pick her up later. I'm sorry about today.'

'Don't be silly,' I say tucking the phone under my chin while I hang the shirts in the wardrobe.

'I'll come on Friday.'

'No worries Jan, if you can't make it, just give me a ring. By the way, Len gave me a drop earring. He found it in the laundry. Have you lost one?'

'I've lost a few,' she laughs.

'I'll put it in the top drawer in the kitchen.'

I hang up after telling her not to worry about Molly. A sudden dizzy spell hits me and I break out in a cold sweat. I lie on the bed and take a deep breath. I'd overdone it again. I'd got things in my head about Vikki Merchant. You've got to stop this I tell myself. You can't say any of this to Adam. He's got more than enough to deal with right now. I lower myself on to the pillows and pull the laptop out from under Kerri's head. I've got commissions to finish. That's what I need to focus on.

April 2017
Seth

Seth stared in shock through the small glass pane of the front door. His view of the body was obscured by the outline of the man leaning over it. His hand was poised to pull the hand bell. He'd seen the cars outside and didn't like to go around to the back before knocking. But now he stepped back, tripping over his tools. He steadied them quickly and walked slowly backwards out of the driveway, his eyes never leaving the front door. At the entrance gate he carefully laid his shovel down and raced from the house, his heart pounding. He'd not got fifty yards before his lean frame collided with someone. He stopped, his eyes wide, his breath in short gasps.

'What's happened?' asked the man. 'Is it something I can help with?'

*

Seth had not followed the man back to the house but instead had hurried round to the gate in Chatterpie Lane. He'd watched, mesmerised, from his hideout in the tree. He'd guessed there was only one place they would put the body and he was right.

April 2017
An Error of Judgement

His brain was numb. He wanted to move, to do something, anything but sit here over her lifeless body. If only he could go back to that moment on the stairs. He should phone the police. But how could he? He'd be ruined. Damn her, damn her to hell. What had he been thinking of?

'What a fucking mess,' he moaned, dropping his head into his hands. He felt like he'd run a marathon. His shirt, soaked in sweat, stuck to his back. Tears rolled down his cheeks. He wasn't kind enough to cry for her, he was crying for himself. All that work, all his plans all that bloody sacrifice down the toilet because of some cheap fuck. Had he been insane? She'd been good in bed, but if this got out, the affair, the pregnancy.

'Oh Jesus,' he moaned. He looked at her lifeless body, her staring eyes that glared at him accusingly. Blood was seeping from the back of her head and he reeled back in shock, clambering to his feet.

'Christ,' he groaned.

Think, he told himself. For Christ's sake man, think. What had he touched? Christ, just about everything. It would take him forever to cover his tracks. It's no good, he was doomed. He'd have to phone the police. With shaking hands he tugged his phone from his trouser pocket. He was about to tap in 999 when the front door swung open. He strained his eyes. It was like a mirage. Standing in the doorway with the sun shining behind him forming a halo around his head stood his saviour.

The man shook his head.

'Let's not do that,' he said calmly, pointing to the phone.

Chapter Fifty-Two

I watch as Seth stacks the paint pots to go into the cellar. The droning of the lawnmower is monotonous and I'll be glad when Earl has finished.

Jan is preparing our clothes ready for London in two days' time when Ralph will resign. Adam will address the nation from outside Number Ten and then go to Buckingham Palace to form a government. I'm still very tired but Doctor Kingsley had said I could go with Adam, provided I take things slowly.

I sit on a stool in the shed doorway and watch Seth tidy up. Kerri wanders close to the lake and I call out to her. Seth looks over and then hurries to pick her up.

'Thanks Seth,' I smile.

'You have a visitor,' Jan rushes to tell me.

I look in to the kitchen to see Rhonda sitting at the table. She stands up as I walk in.

'I just popped by to see if you were okay. We didn't see you at the crochet group and …'

I force a smile.

'I'm fine, thanks for asking. I'm just taking things carefully.'

She spots Seth and waves.

'Would you like some tea?' I ask.

'I can't stop, I just wanted to …'

She looks past me to Jan.

'I'll carry on upstairs,' says Jan tactfully.

'Are you sure you won't have tea?' I ask again.

'You can't imagine what it was like. Katie was a wreck for years. She was terrified of men for a long time,' Rhonda blurts out.

I nod.

'I'm so sorry.'

'She went to America. Seth's a sensitive soul. None of it is his fault. I didn't know about Gerard Meyer's accident. Geoff never told me. I agree with you, they shouldn't have covered it up but … Can you imagine having the press here again, dredging up Kate's rape and …'

'Adam says I'm not to think about it as it will upset me and I have to think of the baby.'

She nods.

'I'm not a bad person,' she says, standing up. 'Peter Snell, it was an accident. Geoff and his mates, well they were angry. Our Katie was only seventeen, just about to have her eighteenth birthday. They wanted him to leave the village. They threatened him and the shock …' she trails off.

'They put a noose around his neck didn't they?' I say with a shudder.

'He had an asthma attack. No one knew he had asthma. It was really quick and …'

She turns again to the door.

'Did you know Vikki Merchant?' I ask.

She turns and her face tells me she didn't.

'I know she was an estate agent and went missing. Why do you ask?'

'I'm just curious.'

I walk with her to the door.

'I hope you'll come back to crochet group sometime, but I expect you'll be in London a lot now.'

'Yes, I expect I will.'

She surprises me by leaning forward and kissing me on the cheek.

'Well, bye.'

I close the door and lean against it. My eyes rest on the flagstones and I remember that I was going to ask Jan to wash them. I look up to call Jan and then see Earl in the kitchen doorway looking at me. I stare back at him. I feel more confident knowing Jan is upstairs.

'It's break time,' he says gruffly.

Jan hurries down the stairs at that moment.

'I'm just about to put the kettle on,' she says.

I stand in the hall, undecided whether to have tea or not. I look up at the monitor but now there is no sign of Rhonda. I think back to the accusations I'd made at the party and cringe. I must have sounded totally insane. But am I? Are my ideas totally crazy? I wasn't wrong about the lake. Maybe a body couldn't be in the shallow part of the lake but it could be in the well. I notice that Henry didn't mention that, and he was so patronising of me. How dare he? He's nothing but a pervert. I wonder if he was like that when his wife lived with him at Claremont Tower. Something about Henry and his wife makes me feel uncomfortable and then I realise what it is. I'd seen a folder on Adam's desk titled *Bluefields*. It's the home where Henry's wife, Rachel, lives. Why is Adam so involved with Bluefields?

Everyone is in the kitchen drinking tea. Even Kerri is drinking from her bowl. I step into the study. The sun shines through the French doors and I glance out to the lake which shimmers under the sunlight. The Bluefields folder isn't on the desk and I sigh in irritation. He must have taken it to London with him. Adam's jumper is slung over the chair and I pick it up and sniff it, the scent of him making me smile with contentment. I open one of the drawers and shuffle carefully through the papers, straining to see what's written on them.

'Do you want a cup of tea?' asks Jan from the doorway.

I jump at the sound of her voice.

'Sorry, did I startle you?'

'It's okay. I'm a bag of nerves. Thanks Jan, tea would be lovely.'

'Be back in a sec.'

She closes the door and I search through another drawer. This time I'm successful and find the folder marked *Care Homes Bill*. I flick through it, not really understanding what I'm seeing. There are printouts of emails and contracts, which I don't understand, but one thing that does make sense. There is only one care home in the folder and that is *Bluefields*.

Chapter Fifty-Three

'Sorry to wake you,' Jan says.

'No, I'm glad you did,' I say rubbing my eyes. I must have dosed off.

'Seth and Earl have gone. The shed looks great. I'm off too if that's okay?'

'Yes, of course. Oh, did you find your earring in the drawer?'

'Oh yes, what a shame, it isn't one of mine.'

'Oh,' I say surprised.

'I put it back in the drawer.'

'How odd, I was sure it was familiar.'

April 2017

'She fell, I tried to catch her,' he said as he rubbed at a bloodstain on his shirt with a tissue.

'It was an accident wasn't it?'

His saviour stepped into the hallway. 'We don't want the police swarming all over the place do we? Nothing you can do for her now.'

'But I can't just leave her there.'

He couldn't bear to look at her broken twisted body.

'What's done is done.'

'I don't know how it happened ...' he stammered. 'One minute she was ...'

'There's no need to explain. We should get you tidied up, clean shirt and all that. Isn't there somewhere you need to be?'

Relief washed over him.

'But don't you ...'

'Leave it to me and we'll talk later. Why don't you go and change. I believe there are some shirts in the wardrobe upstairs.'

He did as he was bidden, relieved to be rescued from a disaster that would have ruined his life.

I carefully climb into the boat. The air is still and there is no sound apart from the cooing of a wood pigeon. Adam isn't due home until eight o'clock. It's now four. The boat rocks as it adjusts to my weight. I wait for it to settle, scanning the bottom of the boat for bloodstains. There are a couple of marks at the head of the boat, the same place I had found the scrunch. A small wave of nausea rises up in my stomach and I take a deep breath until it passes. They could be mistaken for innocent paint marks but I know now for sure that it's blood. I unfold the Land Registry plans and look ahead. The rope slips easily off the mooring and using an oar I slowly push the boat forward. I find myself wondering if Kerri ever made this short journey. The lake is shallow, just as Henry had said, and I can see reeds on the bottom. I stop rowing and check my phone. I have a missed call from Art. I'm about to call him back when I realise I have no signal. I curse and wrap my pashmina around my shoulders. Even though the sun is out, I still feel a chill run through me. I realise that my legs are shaky. According to the plans I should be near the site of the old well but the water is shallow and there is no sign of a well. I feel ridiculous. I have no idea what I'm hoping to find as I prod the bottom of the lake with the oar. I scoop up some weed and dig the oar into the lake again. I convince myself that there is nothing unusual about the lake and row back to the mooring. Everyone is right. These stupid ideas are all in my head. Any number of women could wear Rose Oud, and the bloodstains in the boat could have come from anywhere. It doesn't mean there has been a dead body in it. I reach the mooring and tie up the boat. It is then that I see something glittering in the water. I use the oar to scoop it up. It's Adam's St Christopher pendant. I check the clip and see it is broken. Kerri barks at me, angry that I hadn't taken her.

'It's okay, girl,' I say patting her reassuringly. 'Daddy's lost his chain again.'

My legs are like jelly and I realise how scared I had been of finding the well.

'Let's have a calming cup of tea,' I say allowing Kerri to lead the way back to the house. I click the kettle on and while it boils I go upstairs with the earring and the pendant and drop them in the jewellery box.

'That's it,' I say, 'I'm not going to think about that bloody lake any more.'

Chapter Fifty-Four

I prepare a Bolognese sauce and then try to call Art, but there's no phone signal. I sigh. I check to see if he is on WhatsApp but he isn't. I'm about to try him on the landline when I hear a car scrunch on the gravel.

I hurry into the hall and see it is Adam. I'm relieved he isn't with Tweedledee and Tweedledum, but I have no doubt I will be seeing a lot more of them in the future. I meet him at the front door and he drops his case to hug me. He has a bottle of champagne in his hand to celebrate, even though only he can drink it.

'How are you?' he asks, kissing me. 'God, I've looked forward to seeing you. It's been bloody mad.'

'I've packed a case and Jan made sure everything was laundered. I didn't know what you wanted to take so I didn't pack a case for you.'

'That's fine. I'd rather do it myself anyway.'

He pulls his jacket off and loosens his tie.

'Dinner smells good.'

'It's only spag bol,' I laugh.

I'm pleased to have him home. It will be one of the few nights we'll have in Hunters Moon. Hopefully we'll be here for Christmas. I'll be close to having the baby then.

'I saw Simon today,' says Adam, taking my hand and walking me into the kitchen. 'He's arranging a CVS test for you.'

'Oh,' I say surprised.

'I said it would be a good idea to check everything is okay with the baby. Do it early.'

I release my hand from his.

'Why shouldn't it be okay?' I ask.

He wraps his arm around my waist.

'Don't go getting paranoid, Flora. I'm just thinking after the problems you've had it's probably a good idea to get one done as soon as possible. We don't want there to be anything wrong with the baby do we? Simon agreed it was a good idea.'

'Well, he would agree with it wouldn't he? He's got a knighthood riding on this.'

He sighs and pours whisky into a glass.

'I don't know what you're on about now. I'm thinking of you. There's no harm in a test.'

There's an edge to his voice. He looks tired. He no doubt thinks I'm being awkward.

'I'm not aborting our child, Adam, even if there is something wrong. I can't believe you're even thinking those things. We've waited so long for this baby and ...'

He hurries to turn down the boiling spaghetti.

'Flo,' he says coming to stand in front of me. 'We're not going to be your average couple. In twenty-four hours I'm going to be the Prime Minister. We'll be living at Number Ten. Everyone will love it that we're about to have a baby. You'll be sent tons of stuff. No doubt you'll be asked to endorse all kinds of baby wear and whatnot.'

'I'm not sure what you're trying to tell me Adam?' I say, attempting to keep my voice even.

He pulls a bottle of water from the fridge.

'We have to have a perfect baby.'

I gasp. He slams the fridge door shut and turns to face me.

'We don't want any pity, Flora. We don't want anything that is going to detract from us as a power couple. You'll be entertaining kings and presidents, and God knows who else. You won't have time for a ...' he hesitates.

'For a what?' I ask, feeling myself becoming tearful.

'For God's sake Flo, it's probably perfectly fine, but what's the harm in checking while it's still early. Only a few people know. In a few weeks everyone will know. We'll get the test out of the way, find out everything is okay and then we can announce it. It will be perfect PR. Luke says ...'

'I don't give a toss what Luke says,' I say angrily. 'How dare you talk about our baby like it's a publicity stunt?'

'Flo,' he says, reaching out to me. I shake his hand off my arm.

'It's not like that,' he says tiredly. 'We've got to announce it anyway. Be sensible.'

'I'm not aborting our baby,' I say flatly. 'I don't care if we're hosting Mahatma Ghandi ...'

'He's dead,' he smiles.

'You know what I mean,' I say feeling myself shake with anger.

He drains his whisky glass.

'I think you're being unreasonable,' he says as he walks into the study. 'Let me know when dinner is ready. I've got a few emails to do.'

I throw the sieve angrily into the sink and drain the spaghetti. It was supposed to be our last evening together before our lives changed. I wanted it to be an evening to remember. I follow him into the study, tears pricking my eyelids.

'I'm sorry,' I say. 'If you really want me to have the test, then I'll have it. But we'll have to discuss the results.'

He's sitting at his desk. I lean over him to kiss his neck.

'Of course we will,' he says, taking my hand. I stroke his neck and feel the coldness of a chain. How can Adam be wearing the St Christopher when I'd just found it in the lake?

Chapter Fifty-Five

My hand trembles as I grate parmesan cheese on to the sauce. I can't understand it. I pick at my food as my brain tries to make sense of things.

'You're not eating?' he states. 'You're feeling okay aren't you?'

'Maybe a bit nervous about tomorrow,' I lie.

'It'll be good Flo. It will be the best day of our lives.'

'Yes,' I nod.

'I can't believe we've done it,' he says reaching out a hand to cover mine.

'I couldn't have done any of this without you.'

'How is Ralph holding up?' I ask, meeting his eyes.

He looks at his plate.

'He's doing okay. He doesn't want to resign but what choice does he have. There's only so much I can cover for him.'

I release my hand abruptly.

'How far have you gone to cover for him, Adam?'

'What?' he asks, sipping the champagne.

'Would you have broken the law?' I ask softly.

His head snaps up.

'Don't be ridiculous. Ralph isn't worth that kind of loyalty. I wouldn't be so stupid.'

'Did you know there was a well in the lake?'

'No I didn't. How did you find that out?'

'I got plans from the Land Registry.'

He looks into my eyes.

'You're a sly fox,' he smiles. 'You'll have to show me them.'

'Henry was wrong about it only being three foot deep. Henry isn't always right,' I scoff.

'I don't think he ever said that he was. When's the Best Kept Village judging by the way?'

I shake my head.

'I don't know. You'll have to ask Henry.'

'You're in a funny mood,' he says, topping up his glass.

He's right, I'm acting like a petulant child and I don't know why. I feel something is being kept from me and I don't know what. I feel injured to think that Adam knows what it is.

He pushes his plate to one side and stretches.

'I'm knackered. Are you okay if I finish those emails and then we can go to bed? Have a cuddle and discuss tomorrow.'

I smile.

'Sounds nice, maybe I'll have a bath.'

He scrapes his chair back.

'I'm making a coffee, do you want one?'

'No, I'll feed Kerri and then go up.'

Adam fills the dishwasher while I see to Kerri, and then goes to the study to finish his emails. I wait for Kerri to finish her food and then she follows me upstairs. I check my phone but there's nothing from Art. I look at the signal symbol and curse. No wonder there are no messages. I can't phone him from the landline. It will only set Adam off. I couldn't bear more arguments this evening. I throw lavender oil into the bath and turn on the taps. My eyes wander to the jewellery box. It can't be Adam's chain. It must be someone else's. Adam is wearing his. Whoever it belongs to must have dropped it during our party. I lift the lid and remove the St Christopher I had found. With my heart pounding, I turn it over. The engraving screams at me.

To Adam. Safe Travels, love Mum & Dad.

If this is Adam's chain then what is he wearing around his neck?

Chapter Fifty-Six

I'm passive during our love making. Adam is gentle and considerate. I've told him there is no reason to be. Pregnancy isn't an illness. We don't discuss the test again. Adam is full of excitement for tomorrow. He'd chosen the shirt and tie he would wear for his speech outside Number Ten, and another for Buckingham Palace, and finally his dinner suit for the first evening at Downing Street.

'You can meet all the staff before we leave for the Palace,' he says. 'We can decide at the weekend what things we want there and what we want to leave here. It's all furnished, obviously.'

'Yes,' I say, trying to show some enthusiasm but all I can think about is the St Christopher I had slid under my pillow. I should ask him but I can't. I can't until it makes some kind of sense. I lay awake trying to determine if Adam is sleeping. Finally, it is too much and I slip quietly out of bed. He gives a shallow snore and I hold my breath. Walking on tiptoe I step around to his side of the bed and lift the chain he'd taken off. I turn it over in my hand. There is no engraving on the back. I'm trembling from head to toe. I force myself to calm down, to try and think logically. There has to be a reasonable explanation as to why Adam's chain was in the lake. Perhaps he didn't want me to worry about our luck changing. But that's silly. Adam has always been the superstitious one. Perhaps that's why he bought another one. Maybe it worried him not having the protection. Yes, that would make sense. I slip back into bed and close my eyes. I'm making more of things again. Everything will look clearer in the morning. I feel myself drifting off to sleep when suddenly my eyes snap open and I fight back a gasp. It was the night of the fundraiser. In my mind I can clearly see Adam asking me if I'd seen his St Christopher. How did Adam's St Christopher get in the lake of Hunters Moon if he'd lost it before we'd even moved in?

*

My mind races and I close my eyes. Tomorrow is going to be a big day. Once it's over I'll ask Adam. He'll no doubt explain everything and be really pleased I'd found the St Christopher. We'll celebrate at the dinner. I'm being stupid. I must control my thoughts. I feel myself growing drowsy and as I do, Vikki Merchant's face appears in my mind. What happened to her? I sit up with a start. The earring, I remember why it was familiar. Vikki Merchant was wearing something similar in the photo that was on the wall of the estate agents.

*

I slip out of bed again and creep to the middle bedroom. Using my iPhone I google Lauren and Michael's estate agents. Once into the home page I'm able to scroll down the menu. I click the 'Our Staff' link and take a breath. The web page has the same photos as the display board. I enlarge the photo of Vikki Merchant and gasp. I stare at the earrings and then at the one in my hand that I'd taken from the jewellery box. They're identical.

'Oh God,' I moan with tears streaming down my cheeks. I no longer care what noise I make as I rummage through Adam's clothes that hang in the wardrobe of the middle bedroom. I can barely see through my tears. My head is spinning. I don't know what I'm looking for. I don't even know what I'm doing. I'm confused, scared and unable to think clearly. I have to be wrong. I have to be. There must be something that will tell me I'm wrong. There just has to be. My hands claw through pockets and rip at shirts. But there is nothing. My nose is streaming and I wipe my eyes, on a shirt.

I fall on to the bed clutching it. It smells of Adam's aftershave. I lift it to my nose and inhale deeply. Please God, let me be wrong. It's as I lower the shirt that I notice it is a Ralph Lauren. Adam doesn't like Ralph Lauren shirts. He dislikes their style. I study the label. It's tailor made. Maybe it is Adam's after all. Perhaps they had gifted it to him. He is given a lot of designer shirts but I realise this shirt hadn't been gifted to Adam at all. A small label under the collar tells me it belonged to Gerard Meyer.

*

I don't know how long I sat there holding the shirt but it felt like a lifetime. My tears had dried and all I felt was shock. Finally, I stumbled downstairs, still clutching the shirt. From the study window I stare out into the night. Vikki Merchant's body is in the well, I'm certain of that now. Her body must have been carried from the hallway and through the kitchen. Adam helped cover up her murder, but why? Who was he protecting? The perfume must have dropped from her handbag. I should phone the police but what would I tell them? I think my husband, the Home Secretary, covered up a death in our house.

I drop my head into my hands. There are no tears left. How could Adam have been so stupid? We have a baby on the way. His ambition has made him lose all sense. I somehow always knew it would. I think of Henry's words from the lecture I'd attended. *Every action has its consequences. We can find ourselves in a tangled web of deceit. One error of judgement can, and often does, lead to lies and deceit. Then our moral judgement eludes us.*

I can't let my moral judgement elude me. Adam has done wrong. Vikki Merchant lies at the bottom of the old well in the middle of our lake. I can't leave her there. I grab a tissue from the desk and accidentally knock over Adam's diary. A photo of us together on our last holiday slips out and I stare at it lovingly.

I know he is there before he speaks. I turn, the shirt still clutched in my hands. He stands in his boxer shorts, his hair ruffled from sleep.

'What are you doing?' he says huskily.

'I know what happened,' I say quietly.

'What are we talking about Flora?'

'Vikki, I know what happened to her. We have to phone the police Adam. You can't leave her there. Was it Henry that murdered her? Why are you covering for Henry?'

His eyes harden.

'You don't know what you're talking about,' he says.

April 2017

He hurried to the bathroom, his head spinning. He should phone the police, he knew that, but Christ, what would happen to him if he did ...

'I need your help.'

He looked over the banister. The man was struggling to move her. He was perspiring heavily.

'She's too heavy,' he said, looking up. 'You'll have to help me.'

He felt the bile rush to his throat and had to take a deep breath to stop himself from throwing up. He wouldn't touch her, he couldn't.

'I don't think I can,' he said weakly.

'For God's sake man, we can't leave her here.'

He forced his legs down the stairs.

'Take her feet,' instructed the man.

She was heavier than he imagined. He struggled not to look at her face but thankfully the man had closed her eyes.

'Grab her bag,' barked the man.

He leant down for the bag and saw an earring at the foot of the stairs.

'Oh Jesus,' he groaned. This can't be real. Only an hour ago he'd been fiddling with that very earring.

'Come on,' urged the man.

He shoved the earring into his pocket and then grabbed her handbag. Neither of them noticed the leaking perfume bottle. Between them they struggled through the French doors and out to the lake.

'I'm Henry Dorcas,' says the man between pants. 'I'm the elder of the guild.'

'I ...'

'I know who you are. I wondered when this would all turn sour for you.'

'I can explain ...'

'There's no need. Let's get her in the boat.'

'The boat?' he asked. 'But the lake ...'

Henry threw her handbag in first and then struggled to get the body in.

'There is an old well shaft in the middle,' Henry explained, '40 foot deep. She won't be found. Get yourself washed and changed. I'll tidy up here.'

'How do I know I can trust you?' he asked as Henry wrapped the anchor chain around her body and pushed the little boat away from the mooring.

Henry laughed.

'You can't afford not to trust me. I like to think of myself as a business man. I will look after you if you look after me, and it's not often you get a politician move into the village.'

'We're not moving into the village.'

Henry frowned.

'You have to I'm afraid. You don't want someone else buying this house and digging around finding your secret do you?'

He looked back at the house.

'And what do you want in return for helping me?' he asked, his heart heavy.

'We can discuss that at another time,' smiled Henry. 'The important thing is there's no shame on the village and your life isn't ruined. I hope she was worth it.'

Adam sighed. The truth was she hadn't been worth it at all.

Chapter Fifty-Seven

'What are you holding?' he asks, stepping towards me.

'It's Gerard Meyer's shirt. Adam, you have to tell me the truth,' I say, my voice trembling.

He laughs, sending a shiver through me. It doesn't sound like Adam. Not my Adam. Not the man I love and the father of my baby.

'Ah, I knew I should have got rid of that. Things just got frantic.'

'I love you and I'll try to stand by you, but you can't keep covering for Henry. If you tell the truth ...'

'Grow up, Flora, for Christ's sake. My life will be over. My career and everything I've worked for, all my dreams, gone because of some stupid bitch who meant nothing to me.'

He walks to me with his arms open.

'We've got the baby to think of, our future. We are known as the Power Couple. You've got to put things in perspective.'

I take a step back, hitting my hip against the desk. My mind is reeling. I can't make sense of what he is saying to me.

'I don't understand ...' I begin.

He rolls his eyes.

'I'm going to be the Prime Minister Flora. Forget fucking Ralph, he's history. The papers have enough dirt on him to last for years and ...'

'You were having an affair with Vikki Merchant weren't you?' I say calmly.

He sighs and rubs his eyes.

'It meant nothing.'

'Were you in love with her?' I ask, a lump forming in my throat.

'Don't be ridiculous. It meant nothing. It was a stupid mistake.'

'An error of judgement,' I whisper.

'Flo,' he says, reaching out to me.

'Don't touch me,' I say, stepping back. 'I can forgive an affair but murder …'

'What was I supposed to do? You never wanted it when I did. It always had to fit in around your bloody cycle. I'm only human Flora. You've got to admit that you haven't been much fun lately. I have my needs …'

I shake my head in disbelief.

'Everything has always been about you, hasn't it Adam?'

He shrugs.

'It happened. We went for a drink. It was to discuss houses. I told her we wanted a house in the country and …'

'You did it here?' I say, nausea rising up within me.

'A few times, she had a key for the place …'

'You could at least have gone to a hotel.'

'On reflection you're right,' he says.

'How could you bring me here?' I say, a small sob escaping my lips.

'I couldn't let anyone else buy the house. Who knows what they'd have found. I had to be quick. We wanted a house and what better than Hunters Moon. It was empty and Henry got us a price reduction …'

'You can't leave her in the well. You can't …' I say loudly.

He slams his hand down on the desk.

'Stop telling me what I can and can't fucking do, Flora. I've given you everything and what do you do in return? You dredge this all up. It wasn't enough finding the perfume bottle was it? You had to then wear the bloody stuff …'

'You took the bottle?'

'Of course I did. It was driving me insane. Your talk of a body in the lake and God knows what else. Jesus, I didn't know how to shut you up. I thought the baby would see an end to it but oh no, you just can't stop can you? Henry said …'

I widen my eyes.

'Henry knows about this?'

I wipe the tears from my eyes. My hand is numb from where I had been clutching the shirt to my chest.

'Henry came the afternoon it happened. I'd be in prison now if it hadn't have been for him. He offered to help. He didn't …'

'He didn't want shame on the village, isn't that it? What's the price Adam? He couldn't ask to fuck me like he did Kerri Wilson could he?'

His mouth tightens.

'Henry understands that people make mistakes …'

'Huh,' I scoff. 'Henry only cares what he can screw out of people and their weaknesses. Henry's sick.'

I go to walk past him but he grabs my arm. I shake it off viciously.

'How could you do this to us, Adam? We had everything. I loved you …' I break off as sobs rack my body.

'Flora, it meant nothing. You were never meant to find out.'

'I found your St Christopher in the lake.'

He looks thoughtful.

'Yes, that was unfortunate. I realised later that was how I lost it. She grabbed my shirt. I could have gone down with her. She was crazy Flora. It must have got caught up in her clothes. I bought another as soon as I realised. I hoped you'd forget about it once you saw me wearing it.'

I try not to picture Vikki's lifeless body and her hand clutching at the chain.

I laugh almost hysterically.

'So much for the good luck it has brought you.'

'Actually I think things worked out rather well. Imagine if she was alive, there would be no telling what damage she could do to my career. She was getting demanding Flora.

Why did you have to nose around? Things were going perfectly until then.'

I throw the shirt at him.

'She was pregnant,' I scream. 'You got her fucking pregnant didn't you? You could at least have been careful.'

I stride to the living room and lift the phone receiver.

'Flora, what are you doing,' he barks, hurrying in after me.

'What you should have done months ago. I'm calling the police.'

I start to tap into the phone, when he rips the receiver out of my hand. I gasp in shock.

'I can't let you do that Flora.'

His eyes harden as he looks at me and for the first time in my life I feel afraid of my husband.

'Adam,' I say pleadingly. 'We have to do the right thing.'

His hand tightens on my wrist.

'The right thing is for me to become Prime Minister tomorrow and for you to stand with me. You have to put this behind you, Flora. She was nobody. We can't go back. I can't change it. No one will know. We keep the secret. Henry won't tell anyone. He's too involved and besides ...'

'You'll stop Bluefields from going to the developers,' I finish for him. 'You don't have any other care homes in your bill do you, just that one.'

My stomach has started to cramp and I try not to let it show on my face. I struggle to pull my hand from his grip but he's too strong.

'Bluefields won't close and the bill won't go through. No one will even notice that we only saved one home. Henry's happy. He'll keep his mouth shut if he wants his wife to stay close. It's a small ripple in a big pond.'

I feel sick at his metaphor. Is this really Adam, the man I love? The man whose child I am carrying in my womb. Oh God, please let this all be a bad dream, I plead.

'Flora, please I'm begging you.'

He lifts my hand to his lips and kisses it.

'Think what this will do to my parents. How will they ever cope? You'll kill them.'

I snatch my hand away.

'I can forgive you for fucking someone else. It would mean the end of your dreams, but I never wanted this. You were the ambitious one. We'd have had each other, we could have moved on. But this ... I didn't dump a body in the lake, you did. You should have thought of your parents when you were fucking Vikki Merchant. God knows you weren't thinking of me.'

I think back to our first night in the house when Adam's lust had been uncontrollable and I almost gag as the nausea threatens to overwhelm me.

'You knew that night, the first night here when we made love in that bed that Vikki's body was in the well,' I say sickened with shock.

'Flora,' he pleads.

'Please Adam, let me phone the police. Do the right thing.'

He shakes his head.

'I'm sorry Flora, I can't and I can't let you do it.'

It takes some time for his words to sink in.

'I'd much rather have you at my side tomorrow but if I can't then I can't.'

His eyes are hard.

'You're being ridiculous,' I say. 'If I'm not with you tomorrow everyone will want to know why. I can't lie Adam. It's better if we tell the truth now. I'll do my best to stand by you but it will be difficult ...'

He throws his head back and laughs.

'You're funny, so funny. Are you insane?' he growls. 'I've worked all my life for this. I've struggled. I've bowed down to all those pointless little shits so I could have this one day and you want me to give it up? Don't go all self-righteous on me Flora.'

'You're the insane one,' I snap trying to get past him.

'Flora, don't make me do something I'll regret,' he says, blocking my path.

I let out a nervous laugh.

'Are you threatening me Adam?'

'Everyone knows you've been struggling. The last miscarriage took its toll. Everyone we know will testify to that. You've been low and anxious. Let's face it, I've been worried to leave you alone sometimes. It won't take much to convince people your hormones were all over the place. It's not unusual for people to take their own life when they are depressed.'

The pain punches me again and I take a deep breath. Adam's eyes bore into mine.

'What's your decision Flora?'

Seth

Seth had watched Henry and Mr Macintosh throw the body into the lake. He knew about the well. He'd read about the house in the local history section of the Oxford library, so he'd figured that's why they had rowed to the middle of the lake. Everyone thought he was stupid because he was dumb, but he wasn't. But it benefited him to act that way. People said all kinds of things around him. They thought he didn't know about his father but he did. He knew more than they thought. Henry had thought he'd gone home. Henry was too arrogant for Seth's liking.

'Too much drinking,' he'd told Seth later when they were in the pub. 'I reckon she'll have a real hangover in the morning. She was drunk, lying on the floor. Best not to say anything to anyone, after all, you don't want people thinking you were spying on the house.'

He'd thought of going to the police but knew that no one would believe him. It would be his word against Henry's, his word against a respected Oxford professor. Henry could easily have twisted things and told them Seth was somehow involved. No, he couldn't risk going to the police. He would have been isolated. So, he had decided to bide his time. He knew it would come.

When the new people moved in he had been excited. Maybe he could lead them to the body. He'd guessed it was the estate agent, Vikki Merchant, who they'd dumped. It was too coincidental that she went missing shortly after. She'd been the only one to visit the house after Mr Meyer left. He'd liked her. Sometimes she would be there when he arrived to sweep up the leaves and she'd give him a tenner.

'It always looks tidy when I bring people,' she'd told him. 'I'm dead grateful for that.'

He'd got the shock of his life when he'd seen the new people. It was him. The man he'd seen with Henry that night.

He was going to be the next Prime Minister, everyone said. Then he'd met her, Mrs Macintosh, and Seth didn't know what to do. She was lovely and kind. He had to help her. But he couldn't tell her that her husband was a monster because she would never believe him. He could only lead her to the middle of the lake. There had to be a way to make her think things were not right.

It was easy for Seth to push the boat to the middle of the lake. He could anchor it there. The water was only just above his knees so he could move quickly when he knew he wouldn't be seen. He'd watched her talking to her friends and knew that she was suspicious. He'd tried to look after her. He never wanted to frighten her. A couple of times he'd got into the house through the cellar window. He figured he wasn't trespassing as such. He was just looking for ways to make her think something was amiss. He'd stood at the window. He'd taken a chance but he had to do something. Then they'd changed the password on the gate. When she'd gone into hospital he'd felt so sad. Everyone was saying how sad it was for Adam Macintosh. His wife having a breakdown and all, just as he might become the Prime Minister. If only they knew the truth.

When they'd changed the code on the gate there was nothing he could do. He only hoped he'd done enough to make her look into things more.

Now, it was going to happen. Mr Macintosh was going to be the Prime Minister. He couldn't ruin Flora Macintosh's dreams, not now they had the baby coming. Who would believe him, anyway? He was thinking about Flora Macintosh as he walked back from the pub. He'd been playing darts and it had gone past closing time. It was midnight when he walked past Hunters Moon and as if by magic the gates swung open and Kerri ran out, barking for all she was worth.

Chapter Fifty-Eight

I clutch my stomach and struggle to breathe.

'Adam, I don't understand, I thought we loved each other and ...'

'You're not showing it,' he says petulantly.

'I just need a bit of time alone,' I say. 'Why don't I go and stay with Laurie for a few days and then once you're settled at Number Ten, we can talk again.'

I don't know what I'm saying. I'm rambling and Adam knows it. He runs his hand through his hair.

'Oh Flora, If only you hadn't been so inquisitive. You were all I ever wanted. She was just a passing fling. It wouldn't have happened if you'd been a bit more accommodating.'

I can't believe he's trying to blame this on me.

'Adam, we can go forward. If you explain what happened, I'm sure the courts will be lenient. We can still go on with our lives. It will just be different.'

He scoffs.

'You just don't get it do you? I can't give this up. This is a chance of a lifetime. I'm sorry that you've chosen not to be with me.'

Tears are streaming down my face.

'Adam, please ...'

He leans towards me and I step back but not quickly enough. He grabs my arms roughly and I cry out. Kerri sensing something jumps up at him, barking madly. He turns and kicks out at her, releasing my arm as he does so. I hurry into the hallway as fast as my legs can carry me. Kerri follows, barking constantly. I hear Adam curse as he trips over her. My hand hits the keypad and I pull at the front door. It swings open and I'm about to follow Kerri out when Adam drags me back.

'You're not going to ruin this for me Flora.'

I slap at his hands but it's futile. He imprisons them with his own. He's panting with the exertion of holding on to me. My stomach cramps again and I gasp. I'm going to lose the baby. I lift my knee and bring it up into Adam's groin. He doubles over and releases me. I don't stop to see if he's okay but grab my car keys from the hook and race to the cellar. I'm praying he doesn't see where I'm going. I reach the door and look back to see him struggling to his feet. He has his back to me. I open the cellar door and creep inside, bolting it quietly behind me.

*

I'm too afraid to breathe in case Adam hears me. It's pitch black but I'm afraid to turn the light on in case Adam sees it under the door. My heart is hammering in my chest. I clutch my stomach and whisper,

'It's going to be all right, everything is going to be okay.'

'Flora,' barks Adam. 'You can't hide from me.'

I bite my lip and taste blood. There's a scuffling sound and then I hear his voice.

'She's somewhere. This is a disaster. If I don't find her, the papers will have the best story they've ever had and you'll be in it,' he says harshly.

He's on the phone to Henry, he must be. Oh God, how can I escape them both? My eyes begin to adjust to the dark and I step slowly down the steps to the cellar. My eyes feel gritty and sore from crying. How can this be happening? I push away the image of Adam in our bed with Vikki. Had they had rough sex? Was that what Adam had liked about it? What has happened to him? Or had he always been this driven? He'd been ambitious from the first time I'd met him. I had no doubt then, that one day he would be Prime Minister. But I could never have dreamt it would have been at the expense of my life. I fight back a sob and cover my mouth so I'm not heard. My stomach lurches at the thought of Kerri. Where is she? Will Adam hurt her? I want to crawl into a hole and die but I know I have to survive for the sake of my baby. I have to find a way to escape.

*

Seth scoops Kerri up into his arms and dives behind a hedge when he hears raised voices from the house. The front door is slammed shut. Flora and Adam are arguing. Flora sounds distraught. Kerri wriggles in his arms and he strokes her gently. He needs to get help but who can he go to? There was no one in the village who would believe him.

Chapter Fifty-Nine

Adam

'Damn it,' he cursed.

How could she? How could she ruin everything? They were the perfect couple, the couple who had everything. He'd given her it all and this was how she repaid him.

He punched the wall with all his strength.

'Damn you Flora. I love you, you're the only one for me,' he yelled. 'How can you do this to us?'

He hobbled to the French doors, checked they were locked and removed the keys. He did the same with the back door and then looked frantically around.

'I know you're here somewhere Flora. You might as well come out. See sense for Christ's sake.'

His hand was throbbing and starting to swell. He sighed. Why tonight of all nights. He needed a bloody good night's sleep. There was a rapping at the front door. He opened it to see Henry standing there, just like he had all those months ago. Adam's jaw twitches.

'I don't know if I can get involved in this,' Henry said, looking cautiously into the hallway.

'You haven't got much choice. If I go down, you go down too. An error of judgement, wasn't it Henry, helping me out that night?'

Henry frowned.

'You should have kept a tighter rein on your wife,' he retorted.

'If you don't help me Henry, you can say goodbye to your wife. God knows where she'll end up if Bluefields closes.'

Henry narrowed his eyes.

'Don't threaten me Adam. Let's find Flora and talk to her. She's not stupid. I'm sure we can make her see sense.'

'I've talked to her. There's no reasoning with her. She wants me to hand myself in.'

'Where is she? Let me talk to her?'

'She's hiding somewhere in the house. I've locked the doors. She has to come out sometime.'

'The front door?' asks Henry. 'The gates were open.'

'Shit,' groans Adam, pushing the gate pad. 'No, I was here. She didn't go out the front door. You've got to help me Henry. I take over the premiership tomorrow. I've got a bloody audience with the Queen.'

'This is a bloody mess Adam.'

'Yes, tell me about it Henry.'

'You check upstairs and I'll look down here,' he said as he turned and headed for the kitchen.

Henry watched Adam disappear up the stairs and then called out,

'Flora, it's Henry Dorcas. I'm here to help. Can we talk?'

Chapter Sixty

I hear Henry's voice and take another step down into the cellar. It's cold and musty but it's my safe haven for the moment. I have to fight back the tears that threaten to overwhelm me. I have to get out of the window but how? It's difficult to see in the dark and I stumble, feeling my way until the small glint of light from the window gives me hope. My heart is beating so fast that I can barely breathe and my legs are so shaky that I'm sure it will be impossible for me to clamber up to the window. I curse myself again for not grabbing my phone. Then I remember the torch I'd seen in one of the boxes. It probably won't work but it's worth a try. My hands are trembling so much that it's difficult to find things in the boxes on the shelf. I seem to touch everything but the torch. Finally, after what seems like an eternity, my hand lands on the rubbery base of the torch. With my breath held, I click it on, and fight back my cry of relief when it works. I look up at the window. It seems so high. I felt sure it wasn't that far up before. Using a broom and the light from the torch, I'm able to push it open.

'How about the cellar?' I hear Adam say.

I grab the windowsill and attempt to lift myself up, but it's impossible without something to help me. There's a squeak as the door handle is turned and then the sound of someone pushing against it. It won't take him long to break the door down once they realise I am here.

'Flora,' yells Adam. 'Open the bloody door and stop being so ridiculous. Let's talk about this.'

I look around frantically for something to stand on. Am I being stupid? Surely Adam wouldn't hurt me and the baby. Our child was all we both wanted. Am I losing the plot again?

Should I open the door? I hesitate at the bottom of the steps. Adam's ambition has always come first. I never thought it would come before me. I know Adam well enough to realise he won't give up this chance. The power of being Prime Minister is the ultimate for him and I now know that even I won't be able to stand in his way. I was stupid to ever think I could. Adam won't let me stop his dream coming true.

'Please God,' I pray, looking for something to stand on. My eyes land on the paint tins and I hurriedly pile them on the floor in front of the windowsill. Then carefully I balance on them. There's a thumping at the door.

'For fuck's sake Flora,' barks Adam.

'Let's stay calm,' says Henry. 'You're frightening her.'

Adam mumbles something but I can't hear what it is. I scramble up to the windowsill. I swing my leg over and get the other to move as the door breaks open. I fall on to the ground outside and scramble up the incline, tears blurring my way.

The outside security light clicks on and I freeze like a rabbit caught in headlights. I throw the patio chairs and table across the patio and head to the back gate. I push the keypad but the gate doesn't open. I've hit the wrong numbers in my haste. I try again and it swings open. I stumble into the courtyard and run towards my car. The security light clicks on and I see the flat tyre. A small sob is torn from me. Why didn't I get that fixed?

There are footsteps behind me and I hurriedly clamber into the car only to be dragged from it roughly.

'I really don't need this Flora,' Adam hisses. 'Come back into the house and we can discuss this.'

Chapter Sixty-One

I look pleadingly at Henry as he stands by the French doors.

'Adam,' he warns. 'Let's not be stupid.'

'I think the time for not being stupid has passed, don't you Henry?' sneers Adam as he drags me along the patio.

He is no longer the man I know. Greed and power have taken him over. He can only see the road to success and I'm no longer a part of that. I've become a threat. I claw at his hands but it's futile.

I open my mouth and scream. Adam's eyes widen in horror.

'For Christ's sake,' he says, releasing one hand to silence me. I wriggle free and run to the boat, seizing the oar from it. Adam rushes towards me and I swing the oar but he manages to side step the full force of the blow, but it's enough to topple him and I gain some time to run to the woods.

'For Christ's sake Henry, help me,' yells Adam.

Henry's too slow. I almost make it to the woods but I trip and fall. My stomach cramps and I double over. Adam reaches me and helps me up.

'The baby,' I moan. 'Adam please think of the baby.'

'You need to think of the baby, Flora. Come back in the house and we'll go to bed and tomorrow everything will be fine. You just need to put everything behind you.'

'Henry, you surely can't go along with this,' I shout.

'I'm getting old. I can't get around like I used to. If they move Rachel somewhere away from Penlyn it will be hard for me. I can visit every day now. She needs me, she's always needed me.'

'I'll help you visit,' I say rashly. 'I can drive you there.'

I try to twist out of Adam's arms but I'm too weak and too tired.

'You can't leave Vikki in the well,' I say defiantly.

Adam's eyes soften and for a moment I think he's seen sense. Then he says,

'Flora, why are you doing this? I need you by my side but if I can't have you there, then I'll do it alone.'

'You won't get away with this Adam.'

'I did get away with it and I would still be getting away with it if you weren't so stubborn.'

'Get the boat, Henry,' he orders.

Henry seems to hesitate.

'Henry,' he repeats, irritation evident in his voice.

Adam turns to look at Henry and at that moment I see an opportunity to escape. I jump into the lake, pulling Adam in with me. Henry was quite right, the lake is shallow and I'm able to wade to the other side. Adam splutters and splashes behind me.

My feet sink into the mud at the bottom of the lake and the weeds tangle around my ankles. I wade, stumbling like a drunk through the water with Adam following behind. My lighter frame gives me an advantage as Adam slips and slides in his pursuit. Once I have gained some distance I turn to the bank and make a dash for the opening to the woods. The woods are dark but I have no time to hesitate, I need to get away from Adam.

*

There is the crack of a breaking branch. Adam has no doubt sent Henry around to Chatterpie Lane to trap me in the woods. I've nowhere to go. I can't scream for help without giving my position away. I stumble over the rough ground, my ankle throbbing where I'd scraped it earlier. The cramping in my stomach is getting worse.

'It's okay baby,' I whisper. 'We're going to be okay.'

I don't think about Vikki Merchant. I daren't. I've no idea which way will lead me out to the road. I consider climbing the wall and dismiss the idea immediately. I want so much to stop and rest but I know I can't. I stumble on, tripping over branches and walking into trees. Adam is hot on my heels, I can hear him. I'd dropped the torch on the patio but thankfully the moon is bright, sending shafts of light through the leaves of the trees. There's a snap from a breaking branch and the sound of heavy breathing and I know that Adam is close. I spin round, trying to decide which way to go when suddenly arms encircle me.

Chapter Sixty-Two

A hand covers my mouth as I go to scream.

'Quiet Flora, it's me, Art,' whispers a voice into my ear. 'Seth was afraid for you. He showed me a way into the woods. Are you okay?'

His breath is hot on my face. My body goes limp with relief.

'Adam, he's gone crazy. I'm afraid of what he'll do.'

'Come this way,' he says taking my hand.

'Adam is ...'

He shushes me. I freeze at the sound of a snapping twig and squeeze Art's hand.

'Seth is at the gate with Kerri,' he whispers. 'Keep going that way and you'll see it.'

He points to a clearing in the trees.

'No, you must come with me,' I plead. 'He's insane. I don't know what he'll do.'

'You must ...' he begins.

I scream as the oar hits him on the side of the face, cutting a gash into his forehead. My legs freeze in fear. Adam stands like a monster in front of me, his eyes wild, and his hair wet with sweat. He lifts the oar over Art's body.

'No,' I scream. 'Leave him. I'll come with you.'

He pulls me by the arm and I stumble behind him. I hear Art's groans and sob quietly. Adam stops suddenly and turns to me.

'Do you think I'm stupid?' he growls. 'He'll tell the police. I can't have that. Tomorrow I will be the Prime Minister; the nation will be looking to me. I can't have that idiot getting in my way.'

'Adam, it's gone too far. Even Henry won't cover this for you. Be sensible.'

'Be quiet,' he snarls.

He turns back and lifts the oar again. I struggle to pull it from his hands as Art scrambles up. Adam swings it, hitting me in the face as he does so. I fall on my hands and knees and feel the vomit rise up in my throat. Art races towards Adam and hits him in the chest, knocking the oar from his hand, but it's no good, Art is too weak and I sob as Adam lays punch after punch into him. I force myself up and struggle to lift the oar, but I've no strength left in me and I watch in helpless horror as Art lies slumped against a tree while Adam continues to punch him. He grins, he is enjoying it. A surge of anger empowers me and I take the oar and swing it, knocking Adam to one side. He stares at me. His eyes are glazed over and I don't recognise this man as my husband.

'Why Flora? You used to be such fun. Why did you drive me into her arms?'

My legs won't hold me up. I struggle to lift the oar again but I'm too weak. My stomach cramps and I double over in pain. He takes the oar from me.

'You've lost your mind Flora. You clearly left hospital too soon. It's going to be a terrible blow to me when you kill yourself but I'm sure the public will rally round me. They will feel my pain. The public like a leader that has suffered.'

'You're insane. You won't get away with this.'

I see Art's hand twitch and pray he doesn't make a sound. Adam lifts me up and carries me back through the woods.

'It's a shame, Flora. I really needed you by my side. I'm going to miss you ...'

His voice breaks.

'I loved you. I only wished you had been different.'

'Adam ...'

'We have to get on,' he says, his voice becoming hard again. 'I need to get some sleep before tomorrow.'

I'm too weak to fight and there's a dull pain in my abdomen and I know I'm losing the baby. It's all too familiar. The tears are streaming down my face and I'm hiccupping sobs as he carries me. I realise it is futile to tell him I'm losing the baby. Nothing matters to him now except his career. He's lost all sense. The drive to make it has driven him mad. We finally get back to the house. There is no sign of Henry. Has he gone to get help? Adam wipes the perspiration from his forehead and then points to the lake.

'Get in,' he says roughly.

'Adam,' I plead.

'Get in,' he shouts.

I walk into the lake and he follows.

'Into the middle.'

'No Adam ...'

He pushes me and I lose my footing and fall into the water. He drags me up and I splutter, spitting water from my mouth.

'Is this how Vikki died?' I ask, trying to buy some time.

'You know how it happened. You've had a psychic awakening, remember?' he scoffs.

Had Vikki come to warn me?

'Then it was an accident, Adam. You never meant it to happen.'

'Keep going,' he pushes.

'You didn't mean for her to fall down the stairs.'

'It's done. My life could have been ruined. Bloody women, you ruin everything.'

My foot slips and I feel the lake get deeper. We must be near the old well. Panicking I pull back. Adam grabs me and kisses me hard on the lips.

'Goodbye Flora,' he says as he puts his hands around my neck. I struggle against him but he's too strong. My feet slip from beneath and I gasp for breath. His hands push me down unmercifully. I struggle to find my footing but my feet slip on the sides of the old well shaft. Desperately, I kick hard against the shaft, just enough to surface above and take in another gasp of air. But I'm pushed under again and I begin to feel myself weaken. I struggle and fight but this time I can't feel the well shaft. I writhe under Adam's grip, twisting and turning like a tormented animal. After what feels like an eternity and when I have no strength left to move, a dark peacefulness seems to envelop me. I no longer feel Adam's hands holding me under. I look down the well shaft and see a faint light, then a small hand reaching up to me, and then I see Vikki, she smiles as she drifts up towards me. I reach out my hand to take hers in a moment of surreal tranquillity. A thousand thoughts enter my mind, a thousand images as though my life was being played out on a cinema screen, compressed into one moment of time.

A sudden jolt, like a bolt of lightning, strikes through my body and Adam's hands release their vice grip. I feel the pain flood back into my body as I fight to surface again. It seems as though my lungs are on fire as I gasp at the air. It takes me a few moments to realise that Adam is lying face down in the water, a pool of crimson mingling with the inky black water and spreading like a blanket. There's a figure at the side of the lake and through my blurry eyes I strain to make out who it is.

'Earl,' I try to say, but my vocal chords feel as tight as a vice. He holds his rifle at his side, a faint whisper of smoke emerges from the barrel. And then I see Seth frantically paddling the boat towards me.

'Adam,' I say weakly, 'help Adam.'

He nods and climbs into the water, dragging Adam's body to the boat. Earl wades in and pulls us back to the mooring.

'There's a woman in the well,' I say. 'You have to pull her up. Her name's Vikki Merchant.'

Chapter Sixty-Three

'The police are investigating an incident that happened at the Oxfordshire country home of Adam Macintosh, the Home Secretary,' says the attractive TV reporter standing at the gates of Hunters Moon. 'Ralph Meadows, in a statement this morning, said that no details will be released concerning the incident until police have completed their inquiries.'

Laurie switches off the TV as Doctor Kingsley enters my room.

'Flora, how are you feeling?'

'I don't really know,' I answer honestly.

'The scan results are back and everything is okay. This baby is going to be fine,' he smiles.

'Thank you,' I say tearfully.

Laurie clutches at my hand, her own eyes filling with tears.

'Can I see Art?'

He frowns.

'He's not in a good way, but I'm sure he would be happy to see you. I don't want you getting upset though.'

'I'll be fine,' I say firmly.

Laurie helps me from the bed and together we take the lift to the wards upstairs. Art is in a private room. I'd arranged it. It was the least I could do. His head is bandaged and his face puffy and swollen.

'I'd have made an effort if I'd known you were coming by,' he smiles and then grimaces.

Laurie pulls up a chair and says,

'I'm going to get a coffee. I won't be long.'

I slowly sit down.

'We're a pair,' he says.

I smile.

'I can't thank you enough for what you did. You put your life on the line for me. I'll never forget that.'

He reaches out for my hand and I shyly place mine in his.

'When you last came to see me, you talked about Vikki Merchant and how you thought she might have been killed in your house and … well I didn't like to tell you that I'd seen her with your husband in a pub in Oxford. They seemed friendly but not over-friendly so I couldn't say he was playing around with her, but it made me think. I got the hairband checked out and it was blood. It would have been from a few months ago, at about the time you moved into the house. It freaked me out a bit because I knew you weren't the breakdown type and if you sensed something then it must be real. I also found out that your husband had pulled out all the stops to block a developer from buying Bluefields. I couldn't work out why he'd do that. I looked at other care homes but I couldn't find any others that he was involved with. Bluefields is run down and everyone agrees it should be closed, but there was one person who didn't agree and that was Henry. I realised then there must be a connection between Henry and your husband. I phoned to talk about it with you but I only got your voicemail. I tried again but …'

'I tried to phone you back but I had no signal and then … I found Adam's St Christopher in the lake. He lost it before we ever moved there.'

'I'm so sorry.'

'He was always very driven. Things were difficult for us after the miscarriages, I …'

'It wasn't your fault,' he says squeezing my hand.

He's right of course, it wasn't my fault.

'I hope you'll visit when you come out of hospital,' I say.

'I thought you'd never ask.'

*

The drive to Hunters Moon is different. The sun is shining. It's hot, unlike the first time I'd arrived when the rain had greeted me. I'm in my own little car this time. Laurie had got it repaired while I was in the hospital. My only companion is Kerri who lies contented on her blanket in the back. I stop at the gates and look at the house. I don't believe in ghosts but after what happened I'm now not so sure. Had Vikki come to warn me?

I punch the security numbers in and wait as the gate opens. The house looks welcoming, the grey stone walls bathed in sunlight. My eyes are drawn to the windows but I know there will be nothing there. Vikki is at rest now. Her body was brought up as it should have been and her family are holding a funeral in a few days. They had kindly invited me but I had declined. I've still yet to see Adam. He was taken to a mental institution where he will be assessed. He's claiming diminished responsibility. The front door opens and Jan hurries down the steps. Kerri barks excitedly at the sight of her. Seth appears nervously behind her. It's the first time I'd seen him since that dreadful night. Jan hugs me tearfully.

'Hello Seth,' I say. I wait a few moments and then lean forward to hug him. He holds out a pad. I look to Jan who nods at me.

'He has a lot to say to you.'

I take the pad and begin to read.

Dear Mrs Macintosh, Please forgive me for being silent. I'm the fool in the village. No one would have believed me. I tried to point you to the old well in the lake. I didn't mean to frighten you. I wanted you to think about it. I hope you feel better soon. My gran said I shouldn't work here any more and that you will probably leave. Best wishes, Seth.

'No,' I say handing back the pad. 'I'm not leaving. I'm going to have my baby here and I need you to help around the house. I need you to take Kerri for walks and when the baby is here I will need more help.'

His face breaks into a smile and he nods gratefully. I wait patiently while he scribbles again on the pad.

'I'm sorry for coming into the house and scaring you at the window.'

I take a step back.

'That was you?'

He nods apologetically.

'But how?' I ask.

He begins to sign with his hands and then realising I don't understand, stops and scribbles again on the paper.

'I came through the cellar. I left the window open and bolted the inside.'

I smile.

'It's okay, Seth,' I say, hugging him. 'You must teach me to sign.'

He grins and scribbles, 'Sure'.

I look beyond him to Earl who is eyeing me from his spot among the shrubs, I walk slowly towards him.

'You saved my life,' I say.

He shrugs.

'It were nothing,' he says flatly.

'It was something to me. I'm very grateful.'

He nods and fingers a shrub.

'It was a lucky shot.'

I smile.

'Very lucky for me,' I say. 'You look thirsty; I'll get Jan to bring out some juice.'

'That'll be good,' he says and turns back to his trimming.

'I'll do it now,' smiles Jan.

I look over at the boat and smile. Everything looks just perfect in the sunshine.

Chapter Sixty-Four

I haven't told the police about Henry. I wanted him to explain first. The front door is open and I let myself in. I pass the oak sideboard in the hall and walk into the living room. Henry sits in an armchair holding a photo of his wife, Rachel. Curls of smoke drift up above him. The ashtray beside him is full.

'They're demolishing the home,' he says.

He doesn't look up but I know he's aware it is me.

'Yes, I know.'

He finally looks up at me, his eyes weary.

'I only wanted to stay close to my wife. Surely you can understand that?'

'I don't understand the things you did. Maybe I can understand you covering up the murder of Peter Snell ...'

'It wasn't murder,' he breaks in harshly. 'We only meant to frighten him. We weren't going to hang him. We're not that evil, no matter what you think.'

'You put a noose around his neck?' I say. 'You threatened to hang him if he didn't agree to leave, didn't you?'

'He raped an innocent seventeen-year-old girl, don't forget that.'

'It all went wrong didn't it, Henry?'

'No one knew he had asthma. What we were supposed to do? We tried to get the noose off but it was too late. We tried to resuscitate him.'

I push some newspapers off a chair and sit down, while trying not to recall the last time I had been in this room.

'I bought back the Penlyn Pen issues you lent to me.'

'So where is Peter Snell buried?' I ask, laying the magazines on the coffee table.

'Maggie Snell put his ashes in the garden,' he says, picking up a mug from the table. 'It's vodka,' he says, holding it up. 'I'd offer you some but in your condition it isn't a good idea.'

I look past him to the television and say, 'I saw the DVD.'

'I know you did and you presumed that she was forced didn't you?'

'Wasn't she?'

'No, she wasn't forced. She wanted it. It was the way she dealt with her guilt, like a monk who whips himself to atone for his sins. At the beginning it was this way. They were hedonistic, both of them. You didn't know her or Gerard, for that matter. Gerard thought it would also be a way to keep me quiet. They suggested it, not me. But as time went on she wanted it to stop but he didn't. I think he enjoyed watching it. He filmed it and then gave the DVD to me. They did bizarre things in that house. They were far more debauched than you could ever imagine. Errors of judgement, my dear, they have their consequences.'

'Oh yes, I remember your lecture, Henry. Haven't you made a few errors of judgement yourself? What about the deadly sins that you've committed? Your pride in this village has surely been your biggest downfall. Your lust drove poor Kerri Wilson over the edge. Your wrath pushed things too far with Peter Snell, and in your greed for power in this village you made sure you remained elder of the guild each year. But Adam, what was that about Henry? Was that envy?'

He glares at me.

'You've deprived the country of a good Prime Minister. He was young and popular.'

'And under your control, let's not forget that detail', I interrupt.

'He made a mistake. He succumbed to lust, but whose fault was that Flora? A man has needs and you clearly weren't fulfilling Adam's. His mistake was simply one of carelessness. Having an affair in someone else's house, well it's asking for trouble. But you could have overlooked it. A glittering future down the drain …' he trails off and takes a gulp from his mug.

I stand up and walk to the door.

'I have to tell the police of your involvement,' I say.

'And my wife? What about her, or don't you care about her? She'll have no one if I go to prison.'

'Perhaps you should have thought of that when you threw Vikki Merchant's body in the well.'

I'm at the front door when he shouts,

'You're Miss Virtuous are you? You think Adam didn't know that you lusted after Art Mitchell.'

I fight back my gasp. He stands in the living room doorway.

'I can't let you tell the police of my involvement Flora.'

'I have to.'

'Maybe you've got more self-control than the rest of us, Flora, but you've still made mistakes. You knew all along about Vikki Merchant didn't you?'

I stop in my tracks, my hand on the door handle.

'I don't know what you're talking about,' I say turning to face him.

'I would have kept this to myself but if you're threatening me Flora …'

I don't respond. His eyes harden and he leans against the sideboard.

'You see, Vikki was a touch religious and she liked to confess. I know confession is confidential but I was concerned about this situation. It was too close to the Litha celebrations and the Best Kept Village competition. Scandal was the last thing we needed. Reverend Flynn had no choice but to tell me. After all, I make sure he gets a supply of clean drugs.'

I widen my eyes.

'Oh yes, you were right on that too,' he smiles. 'Gerard put me on to a good supplier.'

'Doesn't the reverend have any Christian morals?' I interrupt.

'If you're going to preach Christian morality, Flora, then you need to read your Bible. It's not our place to judge and Jesus himself said to the moral accusers of his day, *he that is without sin can cast the first stone*. Michael Flynn's sin was a sin against his own body, but he is a good man. He has helped many of us in the village. Regarding his need for drugs, I felt it was best to be in control of the situation. That way it couldn't come out. Of course, we hadn't bargained on you. Vikki told him how you phoned her after the party where she first met your husband. What's your crime Flora, greed would you say? Wanting Adam all to yourself? You never wanted him to be Prime Minister did you? You would have done anything to stop that. What were you going to do, leak to the papers that he was having an affair with an estate agent? I guess that got awkward when you couldn't get hold of her.'

'You're wrong,' I say with a smile. 'He was already wooing her long before I contacted her. You're right about one thing though, I did want Adam to myself. I didn't want thousands of women ogling him. I encouraged her but that's as far as it went. She wasn't supposed to get pregnant. It was Adam's dream to reach the top, not mine. I'm not proud of what I did but a baby needs a father. I would have leaked it, yes and that would have been the end of it. We'd have got through it. He shouldn't have been so weak.'

'You thought it was hotel rooms didn't you? I guess that's the norm. She fell in love with him. I don't think you bargained on that.'

'He didn't love her,' I say angrily. 'Adam only ever loved me.'

'He's gone insane. I blame you,' he says with a snarl.

I shrug.

'He tried to kill me,' I say flatly.

'So what went wrong Flora? How did it all backfire on you?'

'You know what went wrong. She disappeared, dropped off the radar. I couldn't leak a story about the Home Secretary having an affair with a woman that had disappeared. I tried her mobile but never got a reply. Of course I know now that her bag and mobile were in the well. I tried at the estate agents but they just kept telling me she'd left. I didn't for one minute imagine that Adam had killed her,' I say.

'But would he have taken it that far if she hadn't been so willing? Isn't all this your fault? You've got what you wanted. You're having the baby and your husband isn't Prime Minister.'

'He's going to prison, Henry. That's not what I wanted.'

'Errors of judgement, my dear, they don't always end how you'd wish.'

I open the door, relieved to get some fresh air in my lungs.

'Of course, if you tell the police about me, I'd have to tell them about you.'

'Scandal in the village, Henry, isn't that what you dread?'

'It's done, you've shamed us. It could have been kept under wraps. Adam would now be Prime Minister and you'd be happily ensconced in your home with your baby on the way. The successful couple with everything, and I would have Rachel close by. Everyone a winner, but you had to get all righteous didn't you?'

'Except Vikki Merchant,' I say. 'She didn't win.'

'A consequence my dear, can you not see that? If I tell the police that you knew about Vikki Merchant and encouraged the relationship it will occur to them that perhaps you knew more about Vikki's murder than you're letting on.'

'Adam was driven by ambition. I had to do something to stop him.'

'But you pretended not to know about the affair. You would have exposed it if you needed to stop Adam's lust for power, but in doing so you become an accomplice to the crime. I only have to tell them you lied.'

I smile.

'It seems you win Henry, unless of course Reverend Flynn tells on both of us.'

'Oh, he only knows your secret, thanks to Vikki.'

I smile.

'Ah, but I know someone that knows yours.'

I don't mention Seth by name. There is no need to. He raises his eyebrows.

'Touché then, Mrs Macintosh.'

'Goodbye Henry.'

'Rachel will be very grateful,' he smiles.

'You got Earl to rescue me that night didn't you?'

He turns away from me.

'I'm not a bad person. I couldn't let him kill you. That would have been outright murder. I got Earl, yes. He aims well. It was meant to maim not to kill. Earl has his funny ways but he's a good man at heart.'

'Thank you for that Henry.'

'Staying at Hunters Moon are you?'

'I think I will.'

I walk down the drive and hear the front door close. I lift my face to the sun and take a deep breath. It's the Best Kept Village competition at the weekend. I must ask Seth to tidy the drive.

'Morning Mrs Macintosh,' calls Geoff.

'Hi Geoff. Can you tell Rhonda I'll be at crochet tomorrow?'

'Sure thing,' he smiles.

Hunters Moon is warm and welcoming in the sunshine. I believe Vikki Merchant did come to warn me. She came to me in my dreams and I sensed her presence in the house. I hope she is now at peace and forgives me.